T0107317

"The Hall...the estate..."

"Will all have to be sold."

After her fortune is squandered by her drunken gambler of a father, Catherine Davenport must accept the charity of a cousin she has never met. But the household of Phillip Davenport is anything but welcoming. Catherine barely survives a brutal attack that shatters her body and severs her memory. A harrowing rescue on the London docks takes her into the home of two brothers: Rian and Liam Connor.

"Trust him...he will not hurt you."

Mystery and scandal surround Rian, recently returned from a plantation in the Americas. As Catherine struggles to reclaim her identity, she must fight her overwhelming desire for the man who saved her life. But Rian, she learns, has come home for a wedding, and Catherine fears her enigmatic rescuer is already spoken for. How can a woman with no memory, no family, no home, hope to win the heart of London's most intriguing rogue?

Books by Carla Susan Smith

A Vampire's Promise
A Vampire's Soul
A Vampire's Honor
A Vampire's Hunger

Published by Kensington Publishing Corporation

Mischance

Corsets and Carriages

Part One

Carla Susan Smith

LYRICAL PRESS
Kensington Publishing Corp.
www.kensingtonbooks.com

Lyrical Press books are published by
Kensington Publishing Corp. 119 West 40th Street New York, NY 10018

First Electronic Edition: January 2018
eISBN-13: 978-1-5161-0590-8
eISBN-10: 1-5161-0590-7

First Print Edition: January 2018
ISBN-13: ISBN 978-1-5161-0593-9
ISBN-10: ISBN 1-5161-0593-1

Printed in the United States of America

For Sharon

This one is all your fault!

Acknowledgments

This book has taken a particularly long time to come to fruition for reasons that are too boring to mention. However the fact that it has finally crossed the finish line fills me with a great deal of personal satisfaction. As with all my writing, it is never a solitary effort and I owe a great deal of thanks to all the wonderful people who continue to help me achieve my dream.

My family, who are fast learning that Mom trying to meet a deadline more often than not means pizza for dinner.

My great friend and fellow author, Liz O'Connor, who is not only generous with her time and advice when I need it, but totally gets the deadline means no cooking reference.

Ruth Guillot, Karen Smith, and Angel Vandenberg. Thank you for being my first readers. Your comments, insight, and friendship mean more than you know—and I promise if I write another trilogy you can read it one book at a time!

Lynne Harter, who faces the challenge of making each manuscript as close to perfect as possible—a task that would be so much easier with any other writer I'm sure. Thank you for not giving up on me.

Alicia Condon and the fabulous team at both Kensington and Lyrical. Can't thank you enough for your patience in answering my stupid questions, for ignoring my whining over deadlines, and above all, for not losing faith in me. You all rock.

And finally to everyone who reads my books. I can never repay you for your kindness in allowing me into your lives and letting me share a part of myself with you. Thank you.

Mischance

Corsets and Carriages

Carla Susan Smith

At a time when all a woman had was dependent on the men in her life…

Chapter 1

Catherine felt as though she was balanced precariously on the edge of an abyss. The illusion seemed so real that she could almost feel the rush of cold air racing up the chasm wall to lift the hem of her dress and ruffle her petticoats. At any moment her knees would surely buckle, causing her to tumble, head first, into the darkness swirling far below. A voice in the corner of her mind urged her to do exactly that and escape the reality that was about to shatter her world.

But Catherine was a pragmatic young woman who viewed swooning to avoid unpleasantness as not only impractical, but cowardly. Losing consciousness would not improve her situation. She would be just as destitute upon regaining her senses. Slowly she faced the man who had been speaking to her. "Mr. Whitney, how can this be?" She paused, fixing the bearer of her bad tidings with a look that was both bewildered and angry. "The Hall…the estate—"

"Will all have to be sold."

Jacob Whitney had been legal counsel to the Davenport family for more years than he cared to remember. Never treating Whitney as anything less than an equal, Catherine's father had extended the hand of friendship to the struggling young attorney with a family to support. It was a hand that Jacob had clasped eagerly with no regrets.

Until now.

At this moment he sorely wished that he had embarked on an entirely different career. A cabinetmaker, perhaps. But Jacob had not been blessed with the skill or talent required for such a vocation. An aptitude for the law had been his calling, bringing with it both professional and personal satisfaction. But having to relate unwelcome news was never easy, and when personal feelings were added to the mix, the situation became almost intolerable. Retaining a professional demeanor taxed the limit of Jacob's skills, and, for the hundredth time that morning, he silently cursed the name of William Davenport.

Although his advice had been sought by his late employer regarding a number of financial transactions, it appeared the counsel he'd given had been ignored. The full extent of William's fiscal recklessness had remained a secret until his unexpected demise forced everything into the open. And no matter how many times Jacob examined and reexamined the documents placed before him, the result remained the same. The great Davenport fortune was no more. The Hall was mortgaged, the estate bankrupt, and both would have to be sold to satisfy the growing list of creditors.

Jacob silently applauded Catherine for not fainting as the full realization of her predicament became clear. Now he watched as she slowly walked about the perimeter of the room. The only sign of agitation was in the twist of her fingers as she clasped and unclasped her hands. He knew her well enough to know she would have questions, and he had prepared himself to give what answers he could.

Four months had passed since he had last seen her standing as a silent sentinel by her father's grave. He had been saddened, but not surprised, to find himself offering his condolences to a somber young woman who showed no trace of the child he remembered. Jacob recalled being surprised that, while Catherine had furnished the black scarves and gloves for the six pallbearers and officiating minister, she had failed to include any mourning rings. Now he understood why. How she had found the funds to cover the basic funereal service was beyond him.

Pausing, Catherine stood before one of the large picture windows. Afternoon sun streamed through the glass and bathed her in its light, becoming a pale gold halo that caressed her, making her look almost ethereal. The somber color of her mourning dress did nothing to detract from her beauty; if anything, the dark material only enhanced it. As she turned her head, her hair, tied at the nape of her neck with a single black ribbon, cascaded down her back in a champagne-colored waterfall. Her small oval face, normally clear with dusky pink cheeks, was now pale, and dark circles bruised the delicate skin beneath her eyes. Jacob wondered how long it had been since she last slept through the night.

What on earth had been in William Davenport's mind as he squandered the fortune that should have been his child's inheritance? Had he not realized what would happen to his daughter if she were left penniless?

Of course he did, but he was a gambler who thrived on chance and accepted the risks.

No doubt William thought to recoup his financial losses with the next wild proposition that presented itself, or the next turn of a card or roll of the die. But life had dealt him an unexpected blow and Jacob was certain that never, in his wildest schemes, had his patron banked on death snatching him away before he had a chance to repair the damage wrought. Though he could never bring himself to actually speak the words aloud, William did possess a strong, abiding affection for his daughter.

Jacob sighed. Catherine ought to have been married by now, but an ever-shrinking dowry meant the number of potential suitors was also reduced. Matrimony was a business that brought with it certain expectations, and the heavier the bridal purse, the better the prospects. Even with her extraordinary beauty, Jacob knew it was doubtful Catherine would find a husband worthy of her. News traveled fast in their small corner of the world, and bad news had the swiftest feet of all. It was not unthinkable to imagine every family of note in three counties was already aware of her impecunious state.

Catherine, finished with her contemplations, left her post at the window and took a seat across the table from him. "Has *everything* gone?" she asked, a frown creasing her brow at Jacob's confirmation.

"The amount of monies owed is…substantial."

Catherine simply stared at him, her face settling into an impassive mask. She could tell by the way he was shuffling the papers before him there was more he wanted to say. Forming the words, however, seemed problematic. "What else, Mr. Whitney?" She laid her hands on the polished tabletop. They were small, with long slender fingers. Delicate, feminine hands that still managed to convey a sense of strength.

"You are not entirely penniless, Catherine. Your grandmother left you a sum that was originally intended to be part of your dowry, but she did stipulate that should the need arise, it could be released to you. I think, under the circumstances…" His voice trailed off.

"How much?"

Under normal circumstances a sum of one hundred pounds would be cause for celebration; provided she was cautious with her spending, it could keep her modestly for some time. She sighed and mentally pulled up the seed of hopeful expectation before it could take root. "Please use what you must to settle the most pressing of our obligations in the village," she instructed Jacob, "and then divide whatever is left amongst the servants."

"The servants?" He stared at her, flabbergasted. "I'm not sure you heard me, my dear. The sum is one *hundred* pounds."

"Yes, I know." She gave him a tight smile. "I have no need of a dowry, Mr. Whitney, but there are others who could, who *should*, benefit from this unexpected good fortune." The look she gave said she would brook no argument from him. If he didn't want her to use the money, then he should not have told her about it. "Tell me, have you found a buyer for the property?"

He shook his head.

"Then would it not make sense," she continued, "to allow those who serve The Hall to remain until you do? Or at least until they are able to secure another position?"

He nodded.

"It has been well over a year since any of the servants received any wages, and I would like to rectify that situation. But we still must eat, Mr. Whitney, and I cannot expect Mr. Dowd to extend my account indefinitely."

Jacob was not surprised by her words or her reasoning. He was, however, astonished to hear that the butcher had extended her credit. The dour-faced man was not known for his generosity, which meant he thought highly of Catherine. Settling her debts with the village was only right and proper, but, despite his initial impulse to deny it, Jacob also saw the sense in her request. It was reasonable to assume whoever bought The Hall would welcome help that was already familiar with the house and grounds. Still, he couldn't help but wonder how many others, finding themselves in a similar position to Catherine's, would have secured as much of a future for themselves as the money would have provided instead of spending it on others.

"Of course I will see to it as you wish," he told her.

"Good. Is there anything else?"

"Miss Catherine, forgive my bluntness, but have you given any thought to your future?"

Her future? She'd thought of nothing else since her father's death turned her world upside down. "With no dowry, I expect no offers for my hand," she told him bluntly. "Perhaps I could find useful employment administering to the needs of the sick or infirm. I possess a great deal of skill in changing soiled linens, and emptying chamber pots, and of course my personal experience in dealing with those who drink themselves senseless cannot be overlooked. It surely must be an advantage." This last was added with a bitterness that said Catherine expected the lowliest kitchen maid to weather the repercussions of her father's foolishness far better than she. She sighed and smiled wearily at the man sitting across from her. "Forgive me, Mr.

Whitney. Grief has given my tongue an unnaturally sharp edge. I will of course consider any suggestion you care to present."

Perhaps it was simply tiredness, or guilt at her outburst, but whatever the reason, Jacob detected a thread of fear in her voice. He prayed that what he was about to reveal would dispel her fears, and offer her hope for the future. "Have you ever heard the name Phillip Davenport?" he asked.

* * * *

Safe within the confines of his modest carriage, Jacob allowed himself to relax as much as his troubled mind would permit. He rested his head against the buttoned leather back and closed his eyes, reliving the past few hours. After carefully examining his actions, Jacob concluded he had behaved in a manner that was both professional and appropriate. The meeting with Catherine had been conducted with far fewer complications than he had anticipated, although this was mainly due to an odd lack of curiosity on her part.

Any surprise she had shown at her impoverished situation was more a programmed reaction than real shock, but he had assumed she would pepper him with inquiries regarding the existence of Phillip Davenport, a recently discovered cousin. That she remained silent, requesting only the most rudimentary details, concerned him. Could she sense that he wasn't being entirely truthful when he had mentioned Phillip's name? That he knew more than he was alluding to? Even as a child Catherine had been intuitive, and there was no reason to suppose her perceptiveness had been diminished by the passage of time.

But, concerned though he might be, Jacob felt a certain relief that she had not asked him more about Phillip. At least he could state with all honesty he had not lied to her, although it was possible one day he might regret not being more forthright. Still he did not want to add to her burden by issuing warnings that could prove unnecessary. And besides, where else was she to go? Who would offer her shelter if not her recently rediscovered relative? Perhaps he should have insisted she take the hundred pounds for herself, especially as Jacob's correspondence with his colleague regarding Phillip Davenport had not been as reassuring as the attorney might have wished.

While expressing a similar surprise at the discovery of a blood relative, Phillip had dismissed the familial bond out of hand and was completely unreceptive to offering shelter to the penniless girl. Jacob's colleague reported, confidentially, that there was a certain smugness of attitude when the young man learned of Catherine's misfortune. Phillip Davenport, it seemed, was the type of man who took a perverse delight in the misery of others. It might have been different had there been an offer of compensation for his trouble.

Was it any surprise that Jacob had kept this from Catherine?

And then, as if the man's reluctance was not enough, there was the troubling matter of Phillip's character. Jacob was not quite the naïve country attorney some mistook him for. He had initiated inquiries into the young man's background, but all his investigation exposed was a slew of uncorroborated rumors. The city was filled with gossipmongers who, for the right price, would lie convincingly about the Holy Virgin herself. Scandal was not limited to street corners. The finest salons could damage a reputation with equal impunity.

Rumor, no matter how much it twisted Jacob's gut, was still rumor. He dealt with facts, not innuendo. So he decided, albeit grudgingly, to give Phillip the benefit of the doubt. He told himself that all Catherine's potential savior was guilty of was choosing to associate with people of questionable character. Nothing more. As his carriage rumbled on, Jacob soothed his worries with the notion he had served Catherine's best interests by not sharing his suspicions with her. Perhaps if he repeated it often enough, he might even believe it himself.

In the distance thunder rumbled. A summer storm was brewing and Jacob had some miles yet to travel. He hoped to be safe inside his office when the tempest broke.

Chapter 2

How long had it been since Jacob Whitney had left? Catherine did not know, nor did she care. Time had lost all meaning. The room began to darken with the onset of the storm and the glorious sunlight, which had bathed her in its glow, was now obscured by dark, angry clouds. Shadows crept across the floor and hid in corners, but Catherine chose to remain at the window, watching the trees sway and dance with the rhythm of the storm.

Standing still and barely breathing, she became a ghostly figure in the half light. In direct opposition to her physical body, her mind was in frantic turmoil as she turned to the news Jacob Whitney had given her. Believing herself to be alone, Catherine had been given the gift of a kinsman. It was the salvation that snatched her back from the edge of despair, and though the thought was both exciting and confusing, she made herself push it to the back of her mind. It could be taken out and examined later when she could give it the attention it deserved. What she needed to do now was focus her thoughts on the person responsible for bringing such a momentous change to her life. The man she loved with all her heart. The man who had brought her to this crossroad, and who had cruelly abandoned her there.

How many nights had passed since that terrible, awful day? Nights filled with bitter tears for both her loss and the fear of an uncertain future. She had known deep in her heart remaining at The Hall would not be possible, but she had clung stubbornly to the faint hope that a way might present itself. Perhaps she could stay in one of the smaller cottages dotted about the estate. Lord knows there were enough of them, abandoned by tenants who had once shared in the prosperity they had all enjoyed. But now she was faced with having to leave the only home she had ever known, and live her life with strangers. Her daily existence dependent on someone she'd had no idea lived or breathed when she had awoken this morning. A person with whom she had a familial connection, and who, in turn, had one with her. Would it make a difference, or would he resent the disruption her sudden appearance in his life was certain to bring?

The crash of thunder overhead seemed like an ominous warning, telling her she could not hold her father entirely to blame for what had happened. She had to accept her own share of responsibility.

Catherine should never have agreed to attend Edward Barclay's birthday hunt and ball. If she had said no, then her father would be alive still. But wishing something hadn't happened would not make it so, and it had been so long since she had been riding. It had taken her father barely six months to rid the Davenport stable, once the pride of the county, of all its inhabitants, leaving only the scent of hay and horses lingering in the air. Catherine had thought it would take longer to bankrupt the estate, but from what Mr. Whitney had told her today, her father had managed to achieve it in less time than she would have thought possible.

So where had he found the money to have a new riding habit and ball gown made for her? She hadn't thought to ask at the time, and it mattered little now. She sighed, and in the gloom heard her father's voice asking once again, "Would you like to attend a ball?"

"Who is giving a ball?" she'd responded, hesitantly.

It had been a long time since they had received an invitation. All the respectable families in the county no longer thought them suitable to be included at any gathering. Catherine had narrowed her eyes and viewed her father with suspicion, wondering if he was as sober as he appeared.

"Lord Fitzroy Barclay," he answered. He held out the missive so she might read it for herself. "It would seem that young Edward has come home."

Catherine scanned the elegant script addressed to her father, turned it over, and saw the seal remained unbroken. Excitement fluttered inside her like a caged bird desperate to break free. Raising her brows, she looked at her father, who waved a hand, giving his permission for her to break the seal. A hunt, with a ball to follow, in order to celebrate the return of Lord Barclay's only son and heir, Edward.

"Edward has truly returned home?" she murmured, seeking confirmation.

"Apparently so," her father replied.

Catherine smiled. She had fond memories of Edward. Only a few years older than she, he had been her childhood friend. Until Lady Barclay questioned the wisdom of her son spending so much of his free time with a playmate who was rapidly looking less childlike with each passing day. After that, it seemed all of Edward 's time was occupied with pursuits more befitting the station he would one day assume.. And it was no secret her father thought Edward would be a good match, and actively encouraged his daughter in that direction. But Catherine knew whatever affection Edward might hold for her, he would never disappoint his mother. To Lady Barclay, Catherine was disappointment personified. Her ladyship had far loftier goals for her only son.

But now Edward was returned, and no longer a boy, but a grown man. Feeling a nostalgic twinge of regret for what had been lost, Catherine wondered if he had any idea how much she had valued their friendship. He had been her only confidant, someone with whom she shared her hopes and dreams with no fear of ridicule. Easing the pangs of loneliness, Edward had become so much more than a playmate.

She was filled with a certain natural curiosity. How much had he changed? Would she recognize him? Would he recognize her? Could they rekindle their friendship? Would he want to? Sensing the sudden melancholy shift in her mood, William leaned forward in his seat. "It would be a shame to waste your new clothes if you decide not to accept," he told her with a glint in his eye.

The day of the hunt dawned clear and bright with a brilliant blue sky. Lord Barclay had thoughtfully sent a carriage, and Catherine was almost giddy with excitement. Her father had made it a point to remain sober, and seemed equally enchanted by his daughter's enthusiasm and high spirits. It was going to be a good day. Rides had been promised to each of them, and Lord Barclay, knowing Catherine's prowess as a horsewoman, had promised a mount worthy of her.

Although it was spring, it was still early enough in the season for a slight chill to be in the morning air. Catherine gratefully accepted a cup of hot, spiced wine as she joined the milling crowd of hunters and hounds. She noted a few familiar faces and was gracious to those who acknowledged her, while ignoring the more hostile looks thrown her way. It seemed her presence was ruffling some feathers.

At the sound of raised voices, she turned her head to follow the commotion. Most eyes were fixed on the magnificent bay-colored stallion that had appeared, but Catherine observed the groom leading him. No stable boy but an experienced older hand, and judging from the grim line of his mouth, the bead of sweat on his brow, and the straining biceps in his upper arm, his charge was not as easy to handle as the man would have his audience believe. Clearly the stallion was a valuable addition to Lord Barclay's stable. As if on cue, the horse suddenly tossed his head and reared up, snorting loudly as his forelegs danced in midair before his hooves clattered loudly back to the ground.

"High spirited," Catherine murmured in appreciation.

Those standing close enough to hear her nodded in agreement, before suddenly scrambling out of the way as both groom and horse came to a stop. True to his word, Edward's father had found a ride worthy of her. He looked on with an expression of approval as she fearlessly placed her foot in the groom's cupped hands and was boosted into the saddle, taking firm command of the headstrong animal.

Dressed in dove grey silk with an ivory stock at her throat, she was a vision who managed to turn the head of every man present. And not just for her skill at handling a potentially willful animal. The other women present, including those joining the hunt, were not so dazzled, but Catherine didn't care. They could stare and mutter all they wanted. She would allow nothing to spoil this day for her.

Aware that she was now under even more scrutiny, Catherine turned to her host and gave him a dazzling smile. She touched the handle of her riding crop to the brim of her hat, acknowledging the compliment he had paid her. Lord Fitzroy Barclay smiled back, knowing that whatever gossip his favoritism caused, she would treat it with the contempt it deserved.

"Cat!"

Only one person called her by that name, and he had given it to her after witnessing her walk barefoot across rafters in the hay barn as surefooted as any feline. Turning her mount's head, Catherine scanned the crowd for the familiar face. Her mouth fell open. "Edward?" she queried, feeling suddenly shy and awkward as she watched the handsome man coming toward her.

This was not the lanky playmate she remembered. Where was the boy who helped her collect tadpoles while sharing a bounty of wild blackberries that stained both lips and fingers? What had become of the shy lad, barely sixteen, who had plucked up enough courage to kiss her in the hay loft only a few summers ago? Had he really been replaced by the handsome, confident young man before her?

He smiled at her, and suddenly the Edward of her childhood, her one and only friend, was looking at her once more. And this time when she repeated his name, her delight was genuine. Leaning forward in the saddle, he wrapped his free arm about her waist and kissed her cheek.

The newly acquired mustache tickled and made Catherine giggle as she asked, "Edward, is it really you?"

He laughed back. "Of course it's me, you silly goose. Who were you expecting?" His voice sounded the same, though admittedly a little deeper than she remembered.

"You look different," Catherine observed shrewdly.

"I've grown up, Cat," Edward told her, pausing to look her over, "and so have you. You're positively beautiful." His words brought an unexpected blush to her cheeks. "And every woman here wants to scratch your eyes out because of it!" he added playfully.

"That's only because you make them jealous with your foolish compliments," she reprimanded.

Beyond his shoulder, Catherine caught sight of Lady Barclay giving her a piercing stare. It was no secret that many in the county had expected Edward to offer for her, but Catherine knew better. As long as the current Lady Barclay had a say in her son's future, a marriage between them would never happen. Besides, she had heard a rumor that Edward was engaged. It would certainly explain the look on his mother's face.

"So tell me," she asked, deciding to deal with the matter head on. "Which one is your fiancée? Point her out to me so I can be sure to share at least one embarrassing childhood memory."

"Cat, I am not yet engaged," Edward said, sounded genuinely aggrieved.

"Not from lack of trying on your mama's part I'll wager!"

Her horse snorted impatiently and shook his head, deciding he'd had more than enough of their conversation. Nudging him forward, Catherine gave Edward a smile that said she spoke in jest. The grin he offered in return wiped away the loneliness that had been her only companion for far too long.

"Will you come visit me, Edward, now that you are home?" she asked as his horse fell in step and they moved to join the other riders.

"Only if you promise to dance with me tonight," he replied with a mischievous sparkle in his eye.

Catherine's laugh was a sweet sound that carried on the light breeze. "As if I could refuse so handsome a man!" She tilted her head toward him. "Papa has brought me a ball gown," she confided in a whisper.

"I've seen you in a party dress before."

"Not one like this, you haven't!" She urged the big horse forward and left him to stare at the animal's powerful hindquarters as they moved away.

It was in all likelihood one of the last hunts of the season and certainly the last one for Catherine, but she cared nothing for that. All she wanted was the sheer joy of wind in her face and the horse moving powerfully beneath her. Oblivious to the other riders, she laughed out loud as her mount sailed effortlessly over fallen trees and covered the ground with fluid grace. Just when she was certain the day couldn't be more perfect, she heard a cry of alarm, followed by the unmistakable sound of a rider being unseated.

Reining her mount, Catherine wheeled her horse's head around to see who had fallen. She hoped it wasn't Edward because that would be too humiliating, especially as the day was to honor him. Shading her eyes with one hand, she quickly spotted a horse who seemed quite content to graze now he had no rider directing him.

Catherine frowned. The animal looked vaguely familiar, but it wasn't until it raised its head and she saw the white blaze that she recognized it as the one her father had been riding. A chill gripped her, and with a morbid sense of urgency she rode toward the group of riders now milling about the solitary animal. Grasping the hand that reached up to her, Catherine quickly dismounted and made her way past the spectators to the crumpled figure lying on the ground. From the onlookers' stricken expressions, she knew something was wrong. Horribly, horribly wrong. The horse had stumbled and thrown its rider, and in a senseless, freakish accident, William Davenport had broken his neck.

Falling to her knees by his side, Catherine grasped his hand, as if by willpower alone she could pass her own life force into him. But her father did not move. He did not open his eyes to look at her, nor did his chest rise with the intake of breath. Instead Catherine watched as her tears made dark stains on the fabric of his riding jacket. More people had now stopped, and the crowd pressed around her making the air oppressive and difficult to breathe. Letting go of her father's hand, she pulled off her hat and tore the delicate material at her throat. She tugged on the collar of her riding jacket, ripping loose some of the small pearl buttons in her effort to be free of the constricting garment.

A pair of firm hands closed about her upper arms and raised her to her feet. She let out a shuddering gasp as she struggled against them, but Edward pulled her against him and led her away from her father's body. With a grip of iron he held her close to his side, shielding her from the staring faces, until she was standing next to her horse. He let go of her only long enough to boost her into the saddle, and then he mounted behind her, and took the reins. Edward took off the way they had come, but not before Catherine heard a voice refer to her father as a drunken fool.

Wisely, Edward avoided the main house, choosing instead to go directly to the stables, where he took Catherine into the relative privacy of an empty stall. With his strong arms around her, she cried herself out, clinging to him as if she were drowning and he was her only salvation. She had no idea how long they remained there, Edward holding her even after her tears had dried, but by the time Lady Barclay came looking for them, the groom who accompanied her held a lamp to light the way.

As tragic as the event was, her ladyship informed them, Edward had an obligation to his guests and Catherine could no longer selfishly command his time. An escort had been arranged to take her back to The Hall. Unable to speak, she heard Edward speaking for her. He argued vehemently with his mother, the rise and fall of his voice indicating the depth of his feelings. She appreciated how he tried to stand up for her, but it made no difference because he didn't come back. Not then, not the next day, not anytime thereafter. He sent no word, no note of explanation, and when she wrote, over a week later, her note came back with the seal unbroken. Cook told her that Barclay Manor had been closed up, and the family had gone to the West Country with no idea of when they might return. The news produced another wave of grief. Edward had broken his promise to visit her, and in doing so, had shown he was not ready to become the man she hoped he could be.

A sudden clap of thunder overhead startled Catherine out of her reverie, bringing her back to the present. The storm was venting its fury, and rain lashed against the window. Leaning forward, she pressed her forehead against the cool glass, unaware of the hot tears that spilled down her cheeks and splashed onto the bodice of her gown. In a voice filled with an aching loneliness and fear of the unknown, she cried out to the storm raging outside, "Why, Papa? Why did you leave me so?" Only the wind and the rain answered her as the storm continued to beat its own fierce tattoo against the glass.

The abyss that had loomed earlier reappeared, and this time Catherine needed no encouraging whisper to tell her what to do. Stepping over its edge into oblivion, she sank to the floor, swallowed up in a pool of inky black material.

Chapter 3

Isabel Howard considered herself the most fortunate of women. A fortuitous introduction at the age of fifteen had lifted her from obscurity into the bed of a man almost thirty years her senior. She had shed no tears of regret or sorrow when he'd had the good manners to die after six years of marriage, and had emerged from the requisite period of mourning a young, beautiful, and now very wealthy widow.

The generosity of her late husband's estate was such that it allowed Isabel the freedom to live her life exactly as she pleased. In the past five years she had managed to gain a reputation that, though tainted with notoriety, was never risqué enough to exclude her from any guest list. Men found her irresistible, while her own sex was torn between outrage over her latest exploit, and envy at the courage it took to behave as she liked.

With no desire to encumber her lifestyle by the bothersome addition of another husband, Isabel chose to amuse herself with a wide variety of lovers. Young or old, married or single, it made no difference. She would tumble a stable hand as readily as a duke if he caught her fancy, and the encounter could last a single night or longer, depending on how quickly her interest waned.

The men she chose were more than willing to bed the beautiful young widow, and those currently unattached hoped to change her marital status. But Isabel was shrewd enough not to let her heart rule her head. Too many of her sex fell prey to false promises delivered by a silver tongue in a handsome face, and Isabel refused to lose her fortune to either. She'd decided long ago that were she to wed again, it would be to a most remarkable man indeed.

Rian Connor was such a man.

They met by chance at Lady Charlotte Maitling's summer ball. Isabel was between lovers and hoping to change that situation, but had not come across a single gentleman worthy of further attention. She had heard all the latest gossip and exchanged pleasantries with anyone worth knowing, and was now finding herself consumed by boredom. There would be no accounting for the change in her mood if she forced herself to listen to yet another round of the inane society prattle that passed for conversation. If she wasn't careful, someone was going to feel the sharp edge of her tongue, and though she might thumb her nose at society, she was not about to slit her throat. Lady Maitling was well received at court, and Isabel was not so stupid as to risk social suicide by insulting any of her guests.

She quickly made her excuses, and leaving the small gathering of young women around her, she passed through the crowded ballroom and out into one of the receiving salons. As she scanned the crowd, Isabel felt an odd prickle on the nape of her neck. One that said she was being stared at. Casually she turned her head to see what jaded idiot was trying to attract her attention using such vulgar behavior.

At first glance she dismissed him without a second thought, but then she caught the flash of white as he grinned at her, making her snap her head back in his direction. He continued to stare, doing nothing whatsoever to disguise his behavior. The "jaded idiot" was, without doubt, the most handsome man in the room, and Isabel wondered how he had escaped her notice. He must have only just arrived, she reasoned, because it was impossible for her to have overlooked him before now.

He leaned nonchalantly against a pillar near the edge of the room, his arms folded across his chest as he continued to gaze at her with evident admiration. His stare made Isabel feel as if he knew exactly what she looked like wearing only her shift. She glared at him, but instead of being embarrassed at being caught, his smile grew warmer and he nodded at her, issuing a definite invitation.

Flustered by the man's insolent behavior, Isabel turned away and opened her fan, waving it vigorously in front of her. The singular intensity of the stranger's stare was enough to make her pulse quicken and bring a flush to her face. She decided she could not allow the boldness of his behavior to go unchecked. He was an arrogant puppy and would not be the first she had brought to heel with a few well-chosen words.

Snapping her fan shut, she turned back to face him, only to find his attention now otherwise engaged. Lady Maitling was at his side, and, like all well-mannered guests, he gave their hostess his complete attention. Masking her disappointment, Isabel took advantage of the distraction to surreptitiously observe him. He was tall, standing well over six feet she estimated, and the width of his shoulders was clearly emphasized by the simple, yet elegant, cut of his coat. She watched as he leaned down to murmur something in Lady Maitling's ear, his words making the older woman glance up and pin Isabel with an iron stare. It was stupid to pretend not to notice, so Isabel moved toward them without further hesitation, ignoring the handsome stranger until good manners demanded an introduction.

"Lady Isabel Howard, may I present Mr. Rian Connor." The momentary lift of Lady Maitling's brow said she was not fooled by Isabel's show of indifference.

"At your service." The man lifted Isabel's hand to his mouth and lightly brushed his lips across her knuckles, making her skin tingle at the contact.

There was an accent to the rich timbre of his voice, but Isabel was at a loss to place it. She raised her eyes and looked at him, feeling a pulsing throb deep within her. The open expression of admiration said the physical attraction was mutual.

Up close she saw that he was older than she had first thought, and she recalculated his age to be closer to mid-thirties. It was, however, difficult to be certain because the rugged handsomeness of his features was a declaration of a life lived in the elements. If his behavior had not been enough to alert her to his lack of drawing room decorum, then his physical appearance sealed it. But she found herself strangely pleased that he did not find it necessary to display himself like a jeweled peacock. The lack of glittering adornments or intricate, fussy embroidery on either his vest or coat was a welcome relief.

And he wore no wig. Dark, glossy hair, though neatly secured by a length of ribbon at the nape of his neck, fell well past his shoulders. Isabel wondered how it would feel to have its silky heaviness brush over her naked breast. The sudden gleam in Rian Connor's eye said he had read her mind and was wondering the same thing. Her cheeks warmed again, and she quickly looked away. He possessed a roguish charm that was undeniable, and she had to admit she liked the way the corners of his eyes crinkled when something amused him, as their introduction appeared to be doing. Whatever else her feelings, Isabel realized this was no arrogant puppy she was dealing with. It was going to take considerably more than a sharp tap on the nose to bring him to heel.

"Mr. Connor has recently returned from the Americas," Lady Maitling said, regaining Isabel's attention. "Where was it you said again?" The older woman playfully tapped Rian on the arm with her own folded fan.

"The Carolinas," he replied.

That would explain the strange accent Isabel thought as she turned back to smile politely at him. "And what brings you to England, Mr. Connor?" Her manner indicated she couldn't care less why he was here. She was only asking to be polite.

Another grin lifted the corners of his mouth, but before he could answer, Charlotte Maitling interrupted him, delighted to be in possession of facts Isabel was not. With all her connections at court, it was an occurrence that did not happen often.

"Why, Isabel!" she exclaimed. "You did not know Mr. Connor has returned home to attend his brother's wedding?" She paused, raising an eyebrow. "I was certain you could count Liam Connor as one of your many conquests." Turning her attention back to Rian, Charlotte Maitling opened her fan, pretending to use it as a shield to speak behind. "A great many men have lost their"—the pause was just long enough—"*hearts* to our beautiful Lady Isabel," she told him, apparently not caring that the implication included his brother.

Isabel stiffened. The innuendo, magnified by the hesitation, was crystal clear and she wondered if Rian would understand what was really being said. From the undisguised amusement that lifted the corners of his mouth, his understanding was perfect as he looked at both women.

"Oh, Charlotte dear, you know as well as I that Mr. Connor does not come to town as often as many ladies might like, and he is quite ferocious regarding claims on his time. The opportunity has been limited," Isabel retorted with a lift of her chin.

"Ah well, I suppose that would explain how he has managed to avoid your attentions." Lady Maitling laughed as she patted Isabel on the arm. Though her words and attitude gave the appearance of affection, there was a malicious undertone that could not be missed. "But it is a shame we now have to strike his name from our list of eligible young men, don't you agree, Isabel?"

"Yes," she concurred, "a great loss, indeed."

"Of course the addition of a wife is not considered an impediment to some women," Charlotte added slyly.

Rian could feel the undercurrent change as their hostess's remark took a darker turn, and he decided to step in before something regrettable was exchanged. Leaning down, he whispered once more in Lady Maitling's ear, making her laugh out loud while flashing Isabel a triumphant look.

"You really are incorrigible!" Charlotte said, giving Rian the back of her hand, which he kissed with all the grace of a practiced courtier. "Just try not to ruin him, dear," she admonished, turning away with a silky swish of her skirts and treating Isabel's curtsey with complete indifference.

"What did you say to her?" Isabel asked as she resumed an upright position.

"A gentleman never tells," Rian answered gallantly.

"Is that what you are, a gentleman?"

"What do you think?" The grin appeared again.

"Dear God, I hope not!"

Rian burst out laughing. Offering Isabel his arm, he allowed her to steer him through the decorated arch and into the salon she had recently vacated. She was acutely aware that every pair of feminine eyes was now watching them, along with a few masculine ones as well, and she sighed with satisfaction. Perhaps the evening wasn't going to be a total loss after all.

"So tell me, how well acquainted are you with my brother?" Rian asked.

She could hear the laughter behind the question. Did he find everything amusing?

"Truthfully, not as much as I once might have wished to be, which is a pity, as he is most pleasing to the eye."

"But my brother is spoken for, and has been for some time."

"So?" It was Isabel's turn to be amused. "An engagement is not the same as being wed, and, as her ladyship has just remarked, even that is of little consequence if one is so inclined."

"Do you not believe in the sanctity of marriage then?"

"Sanctity of—" She snorted delightfully. "Absolutely not! In my experience, if a man's character is such that he is disposed to constantly seek the company of the opposite sex, then the addition of a wife will not dissuade him from following his nature. I imagine it must be quite liberating to enjoy such freedom," she added with a sly grin of her own.

"Your husband must be a most forward-thinking man," Rian noted as he relieved a passing waiter of two glasses of champagne, "to allow you to voice your opinion so openly."

"I no longer have the bother of that particular inconvenience," Isabel laughed.

"That explains much," he told her.

Unsure whether the comment was one of admiration or disapproval, Isabel decided to change the subject. "I do hope you will not follow your brother's example and seclude yourself in the countryside." Placing her hand on his arm she looked up at him. "To do so would be a terrible waste."

"Perhaps you could suggest some diversion that would require my continued presence in the city."

"Perhaps I could," she murmured.

For the rest of the evening, Isabel made certain to introduce Rian to only the most influential, and affluent, guests in attendance, sharing the most scandalous tales once the danger of being overheard had passed. Some of the stories were true, but most were just fanciful hearsay. Still, Isabel had a quick wit and she sensed that Rian delighted in her company. She also flirted so outrageously with him that he had no other choice but to respond in kind, and at the end of the evening she invited him to her bed.

For Isabel, it was a night of revelation. She had never been so totally and completely satisfied until this moment. With Rian she had found a man whose appetite matched her own, but whose skill was far superior. Dawn was breaking when she finally begged him to stop. His stamina and prowess were beyond all her expectations. Leaning her head against his smooth chest, Isabel heard the gentle, deep rumble as he laughed softly before wrapping his arms about her and holding her to him. Her last thought before she succumbed to sleep was that Rian Connor was surely the most remarkable of men.

Chapter 4

The face Leticia Davenport showed to the outside world was one of calm, untroubled serenity. The truth, however, was far different. Leticia, or Lettie as she was more commonly known, lived in her own particular circle of hell and had done so for the past ten years. Lacking either the resources or courage to change her circumstances, she wore the mask to hide her wretched desperation.

But it had not always been this way.

Once, centuries ago it seemed, she had been filled with virginal fantasies of romance. Dreaming of being wooed and won by a knight in shining armor. The burning, tempestuous passion she longed for was as real to her as the air she breathed even though, in the cold light of day, she knew her hopes of fulfillment were slender. The genetic pool from which Lettie had sprung had not been kind. A plain girl, she had grown into an equally plain and forgettable woman. Eyes set too close together, long nose and thin lips. She looked as if she was being pinched, an image not improved by dull, mousy brown hair that no amount of brushing could make glossy. It was, therefore, a startling shock to all concerned when Phillip Davenport asked for her hand. Startling and, to her parents, most welcome.

Her father, despairing his only child would never find a husband, had been willing to overlook certain proprieties. Discreet inquiries into the affairs of his prospective son-in-law returned assurances that nothing was amiss. Assurances that a more thorough, less hurried investigation would have revealed as being worthless. The result of coin changing hands. But with his own health failing, Lettie's papa was anxious to see his daughter settled and her future secure, so when Phillip formally asked for her hand, her father readily gave his consent.

Generous with his daughter's dowry, Lettie's father had settled not only a sizeable annual income on her, but also gave the newlyweds a townhouse situated in a fashionable neighborhood where they could begin their married life together. It was a beginning the shy girl was ill-prepared to handle.

On their wedding night, Phillip staggered up the stairs and made his way drunkenly to the bedchamber where his nervous bride waited. It wasn't such a bad match, he told himself. His wife was ignorant in the ways of the world and bending her to his will would be a simple matter of course. Moreover her father was ill. Why, the old fool could barely make it through the ceremony, and with any luck he would succumb soon enough. Then Lettie would be very wealthy. Or rather, her husband would be.

The door to the bedroom crashed open and Lettie felt her stomach churn as the strong odor of brandy rolled off her new husband in waves. He wasn't just drunk, she realized. There was something else wrong with him. An intangible that she had no words to describe. Seeing glazed cruelty glint in his eyes, she was suddenly filled with an inexplicable fear that made her mouth go dry. She pulled the bed coverings tightly up around her neck, and in doing so made her husband laugh. It was an ugly sound.

Staggering to the edge of the bed, Phillip sat down heavily and then proceeded to tell his bride, in no small detail, how the only thing he found attractive about her was the wealth that would someday be his. The cruelty of his words cut like a knife and tears sprang from her eyes as Phillip wounded her with every syllable he uttered. Lettie had long ago abandoned any romantic notion of true love, but during their courtship, Phillip had led her to believe he held her in some affection, and promised to treat her with respect. Now she knew it was all lies. Her life was to be lived in complete and total subjugation to his every whim. Nothing else would be acceptable. She existed solely to satisfy his appetites and was granted no voice, no opinions, and no life of her own. With her hopes and dreams shattered irrevocably, Lettie took the first step on her descent into hell.

Attempting to stand, Phillip grabbed the wooden bedpost for support and stared at his wife. "Come here," he slurred drunkenly.

Paralyzed with fear, and unable to move, Lettie watched as Phillip lurched forward and grabbed her by the arm, pulling her out of bed until she stood before him, quaking in terror.

"Undress me," Phillip commanded.

Lettie stared at him uncomprehendingly. What on earth did he mean, undress him? Surely he didn't expect her to remove his clothes? Like a small animal caught in a trap, she stared at him, her eyes wide and unblinking.

"Undress me!" Phillip snapped again, and this time the tone in his voice told Lettie this was exactly what her new husband expected her to do.

With shaking hands she tugged at the heavy brocade coat and then removed the matching waistcoat. Unbuttoning the fine linen shirt, she hesitantly pulled it down his arms, trying not to look at the dark nipples standing out in stark contrast to the pale, almost ghostly white of his skin. He gave a low, vicious laugh as she fumbled with the fastenings on his breeches, keeping her head bent and her eyes fixed on the floor.

The air was filled with an unpleasant odor. The stench of Phillip's unwashed body. His liberal use of cologne could not disguise the rancid smell now he was naked. Lettie felt her stomach roll, and she fought the urge to vomit, suspecting the situation would get much worse if she did so. Closing her eyes, she prayed Phillip would not notice the slight wrinkling of her nose. Pulling her roughly to him, Phillip gripped the neckline of her nightgown and tore it from her body. Her breath left her in a rush of horror. She tried covering herself, but her hands were slapped away as Phillip threw her down on the bed and proceeded to rape her.

It was a night that Lettie would remember in agonizing detail to her dying day. She knew nothing about sex or what to expect from a man, and was totally unprepared. But, as naïve as she was, Lettie knew that what Phillip demanded of her was not normal. It couldn't be. The physical torture and emotional humiliation he forced her to endure was beyond her comprehension. How one person could gain any pleasure from inflicting pain on another was a perversity she had no concept of.

As drunk as he was, Phillip took her three times that night. The last with such violence Lettie prayed to die as he thrust himself inside her broken body, tearing the delicate flesh with each violent lunge. Eventually it was over, and Phillip rolled off her, lay on his back, and fell quickly into a drunken sleep. Lettie shook uncontrollably as she lay next to the man she was now legally bound to. Her body ached all over, and she prayed with all her heart for God to release her from this nightmare. But God didn't hear Lettie's prayers or, if he did, he chose to ignore her. And so she spent night after night in cowering, abject fear as her husband systematically abused her.

She quickly learned that any show of resistance would result in a severe beating, and to spare herself from the worst of her husband's violence, she learned to remain passive and suffer in silence until he was done. She had no idea if this was how it was supposed to be between husband and wife, but she couldn't imagine her father treating her mother in such a way. Compounding her shame was the fact she had not been forced into this marriage. She had entered into it of her own free will, and so to hide her humiliation, she wore a mask of untroubled calm. Refusing to let anyone see how she suffered at the hands of a monster.

Within six months of the marriage, Lettie's father passed away and, as Phillip had anticipated, the bulk of his estate passed to his only child. Lettie's mother went to live with her sister in the country. A separate provision in her husband's will provided for her comfort, for which Lettie was thankful. Phillip, however, made it very clear that there would be no trip to visit her mother to offer consolation for their shared loss. It was characteristic of his cruel nature.

She gained a certain measure of relief when Phillip informed her he had taken a mistress. The affair however, did not last long, and soon he returned to her bed until he found another to amuse him. And so it went on. For ten long, torturous years Lettie's entire existence revolved around the erratic impulses of a madman. The only thing she found to be grateful for was the fact that she had been unable to conceive. Where the fault lay she did not know, but to bring a child into their lives would have been madness indeed. She wanted no flesh of hers to witness the disgrace she suffered. Perhaps God had heard her after all.

But now, into the warped fabric of her life, it appeared as if insanity of another kind was entering.

Phillip had never mentioned any living relatives. In fact, in the early days of their courtship, he had been almost fervent in his declaration of having no family whatsoever. But now the sudden appearance of an unknown cousin filled Lettie with trepidation. This was no child, but a grown woman Phillip was being asked to take in. As starved as she was for companionship, particularly the female kind, Lettie was apprehensive about how her husband would react to another female living with them. Especially if she was attractive. The rapid succession of housemaids was proof that his appetites were not confined to her bed when a pretty face caught his fancy. She offered up a silent prayer that the girl would hold no appeal whatsoever for Phillip, because bearing the familial title of cousin would offer her no protection at all.

Chapter 5

Summer was coming to an end and the light breeze that tugged playfully at the fringe of Catherine's shawl carried with it more than a hint of the cooler days to come. Welcoming the bracing bite, she climbed steadily higher, making her way across hills that were now awash with mounds of purple and white heather. She paused to pick a spray of the tiny flowers, inhaling the fragrant scent before tucking the sprig into her bodice. The wind, having lost interest in her shawl, now concentrated its efforts on her hair. Pulling loose the blond strands held by a tortoiseshell comb, and blowing them across her face. Catherine looked about her. It was more than the wind that brought tears to her eyes as she realized it was time for her to leave, and she could delay no longer. A buyer had been found, and the only home she had ever known was no longer hers.

Carefully she pulled from the pocket of her dress the letter that had arrived almost two weeks before. Smoothing the pages, Catherine scanned the lawyer's precise script, but the words he had written remained the same as when she had first read them.

The Hall had been sold. Jacob Whitney was unable to furnish the name of the new owner as the transaction had been conducted through a third party, but it was the letter's postscript that had incensed her.

"I am discharged on behalf of the new owner's agent to beg your presence at the time possession is relinquished, so certain changes might be discussed with you."

Changes? Why on earth would the new owner think she would want to discuss changes? The Hall belonged to someone else. If the new occupants had a fancy to put a Grecian folly in the middle of the gardens, it was within their rights to do so. The request struck Catherine as odd and rude, and one she was unwilling to accommodate. Aware that news of her circumstances was by now common knowledge throughout the county, she would not permit herself to become an object of satisfaction for another's curiosity.

Angry with Jacob for even considering she might acquiesce, Catherine penned a tersely worded directive stating bluntly that she was not part of the deed. In fact she had no desire to be within the county's borders when possession of The Hall changed hands, and requested that arrangements for her journey south be made with all haste. Details had arrived this morning.

With a sigh she folded the letter and put it back into her pocket, taking one last look around her at all she had ever known. From this distance she could barely make out The Hall through the forest that acted as a natural windbreak. But in only a few more weeks the trees would begin to shed their foliage and the house would be more visible. It was so much more to her than bricks and mortar, and Catherine wondered if the new owner could possibly understand the loss she would feel, knowing this would be the last time she slept beneath its roof. Pulling the shawl over her head, Catherine made her descent. A slight figure burdened by too much grief for one so young.

Early the next morning, as her one small trunk was loaded onto the carriage sent by Jacob Whitney, she said her goodbyes. She felt strangely numb, as if her senses were no longer capable of registering any feeling. And as the carriage made its way down the driveway it took all her resolve not to turn and stare back at the pale faces that watched her leave. Instead, she looked at the road before her and resigned herself to whatever plan fate had in store for her.

* * * *

Lettie was alone in the house when Catherine arrived and it was with an air of barely disguised disbelief she greeted her. The anticipated arrival, having been delayed numerous times over the course of the summer, had made Phillip furious. Questioning his cousin's intentions, he issued threats to withdraw his offer of refuge. Lettie suspected the excuses had been of Catherine's own making, and she did not fault her for them. Even under the best of circumstances it was hard to leave the only home you had ever known to live with strangers.

Now Catherine stood in the hallway, wrapped in a heavy black cloak to ward off the chill, taking in her new surroundings with mild curiosity. Though nowhere near as big as The Hall, her cousin's home was, nevertheless, spacious and elegant. The sound of heels tapping on the black and white tiled floor made her turn and face the woman coming toward her. Pushing back the hood of her cloak, Catherine saw a flash of dismay cross the other woman's face, as if she was disappointed by Catherine's appearance. But then the woman held out her hands, offering a welcome that was warm enough to make Catherine think it was her own anxiety making her see things that were not there.

"Catherine, my dear, dear child," Lettie said, leaning forward to kiss her cold cheek. "We thought you would never arrive. Welcome to your new home. I am Lettie, your cousin Phillip's wife."

The two women looked at each other, assessing both strengths and weaknesses. Catherine sensed at once that the pale, mousy woman before her was hiding something. Lettie's greeting was sincere enough, and Catherine did not doubt she was genuinely pleased to see her, but her cousin's wife could not disguise the glimmer of dread in her eyes. She was keeping a secret, one that weighed heavily on the small woman. Was cousin Phillip already regretting the generosity of his offer? Catherine was too exhausted to speculate. All she wanted was to sleep in a warm bed, and put the past few days of uncomfortable coach travel behind her.

"Thank you," she murmured, squeezing Lettie's hands gently in appreciation.

"Why, you're simply frozen!" Lettie declared, and before Catherine could protest, she found herself being bundled along as Lettie told a maid to bring coffee.

Ushering her into the library, Lettie seated Catherine in an overstuffed chair in front of a freshly made fire. The heat of the flames penetrated her cold, aching limbs, making them tingle, and Catherine sighed. She had thought she would never feel warm again after spending what seemed to be an eternity riding in a most uncomfortable conveyance. Coffee arrived, and she took the cup Lettie poured for her and drank it down. She knew coffee houses were all the rage in larger cities, having been told this by some of the fashionable ladies who had once thought her suitable company to mix with their daughters. Of course if the aim was to impress, then tea would be served. Harder to obtain, and far more costly, tea was a definite status symbol. Catherine had been fortunate to taste it once, and discovered she liked it very much. But she could hardly expect her cousin to indulge her whim for such a luxury. The coffee was hot and chased away the chill, and she accepted a second cup gratefully as she looked about the room.

"You have books," Catherine observed, noting the few volumes scattered about the shelves.

"I must confess this is my favorite room, and reading has become something of a passion of mine." Lettie sounded almost apologetic as she offered Catherine a sandwich.

"I enjoy reading too," Catherine said. Reading material of any kind was a rare commodity at The Hall, and she might have grown up with a complete lack of appreciation for the printed word if not for Edward. Raiding his family library, he made it his personal mission to single-handedly expand her mind and imagination. At least until he was sent away. After that Catherine could only read the newspapers her father sometimes brought home, but more often than not the news was several months old. Unable to stifle a yawn, she flushed with embarrassment. "Forgive me; the journey must have been more tiring than I thought."

Lettie got to her feet at once. "Of course, you must be exhausted. Come dear; allow me to show you to your room so you can rest."

The room that had been put aside for Catherine's use had been tastefully decorated and furnished by Lettie much as she imagined a daughter of her own might have wanted. She was delighted to see from Catherine's expression that her efforts had not been in vain.

"It's a lovely room," Catherine told her. For all its imposing grandeur The Hall never boasted a bedroom as pretty as this one.

Deep rose-colored silk covered the walls while the large four-poster bed was made up with shades of blush and salmon. A pale pink chaise with cerise-colored cushions had been placed before a fire that cheerfully kept any potential chill at bay. Catherine's small trunk had already been unpacked, its meager contents now occupying the drawers of a bow fronted oak chest.

Lettie turned to her. "Now rest, dear. I will make sure that you are woken in plenty of time to dress for dinner."

"I really don't have very much to change into," Catherine said, smoothing the folds of her dark dress. "As you can see I am still in mourning."

Lettie crossed the room to the chest and opened one of the drawers. Lifting out an item, she held it up. Catherine gasped, placing a hand to her face. She had thought the gown her father had bought for Edward's birthday had been beautiful, but it seemed positively shabby compared to the one Lettie held before her.

Silk, the same shade of pink that covered the walls of her room, flowed from Lettie's hands like liquid, begging Catherine to step forward for a closer examination. "May I?" she asked, her hand hovering over the rich fabric.

"Of course."

Everything from the satin bows and seed pearls decorating the bodice, to the elegant lace trim on the sleeves and neckline appealed to Catherine. "It's beautiful," she said, her eyes shining brightly.

"Yes, I think it will suit you very well," Lettie told her.

Catherine's brows pulled together in puzzlement. "But I couldn't possibly wear—"

"It is your cousin's wish," Lettie interrupted, and something in her tone warned Catherine no further explanation would be given.

"But I am still in mourning," Catherine repeated as a feeling of disquiet overcame her. "It would not be proper."

Lettie spoke quietly, but firmly. "If you were a widow then what you say would be true, but as a child suffering the loss of a parent, you have completed a respectable amount of mourning time. You will offer no offense by wearing the gown."

"Regardless, it would not feel right," Catherine said, shaking her head.

Lettie laid the gown across the end of the bed. She placed her hand gently on Catherine's arm. "It is your cousin's wish," she repeated, hesitating before adding, "and he does not suffer disappointment well."

The hand that rested on Catherine's arm trembled slightly, and despite the calmness of Lettie's voice, anxiety filled her eyes. Intuitively Catherine realized that if she did not follow her cousin's wishes, this gentle woman before her would pay the price. Something Catherine did not want on her conscience. "Of course I will wear the dress," she said, "and please forgive me. I was simply overwhelmed by my cousin's generosity."

"Thank you," Lettie said softly. "Now, I will leave you to rest."

Once the door had closed, Catherine walked over to the large window and gazed outside. The room she had been given was situated at the front of the house, and from her vantage point she could easily look beyond the square to the broad avenue filled with traffic passing by. She would have been surprised to know that despite the number of coaches and carriages, this was considered a quiet neighborhood.

What she had seen through the grimy carriage window as the coach approached the bustling city both frightened and thrilled her. So many people and so much noise! She stared in wonder at how close the houses were built to each other. It didn't matter what window she chose to look out of at The Hall; nothing but fields and trees stretched as far as the eye could see. Here it was as if everyone lived on top of each other with no space of their own. How on earth could all these people breathe?

A sudden wave of homesickness threatened, and Catherine felt a tightness in her chest. She told herself in time the feeling would pass, and until then it would serve no purpose to think about what she had left behind. She no longer had any claim on it. Doing her best to brush off her feelings of melancholy, she resumed looking out the window. A carriage turned into the square from the wide thoroughfare, and came to a stop in front of the house. A single occupant alighted, head bent against the rain. A moment later the sound of a man's voice reached her. Though unable to make out the words, Catherine could tell from the strident tone he was angry. This, she assumed, must be her cousin, Phillip Davenport. Perhaps his anger was because she had not remained downstairs in order to greet him upon his arrival. It was a poor beginning, but Catherine was determined he would not find her ungrateful. Turning from the window, she went to sit before the mirror, and stared at her reflection. A dusty and decidedly unkempt visage stared back at her. Moving to the washstand, she poured water from the ewer into the bowl, and quickly washed her face and hands, before returning to tidy her hair. The result wasn't perfect, but given the circumstances, perhaps she could be forgiven.

She waited for someone to fetch her. But there was no knock on the bedroom door, and when the clock on the mantel told her that fifteen minutes had passed, Catherine wondered if she had been mistaken. Perhaps the irate gentleman had not been her benefactor after all. The bed, with its soft pillows looked inviting, and fatigue stole over her. A quick rest, she promised herself. It would refresh her, restoring both mind and body and ensure she would greet her cousin with the proper enthusiasm. Stretching out on the bed, Catherine snuggled against the pillows. A quick rest, no more.

Chapter 6

Phillip was in a foul temper, and did little to hide it. Lettie sat quietly, doing her best not to draw any attention to herself. Drawing on years of experience she willed her limbs not to tremble, her pulse not to race, her breathing to remain calm. When her husband was this enraged, he was beyond reason, and she wished she were invisible. But all she could do was remain still and as quiet as possible, and pray that his rage would burn itself out quickly. It did not always happen. Sometimes her very silence would make the situation worse, provoking his temper down a darker path. Seeing her, so still, so quiet, was all the excuse Phillip needed to strike out either verbally or, as was more usual, physically.

For some inexplicable reason Phillip had been incensed to discover Catherine had already arrived, and was now resting in the upstairs bedroom that had been made ready for her. His rage made no sense. Why should his temper be riled because his cousin was safe beneath his roof? She had, after all, been expected the better part of the summer.

Lettie had tried her best to hide her disappointment at their initial meeting. Despite dark smudges beneath her eyes, and the weary slump of her shoulders, it was impossible not to see how extraordinarily beautiful Catherine was. Something that would not escape Phillip's notice. Now, keeping her countenance calm, Lettie went over all that had happened since Phillip entered the house. His rage had erupted in a profanity-laced tirade with her confirmation of his cousin's arrival. Was Lettie herself the catalyst for his anger? Had Phillip heard something in his wife's voice, a lightness of tone perhaps? Lord knows she had been given no reason in the past ten years to express anything akin to happiness, but was Phillip's anger a perverse reaction to knowing Lettie now had a companion to help fill her lonely days?

She watched him warily, recognizing all too well the signs that warned her what kind of release her husband needed to quell his temper. As his anger burned, so too did the need to slake his lust. Grabbing Lettie by the arm, Phillip jerked her to her feet.

"No, Phillip, not here—the servants!" she begged, revolted by the all too familiar look in his eyes.

"Am I not master in this house?" He growled, turning her around and pushing her face down across the settee's low back.

Lifting her dress and petticoats, he flung them over her head. She offered no protest. To do so would only prolong her humiliation, but she could not stay the silent tears coursing down her cheeks as her husband forced her legs apart. He entered her from behind, making Lettie gasp with each agonizing thrust. She pressed a clenched fist against her mouth, stifling her cries until she heard her husband groan, and a shuddering spasm of his body against hers told her he was done. With his need gratified, Phillip had no more use for his wife. After wiping himself on her petticoat, he readjusted his clothing and left the room.

Lettie silently counted to ten, wanting to be sure Phillip did not return, before pulling down her clothing. The passing years had not diminished the shame she felt, but she hastily wiped away the tears with the back of her hand before settling the mask back into place. The question that had planted itself in her mind the first night Phillip had taken her now crashed inside her head.

What had happened to make her husband the monster he was?

* * * *

The bath water was rapidly cooling so Phillip quickly sluiced himself off and, after toweling dry, lay on his bed to think. Having a hip bath was a luxury few of his peers indulged in, but it had been the first extravagance Phillip had bought with Lettie's money. He couldn't say why such a convenience had caught his fancy, but it set him apart from others. And he enjoyed the distinction, even though he rarely used it more than once a month. Like everyone else, he simply hand washed himself when necessary. Bathing was an indulgence meant more for restoring his humor than cleansing his body. It helped to clear his mind, soothe his temper, and allow him to think.

His focus was now on his newly found cousin. Whatever conflict had resulted in his father being disowned by his family was of little consequence. The man was dead, and his cousin a stranger. As the only living Davenport male, he could have claimed The Hall, but an inheritance so heavily mortgaged was a liability. So he abandoned any claim and decided to let Catherine's home become someone else's headache, especially as he did not possess the means to satisfy the creditors. But even though he had relinquished his rights to bricks and mortar, the damned attorney still had the effrontery to suggest he provide a home for an impoverished girl with no means of support.

He cared nothing for Catherine or her situation, and the idea of giving her shelter filled him with cold indifference. Why should he be expected to support her? It was as if he was being punished because she was not wed. The only reason she even knew of his existence was because she was now destitute. Would she have been so eager to search for his whereabouts had this not been the case? Phillip's derisive snort was answer enough.

It made absolutely no difference that Catherine was equally as ignorant about him. That she knew nothing about the circumstances of his birth or wretched childhood. Or that, even if she had known, she was in no position to change those circumstances. All that mattered to Phillip was knowing she had grown up in a big house with servants, and would, most likely, still be welcome in circles where he would be turned away. Seething at the perceived injustice, he let the bitter taste of revenge coat his tongue and flood his mouth.

When he'd first received Jacob Whitney's letter, he was tempted to burn it, unread, but instead of setting it alight, he opened it. The start of the letter repeated information he'd already been told, but then Jacob made an unexpected suggestion. Perhaps Phillip might fulfill his duty to his cousin by helping to arrange a suitable match for her. He frowned and read the letter again, to be certain he understood. The attorney seemed confidant Catherine would have no difficulty in securing a husband, and there was only one thing that would prompt a man to ask for a hand that came with no dowry. His cousin must be very beautiful indeed.

"Marriage?" he asked Jacob's representative at their next meeting.

The small mousy man, fully apprised of the situation, nodded. "Mr. Whitney assures me that Miss Davenport is most accomplished."

"I care nothing for her accomplishments. Is she so comely that she could tempt a man with no dowry to offer?" He smiled sourly, recalling his own path to connubial bliss.

"I am told she is fair," the other attorney stated. "Very fair indeed."

Phillip gave him a disdainful stare. "All women could be considered fair. I need details." And he proceeded with a list of questions.

Though Jacob's response was favorable, Phillip was still hesitant. The notion of beauty was apt to change according to the viewer, and, if dire circumstances were also a factor, it was reasonable to assume some embellishments would have been made. But Phillip was not interested in finding a suitable husband for his cousin. Marriage was an agreement that depended on far too many variables beyond his control. He looked instead for a simpler arrangement. One where the only matter of concern would be financial, and that was something Phillip could dictate. Especially as he enjoyed an understanding with the proprietor of a certain establishment.

A place where the walls were dark and filled with mirrors.

A place where, for the right price, any depraved appetite could be satisfied.

A place where a girl's virginity could command a king's ransom.

His proposal had been tentatively accepted with the proviso that Catherine met all expectations. The whoremaster was a cautious man, but he sweetened the deal with the promise that Phillip could watch as his cousin was broken in.

And so Phillip had set his plan in motion with meticulous care. To all concerned, the attorney in particular, he gave the outward appearance of helping a destitute relative and, giving weight to the lie, he instructed his wife to decorate and furnish a bedroom for his cousin. But it was never his intention to have Catherine set foot inside his house.

People went missing all the time. They vanished without a trace, and a young girl who was a stranger to the city, traveling with no relative to escort her...it wasn't so difficult to believe. Tragic yes, but not unheard of. Still he had to be careful. Others would know Catherine's destination and Phillip had to make sure that the finger of suspicion was never pointed at him. The pivotal part of his plan was to make sure she was abducted before she ever arrived in the city. So he paid handsomely for her to be taken at the last coaching station where horses were changed. But it never happened, and with no explanation as to why. Phillip's anger spilled over into fury, making him vent his anger and frustration on his wife. His cousin was supposed to have already been on her way to the new life he had chosen for her, not resting upstairs! Now if Catherine were to disappear it might look suspicious.

Unless, unless...it were to happen while she was with his wife.

An abduction in the park perhaps?

Phillip felt his spirits lift. If Lettie were to witness Catherine's disappearance it would give the tragic event credibility, and definitely remove any suggestion of his own involvement. He would just have to make certain that once his cousin Catherine disappeared, it would be a permanent arrangement.

After getting up from the bed, Phillip went to the bureau and put ink to parchment. A few lines confirming his resolve, and explaining how an unforeseen circumstance had forced a change of plan. Quickly he outlined an alternate proposal for delivering Catherine to the man who would ultimately control her fate. The clock on the mantel chimed the hour, the delicate sound totally at odds with the room's occupant. Melting some wax, Phillip quickly affixed his seal and arranged for the letter's delivery before dressing for dinner.

Chapter 7

Staring at her reflection in the tall standing mirror, Catherine hardly recognized the image looking back at her. The gown's pink hue infused her skin with warmth she did not feel, and despite assurances that it was perfectly respectable, Catherine found the décolletage a little too revealing. She bit her lip and frowned slightly. The gown seemed far too extravagant for a simple family dinner, but perhaps, she reasoned, her discomfort was due to a general lack of knowledge as to what was considered socially acceptable. It had been a long time since she had needed to dress for dinner.

The maid, thoughtfully sent by Lettie to assist her, had proved to be quite skillful with arranging Catherine's hair. Now her heavy locks fell in a cascade of curls, interwoven with pink ribbons, over one bare shoulder. The overall effect was an appearance of fetching innocence, and while Catherine might not think the dress appropriate, she knew that she looked pretty.

She glanced at her own dark dress lying on the bed and for a moment was tempted to disobey her cousin's wishes. But then she recalled the look on Lettie's face. One that reinforced the notion such defiance would not go unpunished, except it wouldn't be Catherine bearing the brunt of her cousin's displeasure. Her face crinkled in an expression of disbelief. Surely Phillip would not be so unreasonable over something as mundane as a dress? But a voice in the back of her mind told her not to dismiss his wife's alarm. Who knew him better? If it was important that she wear the gown Phillip had chosen, then she would wear it. If not to please her cousin, then to appease his wife.

It was impossible not to feel the tension in the house. It was so thick and oppressive, it threatened to crush Catherine the moment she stepped into the room. Lettie had warned her that Phillip was almost fanatical about punctuality, particularly at meal times, but dressing for dinner had taken longer than she anticipated. Hearing the clock strike the quarter hour, Catherine kissed Lettie on the cheek, and apologized for her tardiness, seeing a sudden glimpse of unease flare briefly in the other woman's eyes. Whether the emotion had been shared by accident or design, Catherine could not tell, but in any case it was quickly hidden behind Lettie's impenetrable mask.

Turning, Catherine now looked for the first time at her cousin, and her dislike was both instantaneous and vehement. She might not be aware of the current trend in women's fashions, but she knew when a man was looking at her inappropriately. Her cousin wasn't simply looking at her, his stare lingered, fixing on her in such a way she could not help but be uncomfortable at his scrutiny. But had he given her only the briefest of glances, Catherine still would have found his observation distasteful. Hesitantly she closed the distance between them, fighting hard not to let her feelings show. Though she was now dependent on this man's goodwill, she trusted her instinct. She would have to be on her guard, at least until she was able to determine the true nature of her cousin's character.

Swallowing nervously she said, "Cousin Phillip, I can never thank you enough for the kindness you have shown me."

"Dearest Catherine, how could I do anything else?" The sound of his voice made her feel as if something slimy had slithered out from beneath a rock, and she suppressed a shudder when he reached for her hand. "My only regret is that ignorance of your existence made it impossible for the offer to have been given sooner."

The rank odor of his breath assaulted her, and she was forced to turn her head away. All she could do was hope Philip would mistake the movement as an indication of her relief at his generosity. Taking a deep breath she forced herself to look back at him. It mattered not how odious she found him; her debt to him was one that could never be repaid. Something she could never forget. "Your gift is most generous," she told him, gesturing with her free hand to the rose hued cloud she wore.

His expression shifted. A shadow darkened his features and sent a shiver down her spine. "It is most becoming," Phillip agreed. "Come, you must be famished, and the hour is getting late."

Catherine's initial dislike of her only living blood relative did not change with the meal. Whatever manners Phillip may have had, he chose to disregard them at his own table. The soup course was an auditory nightmare of sounds better suited to a farmyard feeding trough. And for some reason known only to him, he abandoned the use of utensils altogether during the main meal. Instead he shoveled food into his mouth with his fingers, all the while insisting on conversing with her, and not caring that particles fell from his mouth onto the table and his clothes. Revolted by his behavior, Catherine felt more than a little nauseated. She wanted to protest, but a glance at Lettie's raised brow was enough of a warning to keep silent.

Her appetite completely ruined, Catherine wondered if it was possible Jacob Whitney had made a mistake about her familial tie to Phillip Davenport. Perhaps having the same name was nothing but a coincidence. Davenport was not so very unusual a name, but as she continued to observe him, Catherine was forced to acknowledge physical similarities between Philip and portraits of her grandfather that she could recall. Davenport blood ran through Phillip's veins as surely as it ran through hers.

Finally the torturous ordeal came to an end, and Phillip joined the two women as they adjourned to the salon. After pouring himself a whisky, he offered a glass of sweet wine to Catherine, which she politely refused. He did not offer his wife anything at all, and continued to ignore her as he had all through dinner. It was as if she didn't exist. Lettie did not appear to be concerned by her husband's behavior. If Catherine had to guess, she would think it was a common occurrence, but it did not excuse Phillip's rudeness and lack of manners. She turned her head to speak to Lettie, but before she could say anything, Phillip quickly drained his glass and came to stand before her. Taking her hand, he raised it to his lips, bade her good night and marched smartly from the room. A few moments later both women jumped at the sound of the front door being slammed shut.

"Did I say something to offend?"

Lettie gave a sigh of relief and patted Catherine's hand. "No dear, of course not. You will, I am sure, soon accustom yourself to some of your cousin's peculiarities."

"What sort of peculiarities?"

"At times his behavior can appear to be quite unfathomable, and erratic." She squeezed Catherine's hand, and the mask slipped. "But you must not let him frighten you."

Catherine narrowed her eyes slightly. "Why would you think he would frighten me?"

"Oh dear, did I say that? That's not at all what I meant." In her haste to try to cover up her blunder, Lettie's true feelings were revealed, making Catherine wonder how many times her cousin had frightened his wife. And why. "You must forgive me," Lettie continued, "Phillip is forever telling me what a silly goose I am, always saying the wrong thing."

She offered nothing further to explain her remark, and Catherine did not pursue it. But she did not think Lettie had misspoke.

"No matter." Catherine smiled, determined to put the other woman at ease,. "I am certain we are more than capable of providing our own entertainment." For the first time since her arrival, Lettie gave Catherine a smile that was free of any restraint, and it lit up her face. "Oh Catherine, I do hope we will be the very best of friends."

"Of course we will. How could we be anything else?"

Whatever was amiss in Lettie's life, whatever secrets she chose to keep to herself, Catherine was positive about one thing. The woman seated next to her was desperately unhappy. And had been for a very long time.

* * * *

Phillip was totally captivated. Having assumed the report of his impoverished cousin's beauty to be somewhat exaggerated, he was stunned to find the truth was a very different matter. The description had been woefully inadequate, so much so it occurred to Phillip that perhaps the fool of a lawyer had been looking at an entirely different girl when he made his account. Or perhaps age was impeding the man's sight. Whatever the reason, Catherine was a vision.

Her voice, thanking him for his kindness, had been a throbbing purr to his ears, and as he scanned her upturned face he found himself consumed with a sudden, overwhelming need. All reason was destroyed by the one strident, demanding thought pounding inside his head. He had to have her! Take her body, possess her flesh, and not be content until he had satisfied himself completely. Never before had such an overpowering urge filled him, sweeping through every fiber of his being, and dominating his senses.

Closing his eyes, Phillip felt waves of lust roll in his belly as he imagined the firm roundness of her breasts filling his cupped palms. All thoughts of delivering Catherine to the man he had already promised her to vanished, especially after he took her hand and pressed his lips against the smooth skin. Though she tried to disguise it, he had felt her shudder at the feel of his mouth on her flesh. It ignited a flame within him. So much the better. It was more than he could have hoped for. And the subtle shift in her body language said she would not willingly let him take her. Which would make the experience all the more exciting.

And now the idea of being *allowed* to watch as Catherine was broken in became ludicrous. No force imaginable was going to persuade him to turn her over and place her in the hands of another. At least not until after he had personally introduced her to the pain and pleasure that would become her reality.

Chapter 8

Catherine wasn't sure what made her wake. There were so many unfamiliar sounds, it could have been anything. The house as it settled or perhaps the barking dog beyond her window. But then the prickly feeling at the nape of her neck told her it was neither of those things. Dread came over her, causing a tight feeling in her chest and a sudden sour taste in the back of her mouth.

Something was out of place.

The room felt wrong, and Catherine had the oddest feeling she was no longer alone. Turning her head, she looked at the bedroom door, which stood slightly ajar, a faint light spilling over the threshold from the lamp that sat on the narrow hall table. A lamp that Lettie told her remained lit through the night. Catherine frowned, certain she had closed the door after she and Lettie had said their good-nights to each other. At least she thought she'd closed the door, but now, with her senses groggy, she could not be sure.

This time a noise did reach her. In the dark it was barely a whisper, and it sounded very much like a breath or a sigh. The feeling of dread intensified, and Catherine knew someone else was in the room with her.

"Who's there?" She peered into the gloomy shadows at the end of her bed, wishing her voice was not so tentative. "Lettie?"

The sound of fabric being rubbed together by movement brought her fully awake, and turning to the bedside table she searched for the candle so she might light it.

"I would prefer you did not do that," a man said.

A shiver ran down Catherine's back. Having been forced to listen to it earlier in the evening, she had no difficulty recognizing her cousin's voice. "Cousin Phillip? Is that you?" Blinking impatiently, she was able to make out a figure standing in the shadows beyond the foot of the bed.

"Indeed, my dear, and I am at your service."

Phillip stumbled forward and sat heavily on the end of the bed. The stench of strong spirits rolled off him in nauseating waves. It was a smell Catherine was all too familiar with, and in a moment of perversity she fought the urge to laugh. She was no stranger to dealing with a man who was drunk.

"It is late, cousin, and I think perhaps you have mistaken which room you are in," she said, keeping her voice firm and even.

The sound that spilled into the darkness was ugly, and it took Catherine a few moments to realize it was Phillip laughing. Only the high-pitched giggle was more suited to a child. Coming from a grown man it sounded obscene. At that moment the moon emerged from behind a cloud, spilling silvery light across the bed and illuminating Phillip's face. His expression caused a spasm of icy fear to snake through her, and realizing she was heading down an unfamiliar path, Catherine felt her resolve begin to unravel. Her father, no matter how drunk he got, had never become lecherous with her. Not even on those rare occasions when he mistook her for her mother.

"I've made no mistake," Phillip told her, "I've come to collect what is owed me."

"Owed?"

She was confused. Had Jacob Whitney told him of the hundred pounds? Was Phillip expecting the money as well? He began to move closer, slithering his way toward her. Catherine shrank back against the pillows, unable to move as he reached out and took a lock of her long hair, rubbing the silky smoothness between his fingers.

"Surely you realize," he said in a voice that suddenly carried no sign of drunkenness, "my generosity comes with a price. You cannot expect to enjoy the hospitality of my home without offering some form of recompense. Make no mistake, cousin, unlike others, I am very much master in my own house, and everything within its walls I lay claim to."

Staring hard into his face, Catherine recognized the same shadow she had seen on his features earlier that evening. A shadow that told her Phillip was more dangerous now than he had been a few moments ago. Her father had been drunk many, many times, but his affliction was due to melancholia. What she knew of drink-fueled lust had come from an overheard discussion between two of The Hall's kitchen maids. Recalling the conversation, she remembered that a quick slap across the face should be enough to thwart any lascivious behavior. She hoped this was true, because she had never faced anything like this before. Fear rose, intensifying the pain in her chest, but Catherine could not allow it to gain the upper hand. It was imperative she keep a clear head.

Struggling to hold her emotions in check, she hissed at her cousin. "If you do not leave this instant, I will scream loud enough for your wife to hear me!"

He let the lock of hair fall from his fingers and sniggered at her like an overgrown schoolboy caught in some mean-spirited prank. The sound made her skin crawl. "Oh, you foolish, foolish girl," Phillip sneered. "Do you honestly think that my dear, sweet, *terrified* Lettie will come to your aid? Even if she were to hear you scream, she has enough sense to place her pillow over her head to cover the sound. No one in this house," he continued, gloating triumphantly, "will come to your rescue."

He leaned forward, close enough that Catherine could smell the odor of his body beneath the stench of alcohol. "Besides, I would like it very much if you did scream. It will make everything so much more enjoyable."

The tenuous grip Catherine had on her courage slipped, and a paralyzing fear threatened to replace it. That Phillip meant her harm was beyond question, and she opened her eyes wide with horror as he reached for the bedclothes she held fast about her. The reality of her situation became very clear. She had to move, and quickly.

Loosening her grip on the coverings, she leaned forward and slapped Phillip across the face. The sound of hand striking flesh seemed to echo in the room, but it was nothing compared to Phillip's start of surprise. Her unexpected attack gave her the time needed to throw back the covers, and scramble from the bed. She ran for the bedroom door, but Phillip recovered more quickly than she realized. With a snarl of rage he barreled into her, effectively using their combined body weight to close the door Catherine had just managed to pull halfway open. She shrieked in alarm and frustration as Phillip pinned her to the solid panel, allowing his hands to familiarize themselves with the contours of her body through the thin fabric of her nightgown.

Don't cry, that's what he wants you to do. Think, Catherine, think!

Her mind was in a frenzied turmoil and, as she tried to anticipate her cousin's next move. Phillip gripped her shoulder and roughly spun her around. The imprint of her hand glowed like a brand across his cheek, and her mouth lifted with satisfaction at the sight. Her cousin, however, was outraged. No woman had ever struck him back, and none dared to strike him first. The idea was intolerable. He was the one who inflicted the pain, and Catherine would pay dearly for her insolence. She watched as he raised his free hand, realizing his intent too late to prevent him from striking her.

Her head snapped back, bouncing against the door with enough force to cause an ocean of stars to explode before her eyes. A master at this game, Phillip used her disorientation to his advantage. Seizing the front of her nightgown he bunched the material in his fist, pulling her toward him and away from any chance of escape.

With an almost casual indifference, he slapped Catherine across the face several more times. Each blow made her stumble backwards. It wasn't until she felt the bed pressed against the back of her legs that she channeled her fear. Curling her own hands into fists, Catherine battered Phillip about the head and shoulders, but her counterattack offered only a temporary reprieve. As she tried to pull away, her nightgown tore, and she lost her balance, leaving Phillip with a handful of lace and a look of almost comical surprise on his face. Ignoring what was left of the torn garment that was now slipping off her shoulder, Catherine tried to run around the bed, hoping to put it between herself and her cousin, but her foot became tangled in the covers on the floor, she stumbled, and struck her head against the carved post. The room tilted at an odd angle as she fell to the ground.

* * * *

A dull, muffled pounding in her head made Catherine moan softly, and the coppery smell of blood made her wrinkle her nose. Moisture on her upper lip would seem to indicate a nosebleed, but whether it was bleeding still was hard to say. Her mouth and one side of her face throbbed painfully. Probing gently with the tip of her tongue she found her lower lip was swollen and even the most careful of movement brought a jolt of pain that spiked along one side of her jaw. She tried raising her head to look around, but the lid of her left eye seemed to be fused closed and would not open. Thankfully, the right one appeared undamaged. Surfacing to total awareness, Catherine realized she was at the mercy of a degenerate. There would be no reasoning with her cousin. He had crossed the line separating sanity from madness, although she doubted Phillip had simply stepped over it. His actions proclaimed his leap across the divide had been conducted with joyous abandon.

She was lying on her stomach, spread-eagle on the bed and was now completely naked. Phillip had torn what was left of her nightgown into long strips which he'd used to bind her wrists and ankles to the bedposts. A cautious tug confirmed the tightness of the bindings, and for the moment escape did not seem possible. Gooseflesh raised across her body and the hair at the nape of her neck stood on end as fear took a downward spiral into complete terror.

Her thoughts became an incoherent jumble of images as she tried to fight through the pain in her head, until with a sudden piercing clarity, Catherine recalled the rest of that overheard conversation between the two maids. The lustful drunk, angered by the slap, had taken his revenge by raping a different girl. Her presence undetected, Catherine had listened to every lurid detail of the rape, and, though filled with disgust and revulsion, she had continued to listen until the tale concluded.

"My love, you have returned to me," Phillip whispered softly next to her ear.

Catherine jerked her head up, a jarring scream of pain making her eyes fill with tears. A series of violent tremors coursed through her as Phillip stroked down her nude body, lingering to caress her buttocks before whispering softly down the back of her thighs. The bed sagged as he bent over her, and, with his tongue, retraced the path his hand had just traveled, alternating between licking and cruelly biting her flesh.

Her tears flowed freely, her humiliation becoming something else entirely at the feel of his hand sliding between her legs. She gasped, biting her tongue as his fingers violated her body, compelling her to cry out. Satisfied that she had given him the reaction he desired, Phillip stopped what he was doing and grabbed a handful of long, blond hair. Twisting it around his fist, he arched Catherine's head and shoulders painfully up from the bed, testing the limits of her bonds. Keeping a firm grip on her hair with one hand, he awkwardly scrambled off the bed and moved into her line of sight.

"Look at me!" he snarled, giving a vicious tug on her hair while his other hand grasped her face. After releasing his hold, he began to undress. Unused to performing the task with no help, Phillip struggled. His efforts made the slack muscles and wasted flesh jiggle obscenely. Sparse, coarse hair covered his pasty white chest before straggling in a narrow line down to the wiry bush from which his engorged penis jutted. Catherine's right eye opened even wider in terror as she watched him wrap his fingers around himself, and move his hand along his shaft.

"Soon, my sweetling," Phillip crooned in a singsong voice.

Like an animal caught in a snare, Catherine pulled on her bonds. But her efforts only tightened the knots and turned the fabric into ropes of steel that cut into her skin. Phillip moved, and she felt a breath across the swell of her buttocks as his mouth slavered over her flesh. His hand moved faster between his legs. Instinctively she clenched her muscles and gritted her teeth as she felt him slobbering. One hand suddenly dug into her flesh, sharp nails cruelly biting into her as Phillip reached his climax. In a series of jerky movements, he ejaculated across her body, moaning and dribbling his semen until his cock began to soften in his hand. Catherine's terror now scaled new heights, but fear of what her cousin might do if she slipped into oblivion that made her fight to keep her senses.

"I must apologize, my sweet, for losing control," Phillip murmured as he stroked her hair. "But do not fret, for I only need a moment and then it will be my pleasure to introduce you to all the secrets of the bedchamber."

Catherine's muscles seized, freezing her in place. The arrogance in Phillip's voice terrified her more than anything else. He could do anything he wanted, and she could not stop him. The realization, delivered on a quick moving wave of absolute panic, roused something inside of her. Awkwardly she raised her head. Her good eye was filled with a deep, bottomless hatred as, with all the force she could muster, she spat in her cousin's face.

Wiping the glob of spittle from his cheek, Phillip narrowed his eyes before telling her coldly, "You can, of course, expect to be punished for that insolence."

Catherine collapsed onto the bed, her moment of defiance taking what little strength she had. She heard the musical clink of crystal as her sadistic torturer poured himself a drink. He had obviously brought the decanter and glass with him because there had been none in her room earlier. His thirst appeased, Phillip smacked his lips and then Catherine heard a sharp whistle that sounded familiar, but one she could not place. The sound came again, and then once more, before recognition suddenly dropped into place. It was the rush of air being displaced by a riding crop.

"I don't think you quite understand the reality of your situation," Phillip said, "but I take full responsibility for the oversight. Allow me to explain, cousin dear. I can do whatever I want with you, and to you, and when I am done you will be given to others who will use you just as thoroughly."

"You're mad!" Catherine said through gritted teeth, ignoring the grinding ache in her jaw. "I will never submit to you!"

The obscene childlike giggle came again. "I do like your spirit," Phillip told her. "Admirable but pointless. How do you propose to stop me, Catherine? There is nothing you can do. Absolutely nothing."

A high-pitched whistle filled the air and made her shudder. She knew all too well what Phillip intended to do with the riding crop, but she had no way of knowing that this was his favorite way to arouse himself. She tensed as she waited for the first blow. Inexplicably she saw Lettie's face in her mind, and she understood the reason for the small woman's fear.

Lettie had suffered—was still suffering—untold abominations at the hands of this brute who called himself her husband.

The first blow drove all thoughts of Lettie from Catherine's mind as an explosion of pain ripped through her. The intense burning sensation screamed that her flesh had been torn open, and a warm trickle of blood ran down her side. Turning her head, she bit down on the pillow, denying Phillip the added satisfaction of hearing her scream. She clenched her jaws together. The searing ache that throbbed along the side of her face was swallowed up by the darker agony overtaking the rest of her body. Hands pulled at her, and Catherine, recognizing the mercy they held, allowed herself to be swept down into a midnight chasm.

Chapter 9

Blow after blow Phillip rained down on the vulnerable body before him, each frenzied swing bringing him closer to his release. Spittle flew from his mouth, landing on Catherine's pale flesh, and mingling with her blood and hair. With each successive strike, his erection grew steadily harder until he reached the point of imminent release. Throwing aside the whip, he took a ragged breath, and looked at his handiwork, blinking slowly as if seeing it for the first time.

From shoulders to calves Catherine was a latticework of ugly red welts and split skin. Her glossy blonde hair was dulled and matted with blood. It suddenly occurred to Phillip that his deal regarding Catherine's future had now been rendered null and void. The proprietor prided himself on his girls having flawless skin. He would be most displeased by such abuse. But Phillip wasn't concerned. If Catherine offended the sensibilities of the proprietor's clientele, there were other brothels where the paying customer was not so fastidious, and a daily dose of laudanum would help keep a potentially troublesome whore agreeable. He stared at the body before him, the throb in his cock becoming almost painful as it demanded release. Phillip licked his lips. Catherine was still, offering no sound or movement. Confident she was no longer capable of resisting, he quickly sliced through the bonds at her wrists and ankles and rolled her to her back.

Catherine surfaced back to consciousness on a violent spasm of pain. Her entire body was on fire, and she bit the inside of her cheek to prevent herself from crying out. She couldn't imagine the horrors Phillip wanted to visit upon her, but she suspected he was nowhere near finished. Instinct, and her will to survive, made her push the agony of her body into a place where it would not compromise her mental focus. She told herself that though she had little hope of overpowering him, escape was still possible if she kept her wits about her.

Continuing to feign unconsciousness, she surreptitiously watched her attacker's movements through the half-closed lid of her one good eye. Repositioning her was causing Phillip some difficulty. Thankfully, alcohol had dulled his senses or he might have noticed the subtle resistance a supposedly inert body was giving him. Catherine prayed silently for God to help her through this nightmare.

Calling on willpower she didn't know she possessed, she forced herself to remain motionless when Phillip moved down her body, and pushed her thighs apart with his hands. The feel of his hot breath on the inside of her legs, and the first touch of his probing fingers was almost too much. It was as if something vile and truly evil was trying to root itself inside her, in a place where it could contaminate her entire being. Realizing this would be her only chance, and surprise her only weapon, Catherine decided to strike.

The movement as she raised her leg made Phillip lift his head, and she kicked him squarely in the face, feeling his nose break beneath her heel. He shrieked in pain, and lunged for her. Ignoring the fiery pain in her back, Catherine scrambled up the bed away from him.

"Bitch!" he snarled in a voice thick with blood as he caught her by the wrist.

Seizing the heavy brass candlestick from the nightstand, she curled her fingers around the stem as her fear spiked, giving her the strength to bring the heavy base crashing across Phillip's temple. Surprise filled his eyes before he collapsed, and his fingers loosened their hold on her.

The makeshift weapon slipped from her fingers and fell to the floor. Catherine's limbs jerked and twitched as violent spasms washed through her. Staring at the still form lying half across her legs, she wondered if she had killed her cousin, but a twitch of his fingers confirmed he still lived. *Pity,* a voice inside her head sighed before telling her with the gravest urgency that she had to get away. After freeing one leg from beneath her cousin's cumbersome weight, Catherine braced her foot against Phillip's side, and pushed until she had enough leverage to release the other. A moan emphasized the need to move quickly.

She tried standing, but a wave of agonizing pain made her collapse to the floor, fall forward on all fours, and vomit up what little she had eaten at dinner. Shakily she wiped her mouth with the back of her hand. She needed to concentrate, and get away from her cousin before he regained his senses. If he caught her again he would kill her, of this she had no doubt. The pain that racked her body was now moving through her in excruciating swells. Something she could not ignore. Crawling across the floor, Catherine was able to reach the door, where she grasped the round porcelain knob with both hands, and pulled herself upright. Though the agony was almost beyond her limited endurance, her legs did not give way this time. Trembling from head to toe, she opened the door.

She refused to look back, afraid that if she did, she would see Phillip looming behind her. Instead she held on to the door, struggling to catch her breath while remaining on her feet. Out the corner of her eye she noticed her heavy traveling cloak now lay across a chair. The maid who had helped her dress earlier must have brushed it out and returned it to the room. Needing something to shield her nakedness, Catherine put it on, and then, with a strangled sob, she stumbled out into the dimly lit hallway.

Escape was her only thought. She had to get out of this house and away from the madman in the room behind her. Put as much distance as possible between herself and this living nightmare, and she needed to move before her strength gave out. Before her cousin came to his senses.

One step at a time.

Each step sent an arc of pain shooting up her legs to her lower back where it exploded in a fireball. Grimly she hung on, making her way, step after step, down the hall, leaving behind, as evidence of her passing, a series of bloody footprints. The staircase provided its own set of problems, but holding onto the banister, Catherine took one torturous stair at a time. When she finally reached the bottom, her lungs were on fire. Each breath felt as if her chest were being sliced open from the inside, and, adding to her misery, a river of sweat rolled down her back, stinging the open lash wounds.

With a hand over her mouth to muffle the sharp rasp of her own breathing, Catherine strained her ears, trying to hear if her progress had alerted anyone else in the house. The fact that her screams had brought no one to her aid did not mean others in the house were unaware of her movements. Nothing but a heavy, ominous silence greeted her, so she made her way across the black and white tiled floor to the front door with as much haste as she could muster. It was difficult to believe that only a matter of hours had passed since she'd first walked over this same floor and accepted Lettie's outstretched hands in welcome. An act that seemed so strange to her now, it might have happened to someone else entirely.

The only obstacle between Catherine and freedom was the heavy front door. She closed her fingers around the ornate iron handle, rotated it first one way and then the other. The door refused to yield. She twisted it harder, but it still did not give. The very real fear of what her cousin would do if he were to appear on the upper landing and see her made her pound her fist weakly against the decorative paneling. Sobs filled her throat, threatening to spill out and break the silence around her. A hand closed over her mouth, stifling the scream that lay just below the surface. Catherine whirled, clenched fist almost striking the smaller woman standing before her.

"Shhh!" Lettie held a finger to her lips, the single flickering candle she had placed on the floor dimly illuminating her face while throwing grotesque shadows on the wall behind them. The mask had dissolved, and Catherine could see her own horror reflected in the older woman's eyes.

From the swollen contours of her face, Catherine used her one good eye to stare in bewilderment as Lettie knelt on the floor, and gently raised Catherine's foot, slipping on a soft-soled shoe. She repeated the action with the other foot, and if she noticed the bloodstains on Catherine's bare legs, she made no comment.

"You cannot go barefoot," Lettie whispered. It seemed the least of Catherine's problems.

Getting to her feet, the smaller woman reached for the bolts on the door and slid them free of their housings. Catherine had never known any door at The Hall to be bolted unless the threat of inclement weather gave cause, so she had not thought to check. Now the iron handle turned easily, allowing the door to swing open smoothly and reveal the fog laden street outside. Rolling in and out, the thick mist hid everything. Revealing nothing beyond an arm's length and also muffling all sound.

Lettie briefly squeezed Catherine's hand. "You must go," she urged. "He will surely murder you if you stay."

"Come with me," Catherine begged.

Shaking her head, Lettie released the hand she'd been holding and took a step back. Catherine frowned, trying to understand why this gentle, kind woman would choose to remain with such a monster. She opened her mouth to ask as much, but, startled by a noise from within, Catherine stumbled out into the night, and was quickly swallowed up by the fog.

Chapter 10

Isabel had no regrets about taking Rian as her lover, but, despite her best efforts, she knew no more about him now than she had the first time they'd tumbled in her sheets. Though charming and attentive, he remained maddeningly elusive when it came to revealing anything of a personal nature. He deflected her questions with ease, leaving Isabel with no other choice but to turn to others to satisfy her own curiosity.

Rudimentary gossip confirmed that Rian Connor had, until recently, been the owner of a prosperous plantation in the Americas. Isabel had no idea what crop he grew, nor did she care, but she was curious as to the reason behind his return to England. That it was a permanent change was confirmed by the rumor he was in the process of liquidating all his holdings in the Carolinas, and, if only half the accounting were true, it would explain why he had no interest in her wealth. It also led to speculation that attending his brother's forthcoming marriage wasn't the only reason for his return.

The man himself would neither confirm nor deny the tales being spread about him, and only laughed good naturedly at Isabel's attempts to wheedle facts from him. Finding her efforts so easily thwarted was a new experience for her, and one she did not enjoy. When pressed by others for details about the enigmatic Rian Connor, she pretended to know far more than she actually did. Putting a finger to her lips, she would smile and shake her head, thus giving the impression she knew a great deal, but was sworn to secrecy. Those who knew her well, a handful at most, saw through the charade and became intrigued. If Isabel could not discover Rian's secrets, then who could? And a man about whom so little was known had to have secrets.

Despite the geographical distance separating the brothers, Rian and Liam had managed to remain close. Well pleased by his brother's choice of bride, Rian knew it was a union that would not only substantially increase Liam's standing as a landowner, but also give him a voice in political circles should he choose to use it. Isabel had never regarded the younger Connor with anything more than a passing interest. His face was handsome enough, she had been overheard to say, but he did not attract her in any other aspect. Now she found it difficult to believe the young man was singlehandedly responsible for his brother's return. Affection for a sibling, no matter how deep, was no reason for a man to turn his back on untold wealth and prestige. Something more significant than a matrimonial union had to be involved. For the time being, Isabel contented herself with the knowledge that if she had no answer, neither did anyone else.

Rian, his mysterious past and unknown future, remained the topic of conversation wherever they went. This suited Isabel perfectly because if he was being talked about, then so was she. In every salon and drawing room someone could be counted on to dredge up and recirculate what little was known of Rian's abrupt departure so many years ago. A violent disagreement between father and son was common knowledge, but the cause less so. It seemed the gossips were undecided whether heavy losses at the gaming tables or an unsuitable love affair was the culprit. Perhaps a combination of both. Still, it was but a matter of days before Rian sought passage aboard ship, and, at barely seventeen, he broke his mother's heart.

With no denial or confirmation from her lover, Isabel was certain the truth differed greatly from the conjecture whispered behind painted fans. It should have been enough that she had managed to capture the enigmatic elder Connor, but Isabel had unwittingly given the gossip mill more grist for the grind.

Having kept Rian longer than any previous man she had been involved with since the death of her husband, Isabel made an astonishing discovery. She did not want her affair with Rian to end anytime soon. In fact she did not want it to end at all. More unsettling however, was finding herself considering the idea of marriage. It was a notion that grew more appealing the longer she thought on it, but she sensed getting Rian before a man of the cloth would be no easy task. In all her other affairs she had been the one to call the tune to which her various lovers had eagerly danced, but this time it was different. The tables had been turned, and though Isabel chafed at the role reversal, she told herself it only served to add to the thrill of the chase. The prize was well worth the hunt, and she had every confidence in the end she would triumph. After all, she had never failed before to get what she wanted. But Rian Connor was no ordinary man, and making him see that she was what he also wanted was going to take every ounce of skill, and every weapon she possessed.

With her considerable wealth of no interest to him, Rian made no secret of the fact that although he found her charming and exciting, and would remain faithful to her for as long as they were together, her body would not be enough to keep him tied to her. She had the impression that should she suddenly disappear from his life, Rian would sincerely mourn her absence, but he would not grieve overlong. It was not indifference on his part, but more a statement of fact. Life was too short to dwell on things that could not be changed, and this was part of his allure.

She consoled herself with the thought that for the present she *did* have him, and he enjoyed her company both in and out of bed. But a lifetime commitment was an entirely different prospect. While Isabel was kept busy with plans to ensnare Rian, her peers wagered amongst themselves on how long it would take for the beautiful young widow to land her prize.

* * * *

At thirty-two years of age, Rian Connor had already tested the waters of matrimony and it had not ended well. He had been amused to find himself declared a most eligible bachelor amongst society, and shocked by the number of young women who were constantly at his elbow. Either of their own accord or because of a firm push from an ambitious mother. Of course his suitability was brought into question once he attached himself to Isabel, but Rian was not in the least concerned.

In spite of the delightful distractions thrown his way, he found no reason to change his current marital status. He knew the joy of giving himself completely to one woman, and had experienced the pain of loss when that same love was scorched by tragedy. He felt no need to relive the experience, and doubted he ever would. Women, he decided, were to be admired, adored and cherished, and he much preferred the role of lover to that of a husband.

His presence at his brother's wedding was going to be a bittersweet experience. It was the first time he had set foot on his native soil since that terrible fight with his father so long ago. He had almost forgotten what had sparked the furious outburst between them. Almost, but not quite. A man didn't truly ever forget the reason for leaving those he loved. But if the same circumstances prevailed today would he behave so rashly? A wry grin turned his mouth. He would not blame the impetuousness of youth for his decisions; after all, they'd helped him become the adult he now was.

As a young man, the seriousness of his manner, coupled with his willingness to work, had convinced the captain of a ship bound for the Indies to take him aboard, and he quickly learned that the life of a sailor was brutal and harsh. Still, luck had been on his side and the captain, though by necessity a hard man, was also a just one. Under his tutelage Rian left boyhood behind on that initial voyage. Unafraid and eager to learn, he earned the respect of his shipmates, and for five years he served on one sailing vessel or another as he expanded his horizons. But it was tales of the Americas that stirred his imagination, and, when the opportunity arose, he seized it with both hands and headed for the New World.

His adopted country welcomed him with open arms and a wealth of opportunities for those not afraid of hard work. From the headstrong youth a man was molded, and with patience, a keen nose for business and a little good fortune, Rian found himself the owner of a modest plantation when he was twenty-four. He thought nothing of working alongside his field hands, and every penny of profit from the crop he helped plant he put back into the rich, fertile ground. In no time at all he was able to add additional acreage, and while still in his twenties he had one of the more profitable plantations in the county. And he might have been content to continue with his new life had not tragedy struck, reminding him how isolated he was without the connection of family.

When news reached him that Liam was to take a wife, it took little coaxing for Rian to put his affairs in order and set sail for his homeland. A voyage infinitely more comfortable as a paying passenger than a member of the crew. Isabel would have been surprised to know the driving force behind his return was nothing more sinister than homesickness.

But his homecoming was not without consequences. His father, with whom he had argued so bitterly, was now dead. What should have been a simple difference of opinion had become a rift too wide for either to cross. In a fit of temper, the patriarch had disowned his firstborn, in favor of his younger brother. The fact he would employ such a tactic only proved how little he knew or understood either of his children. But now, whatever hopes of forgiveness and reconciliation Rian may have harbored lay buried alongside a bitter, twisted man. The fierce need to find a measure of peace was something Rian would have to pursue alone. Even now he could hear the echo of his father's voice inside his head. Embarrassment over a youthful indiscretion had fueled an anger-laced tirade. Unbeknownst to either of them, it was the last time they would speak.

Thankfully, the same could not be said of Rian and his brother.

Over the years they had corresponded with each other and stayed in touch. So when Liam wrote to tell his brother he wanted to marry, it was not a complete surprise to his sibling. His choice of bride, however, was another matter.

Felicity Pelham was not completely unknown to Rian. She was, after all, the daughter of their closest neighbor, but Rian had been astonished that Liam would choose her for a wife. He vaguely recalled a skinny girl who was all elbows and knees and somewhat nearsighted. However, giving Felicity the benefit of the doubt, and allowing for the passage of time, he thought perhaps she might be a good match for Liam. The girl he remembered had a serious outlook on life even at a young age, which would complement his brother's own calm dependability. The added incentive of Pelham lands bordering Connor property made it a sensible match, but Rian hoped this had not been a factor in his brother's choice.

On the surface the brothers were as different as chalk and cheese. Yet it was this difference that strengthened the bond they shared. Knowing his return would cause a great deal of speculative interest, Rian wondered if Liam had requested his attendance as a way of deflecting attention from himself and his bride-to-be. He chuckled at the thought, happy enough to oblige the engaged couple in any way he could. Oakhaven, the sprawling country estate that was the Connor family seat, had not yet been graced with his presence. Wanting to indulge himself first with whatever temptations the city might offer, Rian was residing in the townhouse Liam had had the foresight to purchase some years before. And, as the ceremony was to take place in the city, it made perfect sense for him to remain in town until after the nuptials. He would have plenty of time to visit his childhood home once Liam and Felicity were wed. Then he could confront the ghosts of his past alone, and on his own terms.

* * * *

Isabel took it for granted that she would attend the wedding with Rian. The Pelhams were an old family whose loyalty to the crown could be traced back to the time of Richard the Lionhearted, and while the Connors could not boast the same lineage, a persistent rumor spoke of the family's similar origins down the line of Celtic royalty. In truth no one cared if royal blood was present in either family. The wedding was going to be a grand affair, and anyone of consequence had already been invited. Isabel's own standing, enhanced by her recent connection to the groom's family, guaranteed her new gown would be finished on time. All that was left to decide on were the jewels she would wear.

These thoughts swirled through her mind as she sat at her dressing table attempting to restore some order to the unruly mass of black curls that framed her small, exotic face. Lifting the brush to tease the locks into place, she glanced in the mirror at the man who lay in her bed, propped up on the pillows watching her. Rian stretched lazily and settled himself more comfortably, giving her his complete and undivided attention.

Dressed in a scarlet robe so sheer she might as well have been wearing nothing at all, Isabel delighted in preening for him. She turned one way then the other, ostensibly concerned with her grooming, but an astute observer would see her eyes never left her lover's face in the looking glass. Finished with her task, Isabel gathered up her curls and secured them with a jeweled comb on top of her head. The movement of her arms caused the front of the robe to gape open, offering a tantalizing glimpse of her lush breasts peeking through the scarlet lace. Rian sighed, deciding there was nothing truly more sensuous than a woman brushing her hair.

Dropping her arms, Isabel turned on her seat to face him. The look on his face was the only invitation she needed, and she rose from her seat, and walked toward the bed. Every step was a calculated act of sexual provocation, rewarded by the gleam of lust in Rian's eyes. A slight shrug and the delicate robe fell to the ground, where it shimmered in a red cloud about her feet. She heard his breath catch as he gazed at her, and she smiled. Isabel already knew what an engaging temptress she was.

The normally muted emerald green of her eyes now sparkled with passion. Her cheeks were flushed and the quick intake of breath revealed her own desire quickening through her. Full rounded breasts sat high on a ribcage that gave way to a narrow waist and shapely hips. Her legs were smooth and silky, and she saw Rian's gaze irresistibly drawn to the nest of tight, dark curls that cushioned the top of her thighs. She was the picture of voluptuousness and the scent of her sex filled his nostrils, teasing his own arousal.

"Isabel," he growled, in a voice that was low and husky, "I have a small problem that I think would benefit greatly from your expert handling."

Laughing, she pulled back the sheet that covered him. "Not so small I think, my love, but one that I agree would benefit greatly from my touch." Her face was glowing and she looked almost feline, Rian thought.

Placing one small, perfectly manicured hand against the wide expanse of his smooth chest, she gently pushed him down on the bed, and got on top of him, straddling his hips. A small gasp escaped her as she took him inside her, feeling him fill her completely. For a moment she remained quite still, savoring the sensation, while he lay without moving, content to have her demonstrate how skillful a lover she was.

Leaning forward, Isabel moved her hands to his shoulders, and began to rock herself back and forth. Her hair fell free of the comb and it whispered erotically across his skin as she moved. Gently Rian clasped his hands about her waist and began to match her rhythm, feeling her heat increase as she slid forward to coat him with her own slick passion. A pearly sheen glistened on her skin, and she uttered a barely audible moan as she quickened the tempo. He kept pace with her, and just when he sensed she could no longer endure the sweet agony of their coupling, Rian thrust his hips upward, holding her to him hard and fast as they both exploded in a gratifying wave of sexual release.

Later, after their appetites were sated, it was Isabel who lay back amongst the pillows watching Rian as he dressed. Her eyes roamed over him, drinking in every small detail from the width of his shoulders and well-muscled arms, to his hard, flat stomach and powerful legs. She recalled being trapped by those strong thighs when Rian had playfully pinned her on the bed before persuading her to open for him. Strands of silver threaded the thick mane of his hair, telling her he had known hardship in his life. His hands still bore calluses, and several scars stood out in stark relief against his tanned skin. She longed to know the story behind each and every one.

A strong chin and firm jaw hinted at stubbornness, while his wide mouth gave his face a seriousness he didn't always demonstrate. Isabel knew only too well how quick he was to smile, and, on the rare occasion he did sleep at her side, she hadn't failed to notice a particular vulnerability when his features were relaxed. This was what she wanted to possess more than anything. This side of him she suspected very few ever saw.

By comparison, Isabel now realized her previous lovers had been sadly lacking, and she wondered how she could have ever thought herself satisfied. None could ever claim the hold on her that Rian did, and she was determined no other man would.

Dressed now, he came to her ready to take his leave. The dawn was less than an hour away, but he rarely stayed the entire night. Bending down he brushed a few stray curls from her forehead and kissed her tenderly.

"When will your brother be in town?" she asked huskily.

His forehead crinkled. "Later this week, I think."

"And will he be with you long?"

Rian's mouth curled in a sly grin. "Why do you ask?"

"I'm just wondering how many days I have to be without you."

He laughed and placed a finger beneath her chin, raising her head so he could kiss her on the mouth. "In all probability this will be the last opportunity Liam and I will have to spend together before his duties as a husband claim him. It is his house, after all, and he will stay as long as he chooses," he told her gently. "Besides, aren't you invited somewhere with Charlotte?"

Isabel gasped in mock horror at his familiarity. "*Lady Maitling*," she said with exaggerated reverence, "has done me the honor of requesting my company while she makes a brief visit to her country estate." She pouted and narrowed her eyes. "But if truth be told, I think she is only tolerating my presence so she may satisfy her curiosity about you."

"I have no doubt that a clever mind like yours will find something entertaining to share with her," Rian said, straightening his cuffs.

"Come back to bed. You know you don't have to go." Her voice took on a petulant tone, and to emphasize her point, she sat up and let the sheet fall to her waist.

Sitting down next to her, Rian bent his head and took a tempting nipple in his mouth. Isabel arched her back as he gently rolled his tongue over its surface, licking and teasing until a stiff peak formed. He scraped the swollen flesh lightly with his teeth before letting go, and her eyes became glazed.

"Nothing would give me greater pleasure, my dear," he said softly, "but there is a reputation that needs to be protected, and you have placed that burden squarely on my shoulders." Giving a theatrical, exaggerated sigh, he stood and began backing away toward the door.

"Reputation be damned!" Isabel shouted in frustration as she threw a pillow at him. "I care not one whit for my reputation."

Laughing, Rian easily dodged the missile and opened the door. "That is something I am all too well aware of, but it isn't your reputation I'm trying to protect." He blew her a kiss, leaving her to fume in her bed.

Chapter 11

The pale fingers of dawn made busy pushing back the mantle of night. The fog that had stolen through the streets earlier dispersed, although pockets still lingered here and there. And there was enough of a bite in the air to herald the forthcoming change of seasons, but it was not cold enough to discourage Rian from walking. It was, he decided, perfect thinking weather, and the distance to the townhouse was a comfortable stretch for his legs. Turning his collar up against the morning breeze, he set off. At this hour of the morning there was little to disturb him.

His thoughts centered on the woman he had just left. There was no denying Isabel was a delightful creature, and he was quite taken with her, but he had also heard the rumors circulating about the two of them. According to the gossip, Lady Howard would not be opposed to receiving an offer of marriage were he to propose one. A change of attitude so remarkable it had raised many a painted brow, especially as Isabel had made no secret of her aversion to matrimony. That she would consider taking a husband had set more than tongues wagging. Wagers were being made on how much longer she would retain the title of Lady Howard. Acutely aware of the tales being spread, Rian knew it was time to address them, and so he pondered the question.

Would marriage to Isabel be such a terrible thing?

There was no denying she was beautiful. Blessed with a sharp mind and a quick wit. And she was an exhilarating lover. She was also the first woman he had met in a long time who made him realize how much he missed the daily interaction of female companionship. Perhaps it was a sign telling him to put the past behind him, settle down and take a wife again. But was Isabel the woman to fill that empty place in his life? Rian knew she certainly thought so. He was not so sure.

A dog trotting down the street captured his attention. It stopped and looked at him, canine curiosity cocking its head to one side with ears pricked before deciding Rian was no threat. Ignoring him, the dog carried on, intent on his wanderings. Watching the animal go about its business, Rian smiled. Sometimes he wished his own life could be that simple, devoid of needless complications. He sighed. He wanted his relationship with Isabel to continue exactly as it was, but he already knew that would be impossible. Despite all her protests to the contrary, Isabel was subtly asking him for more. It was nothing overt on her part; indeed to an outsider their relationship had not changed a whit, but Rian could sense a certain restlessness growing within her. No longer content with the status quo, Isabel wanted to know whether he was going to make her a more permanent part of his future. Late night suppers and afternoon trysts, while still delightful, were a temporary diversion that would bring satisfaction for only so long. With Isabel it would have to be all or nothing.

In the quiet of the early morning, Rian examined his own feelings with an honesty that was brutal, before considering the qualities he desired in a partner. He sighed with disappointment at the realization that, for all her charm and beauty, Isabel was not the woman he wanted as a wife. He couldn't explain why he felt this way, or what necessary element she lacked, but he trusted the feeling within himself that said it was so.

While many marriages, particularly arranged ones between great families, endured without the benefit of love, it was an understanding he had no wish to be a part of. He despised the idea of a loveless match. He wanted children, and he wanted to love them in a way his own father had never been able to do. How was he going to do that if he felt only a modicum of affection for their mother? Isabel teased his body and delighted his mind, but Rian felt nothing that made him want to open his heart and share his hopes and dreams with her. A long-term future with the dark-haired beauty was doomed. They would drift apart until they were nothing more than strangers who shared a house and politely greeted each other whenever their paths crossed. Any affection they felt now would fade until it was nothing but a bittersweet memory.

Both of them deserved more.

As the early morning breeze stiffened, tugging at the hem of his coat, Rian knew he could never love Isabel the way he believed a husband should love his wife, the way he had once loved. Without any reservations, and with a depth of feeling that would continue to grow as the years passed.

The love that his brother already shared with Felicity. Liam not only loved his bride to be, he was also very much *in love* with her. To offer any woman less would deny both of them the chance of finding true happiness, and that was something Rian was not prepared to do.

Finding the answer to a problem he didn't even know he'd been subconsciously wrestling with, Rian acknowledged the necessity of ending his relationship with Isabel. He would be as kind as possible. He did not want to hurt her, but it would be a greater cruelty to allow her to think he might ask for her hand. For him she would always be a beautiful, cherished memory, but he could offer her no more.

He could not have said what unknown hand steered him toward the docks, but he was not terribly surprised to find himself there. The sight of the great ships always stirred something deep within him, and he took a measure of comfort in their presence. They had provided the key to his freedom a lifetime ago. Now, standing quietly in the shadows, he closed his eyes, listening to the sounds of the wharf coming to life. No gentle bird song awakened those needing to be about their business. Instead the raucous shriek of gulls, dipping and soaring overhead, mingled with the sound of early morning human activity. In a short while the area would become a center of controlled commotion as people went about their daily lives, their purpose set.

Rian's mouth was fixed in a grim line as another problem poked at his brain, demanding his attention. What was he to do now he had returned home? He needed a purpose. Their father had kept true to his promise and disowned him. Oakhaven now belonged to Liam, though that was of little consequence to Rian. If their father had not taken charge of the matter, Rian would have found a way to legally renounce his claim to the estate. He had no need of the property or the income it provided, and his brother had more than earned the right to it long ago, but being a landowner was in their blood. Both his and Liam's. They derived a great satisfaction from growing crops, raising livestock, and being responsible for the well-being of those who worked the land. It was something passed down the Connor line, and an occupation Rian was good at. Perhaps Liam knew of some land he could buy.

With a satisfied smile on his lips, Rian took in a deep breath. The tang of salt in the air was strong, and he savored the scent like the sweetest perfume. There would be time enough to decide his own future after Liam and Felicity were settled; for now it was enough to enjoy the crisp freshness of the morning before it became polluted by the day's wear. Listening to the rhythmic slap of water against the stone wharf, Rian let his mind wander as the water sang to him. He thought of everything, and he thought of nothing.

* * * *

Catherine had lost all concept of time. Her mind was now locked in a secret place, and she no longer possessed the key to free it. Moving almost mechanically with a will of its own, her body slipped in and out of the fog-shrouded streets and dark alleys. Instinct drove her as she heeded the overwhelming urge to flee and put as much distance as possible between herself and the nightmare that sought her destruction.

Muddled, vague images floated before her eyes, but she could not tell if they were real or imaginary. Shadowy figures called out to her, their singsong lilt haunting, but the grip she had on reality was tenuous, and she did not trust herself to answer them. The ability to make sense of the past few hours, what little she was able to remember, was failing fast. The effort needed to recall the details was a struggle that threatened the last reserves of her depleted strength.

In the beginning each step had brought spasms of pain that screamed up her legs and clawed across her back, but after a while the chill of the night acted as a balm, numbing her to the point where she now felt nothing at all, not even the sharp stones and pebbles that cut into her bare feet. What had happened to her shoes? When did she lose them? She vaguely recalled a kind face with gentle hands slipping them on her feet. A woman who'd helped her, but who she was, Catherine no longer knew.

She told herself that it was important to remember why she hurt, but the harder she tried to grasp the reason, the further away it slipped until it disappeared entirely, and could no longer be brought to mind. She bit her lower lip in frustration, and winced at the pain. Gingerly she touched her mouth, staring at the bloodstains on her fingers in confused bewilderment. Had she bitten herself that hard? For a moment the memory danced just within reach, but it filled her with fear and so she let it slip away as silent tears spilled down her cheeks.

She reeled like a drunk through the streets and back alleys of a city she did not know. Landmarks had no meaning, and she had no idea in which direction she was going. All she could do was trust her inner compass, hoping she would recognize her destination when she arrived. She cried, muffled sobs echoing off stone bricks, but no one heeded the distorted sound carried through the dense fog. Weeping was an all too familiar sound. A man, taking her for a whore, approached only to realize his mistake after seeing her bruised and bleeding face. She clung to the shadows, waiting until the sound of his boots ringing on the cobblestones had faded before trusting herself to move. Catherine saw no one else, and if others saw her, they stayed silent and kept to their own shadows.

Onward she walked, obeying some involuntary pull, one bloody footstep in front of another until she found herself at the docks. Like a phantom she glided in and out of the shadows until she was standing at the far edge of the wharf, at the farthest point away from the ships, where she stared into the murky depths of the river. Dawn was breaking, and in a short while this place would be bustling, and people would notice her. But for now an eerie quiet filled the air, as if each block of stone beneath her feet shared her pain, and promised to act as her witness. Her body ached from the cold, injuries, and sheer, bloody exhaustion. Catherine had never felt so tired. She needed to rest but her functioning eye refused to close, and a voice in her head told her to stay focused. There was a reason she was here.

The small waves that slapped against the huge stone slabs commanded her attention. Catherine peered into the water and saw something shimmering just below the surface. Her brows knitted together as she forced herself to concentrate, but she was tired and it was difficult. But then she saw it again, and the watery reflection revealed itself. It was a face, and one that she recognized and could remember only too well. The countenance below the surface belonged to a handsome man who was strong and vital and in his prime. A man whose life held purpose. It was the way she remembered her father looking before her mother had died. A time when they had all been happy.

Seeing her father smile at her, Catherine tried to smile back, but her swollen mouth could only produce a grotesque leer. She feared the image in the water would turn away from such ugliness, but it did not. Instead her father opened his mouth and called her name.

Catherine.... Catherine....

The sound of his voice carried on the waves slapping lightly against the wharf, whispering inside her head.

Catherine...child...come to me.... Come...Catherine. Ease your pain....

She shook her head as bewilderment and confusion sought to cloud his meaning. As if sensing her difficulty, her father spoke to her again, only this time his voice carried a shaper sense of urgency.

One step Catherine.... One small step.... Then you will be with me. Come, child....

William held out his arms, his intention perfectly clear. All she needed to do was step off the edge of the dock, and she would be carried down to the murky depths of the water below. Her bloodstained feet moved her forward until she could feel her toes curl around the rough edge of the stone block. The river would surely take pity on her. Carry her to a place where she would find peace, and someone who would love her.

A dull throb pounded in her temples, forcing her to close her eye and sway as a wave of nausea roiled from the pit of her stomach. She fought off the sickening sensation, but when she was able to open her eye again, she saw her father's face was fading along with his voice.

Come, Catherine. Hurry, child.... There isn't much time....

The ghostly image in the water disappeared.

"No!" she shrieked hoarsely, not knowing if she spoke the word aloud or if it was nothing more than an echo inside her head. "Don't leave me, Papa! Come back to me. Don't leave me. Not again."

Tears filled her eye, making the surface of the water swim before her, and as she struggled to focus on her father's words she did not hear the approaching footsteps. One small step, her father had said, just one small step, and she would be released from the pain that now twisted itself around her heart. Free of the fire that burned her limbs. The peace she craved was a step away. It was all so easy, but as Catherine went to move forward, destiny placed its hand on her shoulder, and turned her away from a watery grave.

* * * *

Rian couldn't have said what drew his attention to the figure standing at the far edge of the wharf. At first he thought it was the early morning light playing tricks. The remnants of morning fog producing a phantom in the mist. Something that wasn't really there. But then some unfathomable sense tugged at him, and he began to walk toward it.

The figure was no phantom, but it was difficult to tell if it was male or female due to the folds of the cloak draped about its shoulders. Still, Rian's curiosity was pricked, and as he grew closer a shift in movement revealed the outline of feminine curves. His brow wrinkled with concern. It was too early for a dockside whore to be plying her trade, and it made no sense to be so far away from the wharf-side taverns and inns. Paying customers did not stray this far at any time of the day or night, so what reason had brought her to this lonely place?

It struck him that perhaps the girl was in some trouble, and too frightened to return to whoever claimed responsibility for her. Perhaps she had been robbed, or a customer had refused to pay for her services. Generous by nature, Rian decided if a few coins could make the difference, then he would gladly give them. He was not ashamed to admit that as a young man he had eased his loneliness from time to time by taking comfort in her profession. It would be a small token of his appreciation for kindness received when he'd had need of it.

Going closer, Rian happened to glance down, noticing the paving stones were stained with blotches that looked remarkably like footprints. Bloody footprints. His frown deepened when he saw bare feet beneath the hem of the cloak the girl wore. And this was another curiosity, for even in the early morning light he could see that the quality of the garment was too fine to belong to a common streetwalker. Was this the source of the girl's woes? Had she stolen the cloak? It would not be unheard of: Thievery and prostitution were more often than not two sides of the same coin.

He continued his approach, making no effort to disguise his footsteps, but the girl gave no indication she heard him. Whatever problem she wrestled with, it was weighty enough to render her oblivious to everything around her. Seeing how close she was to the edge of the wharf, Rian prayed he did not startle her. A sudden loss of balance would send her tumbling into the murky water, where she could easily be carried away by the river's strong undercurrent.

The inexplicable sense that had tugged at him before now increased in intensity. Rian could almost smell the scent of despair clinging to the girl, and the thick, cloying perfume filled his nostrils. Intuition told him a handful of coins, no matter how generous or well intentioned, would not ease the girl's misfortune. And that did not sit well with him.

He was behind her now, and yet she still seemed completely unaware of his presence, her attention firmly fixed on something in the water. She cried out, her words garbled and incoherent, but Rian had no difficulty in recognizing the anguish behind them. It was the most pitiful sound he had ever heard, and it set his course. Carefully he reached out a hand and grasped her shoulder. Keeping his hold firm and true in case she might still stumble, Rian slowly turned her toward him.

Very few things in life took Rian by surprise, but this was one of them, and he found himself uncharacteristically struck dumb. With one sweeping glance he took in the white blonde hair that tumbled about her face, the swollen, bruised mouth and the discolorations along either side of her jaw. But what troubled him most, set him back on his heels, was the fear, distrust and pain that were so clearly reflected in the one eye that gazed steadily at him. An orb of deep, infinite blue, it held him fast, refusing to look away despite the horror Rian could see there. But then she blinked, thick lashes sweeping downward, and this time when she looked at him, Rian saw something else.

Beyond the terror he saw a need that called to him. A want that awakened an unexpected impulse, inflaming a need of his own. This one more basic, more primal, shocking Rian with the sudden protective impulse he felt. Whoever she was, she was no dockside whore, but as he opened his mouth to reassure her, that disturbing blue eye rolled back in her head, and she slumped against him.

Chapter 12

Lettie sat on the edge of her bed nervously twisting the sash on her robe over and over until the smooth material resembled a piece of coarse string instead of fine silk. Her nerves were on edge and she jumped at every sound, both real and imagined. It was almost a relief when her bedroom door was finally thrown open to reveal her husband standing on the other side. He had dressed in a hurry and his clothing was askew, the waistcoat open and his shirt buttoned incorrectly. Lettie was thankful that he had managed to fasten his breeches but she frowned at seeing him barefoot. Dried blood matted his hair and the ugly purple bruise above his temple was hard to miss. His nose had been bleeding and it now possessed a crooked appearance.

"Bitch," Phillip said in a voice that was oddly thick but nevertheless calm.

Lettie's fear escalated. If her husband had been raging and screaming, she would have stood a chance, but she knew from experience his ice-cold demeanor meant he was at his worst. She had no doubt that if Phillip were ever to commit murder, and at this moment she could not state with any degree of certainty that he had not, it would be as the chilling figure now standing before her. Unable to move, she watched as he went to the washstand and poured water from the ewer into the basin. After soaking a linen cloth, he proceeded to wipe away most of the dried blood from his temple before sitting next to her on the bed.

"Did you plan this?" he asked with no change to his tone. "With her?"

Lettie clutched at her throat, barely able to breathe, much less speak. "P-p-plan w-w-what?"

"That whore's escape," Phillip said. His voice may have been calm, but his eyes were murderous. "I know you helped her find her way out of this house tonight. She could not have managed it alone."

Lettie's throat constricted, rendering her unable to utter a word. She stared at her husband like a mouse hypnotized by a snake, knowing it was in imminent danger, but completely powerless to save itself.

"There is no one else who would dare defy my authority, although"—Phillip reached out and caught a lock of her hair, idly twisting it in his fingers—"this act of rebellion on your part has quite surprised me." He jerked his hand suddenly, pulling her hair tight and forcing her face closer to his. "I really didn't think you had it in you," he whispered as a cruel smile twisted his mouth. "But such disobedience will, of course, require punishment." And loosening her hair, he gripped her upper arm and pulled her from the bed.

"I hate you!" Lettie screamed, finding her voice and surprising both of them as years of pent up fear and revulsion were released with those three words.

"I had no idea you were capable of such passion," Phillip sneered, "but I would ask you not to flatter yourself, madam, by presuming I share the sentiment. Believe me when I say you mean nothing to me."

Phillip punched his wife in the face, smiling in satisfaction as she dropped to the floor, gagging and retching on the blood that gushed from her nose. Reaching down, he grabbed her by the arm once more, and jerked her to her feet.

Shrieking, Lettie tried to pull away, but Phillip's grip was strong, and he easily ignored her feeble efforts. All she could do was try to keep up as he marched her down the hall to Catherine's room. Opening the door, he flung her to the floor, where she barely missed the puddle of vomit on the carpet. Tears streamed down Lettie's face, mixing with the blood and mucus that ran from her nose, and forcing her to spit out the contents of her mouth with each breath she tried to take, lest she choke. She struggled to her knees, only to be sent sprawling by a vicious kick.

"She was mine," Phillip snarled, standing over his prostrate wife. "Mine! To do with as I pleased, for as long as I wanted."

"You're mad!" Lettie said thickly, turning her head and spraying him as she spoke.

Phillip looked down at himself, curling his lip in distaste at the globules of bloody mucus splattered on his clothes. "Mad, am I?" It wasn't a real question, and he leaned closer, making his wife cringe in terror as his voice dropped to an icy calm. "You forget yourself, my dear. The state of my mind is of no consequence because, regardless, I am still your husband, which means I can do with you as I will."

The look in his eyes was pure evil. A malevolence so deep that Lettie, fearing for her life, curled into a ball. She covered her head with her arms, and so did not see Phillip fetch the iron poker from the fireplace. The first blow carried all the weight of his frustration and rage, and she was unable to stifle the scream of agony as she felt the bone in her thigh break. The years of abuse at her husband's hands had taught Lettie to hold her tongue, knowing Phillip took pleasure in hearing evidence of his mistreatment. Screams, whimpers, even a stifled sob would only guarantee a continuation of the torment. So though he rained down blow after blow on her unprotected body, Lettie kept silent, almost biting through her lower lip in order to do so.

Finally the events of the night caught up to Phillip, and the ache in his arm forced him to drop the heavy poker and stagger out of the room. Uncovering her head with her arms, Lettie fought the lightheadedness trying to suck her down and take her to a place she didn't want to go. She was in acute physical distress. Phillip had hit her before, but he had never before shown such savagery. She had been certain he meant to kill her, and for the life of her, had no idea what had stopped him.

Excruciating pain ripped through her shattered leg. The throbbing, fiery ache spread from her foot to her hip, and halfway up her back. Raising her head slightly, she caught sight of the bed, and the bloodstained sheets half pulled off, and the strips of fabric still wrapped around the bedposts. She stared in horror as she realized what they had been used for. Too weak to move, Lettie was unable to prevent the vile images that filled her head, revealing all too clearly what Phillip had done to Catherine, reminding her what she herself had experienced at his hands.

But never this, oh dear God, it had never been as bad as this!

As the bed began to swim before her, Lettie allowed a brief moment of satisfaction to fill her. It blossomed like a flower in her chest, infusing her with a sense of rightness, knowing she had helped Catherine escape.

"God lead you to a safe haven, Catherine, and keep you in his hands," she whispered just before she plummeted into the realms of darkness where only agony waited.

Chapter 13

It was early enough that most of the household staff were still enjoying their breakfast, and had not yet set about their daily chores. As luck would have it, one of the housemaids had been sent to fetch the housekeeper's shawl. Not expecting any of the family to be awake at such an hour, the girl had taken the liberty of using the main staircase instead of the one at the back of the house. She was crossing the tiled lobby when the sound of Rian's boot kicking loudly against the front door startled her. Her mouth fell open as he strode past her, carrying an unconscious woman in his arms.

"Tell Mrs. Hatch to send for a doctor immediately," Rian barked as he continued up the staircase. Too surprised to curtsey, the girl ran to do as he had ordered.

Once in the master suite, Rian carefully placed his burden on the bed. His release drew a reflexive moan from the insentient girl as he carefully rolled her out of his arms. The room's interior was still dark enough to warrant lighting a candle, which he did before taking off his coat, throwing it carelessly over a chair. Rolling up his shirt sleeves, Rian went to the washstand and poured water into the basin. He picked up a wash cloth and returned to the bed, where he began to gently wipe the girl's face.

Always the more volatile of the two brothers, Rian was having a difficult time keeping his anger from spilling over as he saw the ugly discolorations that mottled her pale skin. Her lower lip was swollen, and he dabbed carefully at the dried blood that clung stubbornly to the corner of her mouth. With a practiced eye he assessed the swelling and bruising along the edge of her face and, after probing cautiously with his fingertips, he determined her jaw did not appear to be broken or dislocated. But the bluish-purple shade that now colored the delicate skin of her right eye made him seethe. He knew from experience that a blow of some force was necessary to produce such bruising and make the skin swell closed.

As he moved the cloth across her skin, she began to make fretful, mewling sounds and attempted to bat his hands away. It was a feeble protest which Rian ignored. Having seen the damage to her face, and also noting the condition of her feet, he made the prudent decision to see if these were the extent of her injuries. Unhooking the decorative clasp that held the cloak closed, he pulled the garment open, only to let out a particularly unsavory curse as he quickly closed it again.

From the moment he'd scooped her up in his arms, Rian had known she wore no gown or even a petticoat, but he had supposed that she was wearing *something*. He was shocked to find she was completely naked, and his brain began to conjure up scenarios to account for her nudity. All of them highly disturbing. Knowing the image he had seen would be forever branded in his mind, he got up from the bed and turned away.

"Master Rian?" The housekeeper stood in the open doorway, hands folded before her as she addressed him in a quiet voice. "The doctor has been sent for."

Rian motioned for her to enter, and as she did so he was struck by the notion that no matter the hour, Mrs. Hatch was always properly dressed, with her hair neatly tucked beneath a starched white cap. He could not recall a time, even as a boy, when she was not impeccably turned out. Liam had been convinced she didn't sleep. Instead, he informed his older brother, she rested in an upright position, propped against the wall and fully dressed in order to be ready for any eventuality.

"Prepare yourself," Rian murmured. "She is wearing no clothes."

The unflappable woman said nothing, except to ask Rian to send the maid waiting in the hallway for hot water. He had just dispatched the young girl when the housekeeper's gasp filled him with concern.

"Oh, my Lord!" the matronly woman exclaimed, keeping her eyes firmly fixed on the bed. "What monster could do such a thing?"

It was not the girl's nakedness that prompted the housekeeper's reaction. Though she appreciated Rian's warning, it had been unnecessary. Having borne eight children of her own, and prepared three, along with her husband, to meet their maker, the human body, male or female, did not offend her. It also held very little mystery. But she had not been prepared for the shocking brutality inflicted on the still form lying before her.

In her semiconscious state, the girl had sought to ease her discomfort by rolling onto her stomach. Mrs. Hatch, seeing the girl's arm entangled in the folds of the cloak, gently pulled it away from her shoulder and, in doing so, revealed the girl's upper back. The welts that marked her skin had made the housekeeper roll the cloak further down, and the sight of ripped and bleeding flesh had been responsible for the older woman's audible reaction. She turned her head to look at Rian, and he saw anguish etched in every line of her face. As he returned to the bed, his own anger quickly turned to a furious rage.

"A hand if you please, Master Rian," Mrs. Hatch whispered, once more in control of her emotions.

With his help, she carefully slid the cloak away, freeing it until she was able to drop it to the floor. Seeing the housemaid return, Mrs. Hatch moved quickly to the door, where she relieved the girl of the kettle of hot water she carried while issuing further instructions in a low voice. Unable to tear his eyes away, Rian simply stared at the naked figure lying face down on the bed. She was still insensible, for which he was grateful, but he now had an idea of what had driven her to the water's edge. He made a silent promise that when he found the person responsible for such a heinous act, he would make sure they paid dearly for it. Turning to face his housekeeper, he watched as she swallowed a couple of times before finding her voice.

"Master Rian, I must ask, sir. Do you know the lass?"

He shook his head, not at all offended by her question. "I have no idea who she is."

She paused for a moment. "Then how is it that you have brought her here?"

He quickly told the housekeeper how he had come across the girl down at the docks. It took no more than a few sentences, and if the older woman was curious to know what cause he had to be there, she did not ask. "I think she meant to throw herself in," Rian told her.

"Good Lord, no!"

Unable to continue looking at the figure on the bed, Rian went to the dresser, poured himself a brandy, and tossed it off in one go. He grimaced as the liquid burned a fiery path down to his belly, but the alcohol did its job. It enabled him to push his anger to one side, where it could be dealt with later. Right now he needed to remain objective, and as calm as possible. The low voices coming from beyond the open door made him turn his head in time to see Mrs. Hatch pulling a sheet over the girl.

"Ah, that will be the doctor," she told him. "I think it would be best if you left the lass to us now, Master Rian." Her frilled white cap bobbed in the general direction of the bedroom door. Mystified by her directive, and even more so by the firm hand that pushed him across the room, Rian tried to protest. But found no words to do so.

"Best leave the girl to the doctor, sir. I'll send word when he's finished with his examination, and in the meantime I've had breakfast set out. Why don't you go down and get a bite to eat?" She emphasized this last by taking the empty brandy glass from his hand, and giving him a reproachful look.

"How do you think I could possibly be interested in food at a time like this?" Rian hissed.

The woman before him had the advantage of having dealt with Connor men all her adult life, and took no umbrage at his snappish tone. No matter how long he had been gone, some things didn't change. The firm hand that she placed in the small of his back now felt like a steel fist. "I think you will find your appetite has returned, Master Rian," she said in a tone more curt than his. "It isn't proper for you to see the lass like this."

He opened his mouth to utter one last protest, but found himself brushed to one side as a smaller figure stepped past him. *The doctor*, Mrs. Hatch mouthed, right before she closed the door in his face.

Rian stood on the other side for a few moments, staring in disbelief at the intricately carved wood paneling, before realizing his housekeeper was absolutely right. Even if he could claim the right of a husband, it still would have been inappropriate for him to remain. He had not been gone so long that he had forgotten Mrs. Hatch was a kindly, God-fearing woman with a strict moral code. One that was respected by all the staff. Which explained why he had never considered bedding Isabel in the townhouse. He was too terrified of having his ears boxed by the matronly chatelaine if she found a woman in his bed who was not his wife. It made no difference that he was now a grown man. She had known him since he was a child, and his brother would be absolutely livid if he was the reason they needed to find another housekeeper.

When he entered the dining room, the enticing aroma of a freshly prepared breakfast made his stomach rumble loudly. It had been too long since he last ate. Rian was on his third cup of coffee when the doctor was shown in.

Dr. MacGregor was a compact man who had lost none of the highland burr of his native Scotland. It rang out pleasantly as he gratefully accepted the invitation to breakfast. Rian couldn't help the smile that tugged at the corners of his mouth as he watched the man demolish the contents of his plate with clinical precision. He imagined the doctor did not get many chances to start his day so well fortified, and found it no hardship to wait until the man had eaten his fill before speaking.

"Well?" he asked as the doctor pushed his plate away and spooned a generous helping of sugar into his coffee cup.

"I've done all that I can, Mr. Connor. The wounds have been cleaned and dressed and I have left a salve with your housekeeper along with instructions for its application. I have also given the lass something to help her sleep." He stirred the contents of his cup as a worried frown creased his already wrinkled brow. "There was, however, one verra nasty wound that required stitching. It canna' be helped, and I'm heartily sorry the lass will be scarred."

Rian nodded in understanding. He had no doubt the physician had done whatever was best for his patient. "Is there anything we can do to make her more comfortable?" he asked.

Dr. MacGregor sipped his coffee, his face momentarily blissful before resuming a more professional expression. "Infection is always the biggest concern," he replied.

"The wounds on her back?"

"Aye, but I am more concerned about her feet."

Rian raised a brow as he stared across the table. "Her feet? I'm not sure I understand you."

"From the poor condition of her feet, I would say the lass has traveled a fair distance without the benefit of shoes. Something, in my professional opinion, she is not used to doing. She has lacerations on both soles, and, despite my best efforts, I fear I may not have been able to give them as thorough a cleaning as I would like." He shook his head as he replaced his cup in its saucer. "It's nigh impossible to know what muck she's walked in, but it would be best if she stays off her feet as long as possible...." He trailed off and looked pointedly at his host. Unasked was the question of the girl's status in the household.

"Of course," Rian answered. "She will remain with us as long as is necessary." Dr. MacGregor nodded with both relief and approval. Rian raised a hand and gestured to his face. "What about these injuries?" he asked.

"There is too much swelling to know if she has suffered any permanent damage to her eye. Hopefully I can make a better diagnosis in a day or two. She will be sore, and in time the bruises will fade. I have recommended to your housekeeper she only eat soup and perhaps soft puddings. Though her jaw is not broken, I am certain it is verra sore, and it may be a while before she feels up to tackling solid food."

Rian grunted. Leaning back, he placed his elbows on the arms of his chair and steepled his fingers, lost in thought. The sound of throat clearing made him look up.

"Please understand, Mr. Connor, I mean no offense," the doctor said with a troubled look, "but I feel it is my duty to ask—"

"I have no idea," Rian said, cutting off the question in a tone as grim as the expression on his face. He quickly repeated the same story he had told his housekeeper, certain the pertinent facts would already be known. There was silence as the physician digested Rian's fuller accounting.

"I don't know if it is a concern of yours, but your housekeeper does nae think the lass is a working girl. It is an opinion I support."

It occurred to Rian that Mrs. Hatch was indeed a woman of many surprises. How she was familiar enough with prostitutes to know the girl lying in the bed upstairs was not one, was beyond him. "It makes no difference at all, but I would be curious to hear your reasoning," he said, picking up the coffee pot and refilling both their cups.

"I can only speak for myself, Mr. Connor, but in my profession I have seen too many lassies who, due to harsh circumstances, believe this is the only way they can survive. Many are barely more than bairns their first time. Though the young lass upstairs has not known that type of life, someone has used her most cruelly."

"I saw the lash marks," Rian admitted.

"Aye, but did you know she was also bound?" Rian felt himself go cold as the doctor continued. "There was a strip of cloth still tied about her one wrist, and the bruising on her ankles would suggest movement was restricted." The Scotsman paused before adding, "However, she does not appear to have been raped."

"You…examined her?" Rian sounded slightly shocked.

"Mr. Connor, it is not often that I am called upon to treat the kind of injuries sustained by young woman you have upstairs—"

"You surprise me, doctor. From the way you spoke I assumed you were familiar with such injuries."

The doctor gave him a cross look. "You misunderstand my meaning, sir. The lass in your care has all the appearance of being strong, and for the most part, healthy. As I can find no signs of previous ill treatment about her person, I must assume this is a singular event. How she came to be the victim of such abuse is unknown, but I would stake my reputation that she was held against her will. I saw no evidence of a wedding band, sexual intercourse, or any indication of having birthed a bairn, so I would rule out the probability of a husband or family of her own. And I believe the status of her virtue would be very important to the lass."

Feeling thoroughly chastened, Rian apologized.

"Aye, well you're not entirely wrong," Dr. MacGregor told him. "Black eyes, split lips, bruises and broken bones I deal with on a regular basis, but injuries like hers?" He paused and shook his head. "It takes a particular type of wickedness to revel in such vicious cruelty. Be thankful, Mr. Connor, that she was spared the additional degradation of rape."

Rian felt his stomach roil at the thought of all that single word entailed. Life aboard ship had introduced him to some of the uglier aspects of what men could do to each other and, even though his size and fists made sure he was never touched, he had witnessed others who were not so lucky. One youth, cursed with features better suited for a drawing room, had thrown himself overboard one night. An alternative more welcome than the attention forced on him by some of his crew mates.

"Thank you, doctor, for your candor," Rian said. "What is your prognosis regarding her recovery?"

"That all depends on the lass. There is no reason to suppose, with rest and proper care, she will not make a complete physical recovery. But who can tell?" He shrugged slightly.

"Physical recovery?" Rian repeated, turning the distinction over in his mind. "What is it you're not telling me?"

The older man sighed and stared frankly at Rian as if trying to decide how best to phrase his reply. "I canna vouch for her state of mind. 'Tis impossible to know what effect such violence to a body will leave on the senses." Dr. MacGregor tapped his temple with his forefinger and paused, wanting to be certain he had Rian's full attention before continuing. "I have heard of cases where a complete recovery, in the wholeness of the meaning, is never achieved. It would be remiss of me not to make you aware of the possibility."

"You're saying she may never get over the attack, in her mind?"

"It would not be unheard of."

Rian thought for a moment, and then gave Dr. MacGregor an unflinching look. "That," he said firmly, "is a bridge we will cross when, and if, we come to it."

Chapter 14

Standing by the side of the bed, Rian looked down at the sleeping figure. Dr. MacGregor had left with a promise to return the following morning to check on his patient. Rian had a feeling he would be in time for breakfast.

"How is she?" he asked softly, addressing his question to Mrs. Hatch.

"Calm enough for the present, Master Rian," she answered. "The doctor gave her a draught to help her sleep, and left me some ointment for her back."

The patient was lying on her stomach, the best position for her, and her head was turned toward him. Her eyes were closed and her breathing was now deep and even. Mrs. Hatch had managed to wash the matted blood from the girl's long hair, and it lay spun out on the pillow to dry. Rian couldn't remember ever seeing such a color before. It reminded him of a field of winter wheat waiting for the kiss of the harvester's scythe. A sheet had been modestly pulled up to her shoulders to cover her, but it did not hide the bulky strips of linen that crisscrossed her back, and continued down her legs.

Following the contours of her body, Rian allowed his eyes to linger on the hollow in the small of her back, continue over the rounding curve of her buttocks and the long tapering legs that ended with unnatural looking lumps. It took him a moment to recall the doctor's words, and realize he was looking at her heavily bandaged feet.

"Dr. MacGregor said you don't think she's a working girl." Rian kept his voice low and gave his housekeeper a wry smile.

"That's right, Master Rian," she confirmed in a voice that remained firm in spite of the heated blush fanning her cheeks.

His own curiosity got the better of him, making him ask, "What makes you think that?"

"It's her hair and hands."

He raised a brow, a sign that further clarification was needed.

"Her hair is clean, much cleaner than a girl working the docks would have, and her hands are soft. Though she has a few calluses, they're the kind a lady of good breeding would have. The kind your mother used to have."

Rian could remember the feel of his mother's hands soothing his brow as a child, but he had no memory of whether her hands were calloused. He was amazed that Mrs. Hatch could recall such a detail. "I had no idea ladies got calluses."

"Those who refuse to be idle do."

Unable to fault the housekeeper's logic, and knowing this was all the explanation he was going to get, Rian turned his mind to a slightly more mundane, but no less pressing concern. He hadn't considered where to put the girl when he first entered the house. He had simply taken her to the only room that made sense to him. The room he was using. Obviously he needed to move out, but had no idea which bedroom to use. Glancing at the dresser, he noted the absence of his personal items. Mrs. Hatch, it would seem, was a step ahead, as usual.

"Your clothing and personal belongings have been moved to the suite down the hall, if that will be satisfactory," she told him, noticing his look, and grateful to change the subject. "The doctor advised not moving her for a day or so."

Rian nodded. "For as long as it takes, Mrs. Hatch."

He turned to leave, and then turned back and spoke in a low voice. "I think, for the time being, it would be best if news of our guest did not travel beyond this house. I leave her well-being entirely in your care, and I trust you to deal with questions from the rest of the staff as they arise, but until she can tell us who she is, and what happened to her, I see no reason to broadcast her presence."

"Of course, Master Rian. No one will breathe a word about her," the housekeeper assured him. She did not need to add that anyone foolish enough to disobey her instructions would soon be looking for another position.

He gave a satisfied nod. "Well, I will leave you to your patient then."

It had been a long night, and, thanks to Isabel, he had gotten little sleep. Making his way to the room he had been moved to, he quickly undressed, got into bed, and fell asleep almost immediately.

* * * *

When Rian opened his eyes the lengthening shadows on the wall told him he had slept through the entire morning and much of the afternoon. Far longer than he had intended. He swung his long legs over the edge of the bed and shook his head to clear away the last cobwebs of sleep. With a yawn, he walked to the washstand and poured cold water into the basin provided. After washing his face and hands he dried off and quickly dressed. He wanted to check if there had been any improvement in the girl's condition, even though he was confident that Mrs. Hatch would have woken him if there had been.

Seeing the door to the master suite ajar, he paused. The sound of low moaning came from within the room. It was similar to the fretful mewling he remembered from earlier; although more agitated it seemed to him. It was possible the girl was being attended to, having her dressings changed, and he did not wish to disturb the process. But he did not hear any sounds that would have accompanied such a task. There was no soft rustle of the housekeeper's skirts as she moved, no gentle murmur offering comfort. Rian heard nothing save for the girl moaning.

Concern got the better of him. He pushed the door open and stepped over the threshold. The girl was completely alone, moving restlessly beneath the sheet, and the sound of her distress was turning more insistent. Rian occupied the vacant chair at the bedside, watching as the girl rolled onto her back, tossing her head from side to side, and drawing a labored breath between clenched teeth. His initial anger at finding her alone was now replaced with alarm. A basin of water was on the table next to the bed. Using the cloth left for such a purpose, Rian dipped it into the water, wrung it out and then wiped it across the girl's brow.

His effort seemed to soothe her a little, but as he smoothed the cloth over her forehead and across her cheeks, he could feel an unnatural heat coming from her. Placing his hand on her forehead, he confirmed the burn of fever. Her cheeks were flushed, and her breathing became even more labored as he listened. He began to hum softly. A tune he recalled from his childhood. One his mother had turned to if ever he or Liam had difficulty sleeping. The sound seemed to ease the girl. Rian did not think it was his slightly off-key crooning she responded to; rather he imagined the melody was familiar. In his experience almost all lullabies sounded the same.

He was concentrating on wiping the perspiration from her brow when she took him by surprise. Gripping his wrist with an unexpected strength, she turned her one bright blue eye to him, tears sparkling on the thick lashes like small diamonds. Her swollen lips moved painfully as she tried to speak, and Rian leaned closer so he might catch her words.

"Please…no more. Please…don't hurt me."

It was the most harrowing plea he had ever heard, and as he gently unclasped her fingers from his wrist and held her hand, a strange sensation engulfed him.

The feeling of rage that had coursed through him earlier now returned, racing fiercely through his blood, its fury directed at her unknown assailant. But moving alongside it, with an equal intensity of passion, came a sense of protectiveness that was so strong it threatened to overwhelm him. Staring down at her, Rian saw not the injured girl in the bed, but the woman she really was. It wasn't that hard for him to look past the swelling and discoloration, to imagine her cheeks flushed with joy, her eyes sparkling, and her generous mouth lifted in happiness. And he knew he wanted to see her look like that with his own eyes. More importantly, he wanted to be the one responsible for making it so.

Holding her hand, he brushed a stray curl from her damp cheek and as he did so, she opened her eye again and looked directly at him. Her gaze was steady, even though the blue iris glittered wildly with an unnatural light as her fever ran its course. For a moment that seemed to last an eternity, the two of them gazed upon each other, and Rian felt his throat tighten. Any words of comfort he thought to offer died in his throat as the girl struggled to speak.

"Help…me," she begged, as more diamonds fell from her lashes and glistened on her flushed cheeks. "Help…" and, as if to emphasize her plea, she squeezed his hand with what little strength she possessed before her eyelid closed, and her hand grew slack in his palm.

"I promise," Rian whispered, laying her hand gently back on the sheet. He had no way of knowing if she heard his words, or if she understood the significance of the husky emotion with which they were delivered.

At that moment a housemaid appeared in the open doorway and apologized profusely for leaving her charge alone. "'Twas only for a moment, sir," she said, shifting from foot to foot, nervously awaiting the reprimand she was certain was coming.

"It's all right," Rian said, his voice unexpectedly calm. He would gain nothing by being angry, and whoever she was, Mrs. Hatch trusted her enough to have her attend the girl. A longer look revealed her as the maid who had opened the front door to him earlier. "What's your name, girl?"

"Tilly, sir." She dipped a hesitant knee to him.

"I want your promise, Tilly, that you won't leave her alone again. If you need to leave this room for any reason, then you stand in the doorway, and you call until either Mrs. Hatch or I come to you." The words were kindly spoken, but there was no mistaking the firmness behind them. "Can you promise me that?"

"Yes, sir, it won't happen again. I give you my word."

Rian nodded and thanked her with a grave look. Outside the room, with the door firmly closed behind him, he leaned against the wall. His head was swimming and his heart was pounding in his chest. Damn! There was something about this girl that was affecting him in a way he had never imagined could happen again. Something he had long forgotten. The seed of an emotion buried deep inside him had taken root, and was pushing up a delicate shoot, waiting to see if there would be any encouragement to grow.

It wasn't possible. Was it?

Rian shook his head. It was a ridiculous notion. He knew nothing about her, who she was, where she came from, or the reason behind her horrific injuries. Did he really want to add to the confusion of the situation? Better to put a stop to any wild imaginings on his part before they got out of hand and he made a fool of himself. Refusing to think further about this possible predicament, he headed for the staircase, where the sound of rising voices told him a visitor had arrived.

Chapter 15

Liam's arrival, as already shared by Rian with Isabel, was not unexpected, and his timing could not have been better. The two men embraced warmly, and the younger Connor prudently chose not to comment on either the hour or the fact that his sibling appeared to have only recently arisen. Once settled in the study, and minor pleasantries exchanged, Rian wasted no further time with small talk. "So, brother mine, do you have another reason for being in the city, or are you simply here to see what mischief I am up to?"

"Actually, Felicity sent me."

Rian raised a brow. "Really? For what purpose?"The younger man's expression was one of mild amusement. "My fiancée wonders if your continued absence is a deliberate ploy on your part. A willful attempt to avoid her." Amusement bloomed into a grin. "She has sent me to reassure you that you are quite forgiven for the unfortunate duck pond incident."

The frown Rian wore cleared as his memory returned. He chuckled, recalling the sound of alarmed quacking from displaced waterfowl as a skinny girl lost her balance and entered their habitat uninvited, and with a great deal of splashing.

"I'd forgotten all about that," he admitted with a sheepish look. The skinny girl wouldn't have lost her footing if he hadn't startled her by putting a very large frog in her hands.

"Ah yes, well, Felicity remembers everything," Liam told him.

"I'll bear that in mind."

"Truthfully, we were wondering if you intended to visit Oakhaven before the wedding," Liam continued. "It would be nice to spend some time with you, and to be perfectly honest, I'm feeling a little overwhelmed. I need to be able to converse with someone who isn't going to badger me about feminine frills, as if I could tell the difference between ivory and ecru colored lace!"

"Ah, Liam, what have you got yourself into?" Rian teased, enjoying his brother's discomfort.

"Nothing really. I just fell in love with the girl next door."

Both men looked at each other and laughed aloud. It was a warm sound full of life and joy.

"Are you happy, Liam, truly?" Rian wondered, his tone becoming reflective.

"I never knew what was missing from my life until Felicity became a part of it, and now," he paused searching for the right words, "now I can't imagine living a single day without her."

"Then you are indeed a lucky man."

Always the sensitive one, Liam became empathetic. "It will happen for you again, Rian. The right woman is waiting for you. Don't ever give up looking."

The thought that the right woman could very well be lying upstairs in his bed suddenly galloped across Rian's mind. He found the idea unexpectedly exhilarating, and mildly disturbing. He got up from his seat and poured them each a drink. Handing Liam his glass, Rian looked at his brother as if seeing him for the first time.

This was not the boy he remembered leaving behind, but a grown man, secure and confident as to his purpose in life. Not as tall as his brother, Liam could still boast a height of over six feet, and as fair as Rian was dark; he favored their mother's side of the family. At first glance a stranger might not think them related at all if his observation were based only on their physical attributes, but a keen eye could find the similarities. The same wide forehead; heavy-lidded, wide-set eyes, and the strong jaw that pointed to a Celtic bloodline.

Sensing a shift in Rian's mood, Liam spoke quietly. "Has something happened, Rian? Your thoughts seem occupied elsewhere."

Taking a healthy swallow from his own glass, Rian let the amber liquid flood his mouth with fiery warmth as he stared at his brother. How was it Liam could be so attuned to him even after so long a separation? He didn't know and he would not ponder the fact. He was just grateful that the bond between them had survived the intervening years.

"I had fully intended to travel by week's end, but it now appears that I may have to delay my journey." He paused and took another generous swallow from his glass.

Liam was filled with curiosity, and correctly guessed his brother's delay was because of a woman. "I am certain you have seen all the sights the city has to offer by now, so share with me the name of the seductress who keeps you here? Lady Isabel Howard perhaps?" Rian pretended to look shocked as Liam continued. "We may live in the country but that doesn't mean we are provincial. Gossip reaches us even at Oakhaven, and, according to my fiancée's mama, you and Lady Howard have been fodder for many wagging tongues."

What Rian thought about the folly of gossip, and those who indulged in it, was summed up in a disgusted grunt.

"She's a very beautiful woman," Liam continued. "It is easy to see how a man could find himself...distracted."

Rian arched a brow. His brother was being generous, but nevertheless. "And just how familiar are you with Isabel's talent for distraction?" he asked.

"There have been occasions when we have been on the same guest list. Did you suppose I kept myself in hiding while you were sailing the seven seas in search of your fortune?"

"Of course not," Rian said, surprised at the indignation in his brother's tone, "but I had no idea Isabel had made such an impression on you. Tell me"—he dropped his voice to a sly whisper—"does Felicity know of your association with Lady Howard, and would she approve, given her ladyship's reputation?"

For a moment Liam was confused, his expression puzzled, until he realized what was being implied. He quickly turned a deep crimson. "Good God, man! We were introduced, had a few conversations, but I swear that is all. I would never—and Felicity would never forgive me if I had!"

Liam's horrified expression was too much, and Rian began laughing. Realizing he was being teased, Liam joined him. The opportunity had been too good to pass up, and Rian was pleased to see Liam did not take offense, but shared in his mirth. He had not realized until now how much he had missed his brother's company, and as their laughter faded it was replaced by an easy, companionable silence.

"So, is it Lady Howard who keeps your attention?" Liam asked, swirling the remnants of his drink in his glass. "Has your affection for her taken a more serious turn?"

"My affection for Isabel has not changed. She is a delightful companion whose company I enjoy a great deal, and that is all. But you are not wrong in thinking a woman is keeping me here, just not Isabel."

Liam leaned forward, intrigued by this unexpected admission. His brother's name had not been linked with any other female, and he wondered when Rian would have found time to seek the company of another. "So what is the name of this mysterious beauty?" he asked.

"I've absolutely no idea."

Liam was flummoxed. "Forgive me, did I misunderstand? You say you are involved with another woman besides Isabel, but you don't know her name?"

"Involved is too strong a word," Rian stated. "In truth we have no connection, at least not in the way you're thinking."

"Perhaps you should start at the beginning," Liam suggested, looking more confused than ever.

At that moment Mrs. Hatch appeared to say dinner was waiting for them. Rian stopped her as they headed through the doorway.

"Any change?" he asked, and she shook her head. "You'll let me know immediately if there is."

"Of course I will, Master Rian."

"Any change in what?" Liam queried, as he bent to kiss the housekeeper's cheek. She returned his regard with a smile filled with maternal affection. It was a comfortable fondness that existed between them and one that was only offered, or accepted, in private. Rian did not mind or feel put out. Liam had always been her favorite, even when they were boys.

Clapping his brother on the back, Rian led him out of the room. "You're right, Liam. I think I should start at the beginning."

* * * *

The younger Connor listened as his brother shared his tale in a low and thoughtful voice. When it was done he became reflective, pondering all he had heard. "So you have absolutely no idea who this young woman is?" It was a purely rhetorical question.

Rian shook his head, dark hair flopping untidily across his brow. "I am confident once she regains her senses we will know both her name and what happened to her. For now she really is in no condition to be moved, and I do not feel comfortable leaving her here alone."

"No, of course not," Liam agreed, "but Rian, do you suppose she might have a family? A husband? Someone who is even now searching for her?"

He watched as his brother frowned, considering the possibility.

"She wears no wedding band. Of course there is the possibility that if a husband exists, he might be the one responsible for her condition," Rian added in a grim tone.

Both men looked at each but said nothing. Rian's brief description of the girl's injuries had been horrifying, and Liam could not imagine someone intentionally inflicting such a punishment. "You say she was restrained?" He grimaced as Rian nodded.

"So it would seem. Mrs. Hatch had to use scissors to remove the one strip that was still bound to her wrist, it was so tight. The bruises suggest she struggled to free herself."

Neither man wanted to speculate on what must have been going through their housekeeper's mind as she removed the remnants of the girl's bonds.

"And you did have her examined by a physician?" Liam asked.

Rian shared the doctor's tentative prognosis, but he did not disclose Dr. MacGregor's concerns about any possible mental instability as a result of the assault. "For the time being I thought it best that no one outside of this house know she is here," he continued. "Until we have any details, I think it would be prudent to remain cautious."

"What can I do to help?"

Rian smiled in gratitude at the offer. "I need someone who can find information, discreetly of course; only my absence prevents me from knowing the best place to obtain the services of such a person." He hesitated a moment before continuing. "And while I'm not suggesting you have ever needed to make use of such an individual, is it possible you might know someone who could offer such assistance?"

"What kind of information are you looking for?"

"The girl's identity, of course, but if anyone is searching for her, I want to know what their intentions are."

Propping his elbow on the table, Liam stroked his chin as he thought on his brother's request. "I do know someone I could ask. He is competent and discreet, but I might not be able to speak with him until later tomorrow."

"Well, I don't think our guest is going anywhere, anytime soon," Rian told him. "Tomorrow will suit just fine."

"I will need her particulars for a general description. Height, hair and eye coloring, that sort of thing. I want to be sure that if our inquiries bring results, they are for the correct person."

Rian nodded in agreement. "Mrs. Hatch can provide the information you need."

The past twenty-four hours had been eventful, strange and significant somehow. Rian wasn't able to put his finger on it, but he had the inexplicable feeling that this was a turning point in his life. It did not matter what happened tomorrow or on any of the other tomorrows that would follow; something told him that he was supposed to find this girl. He grinned, seeing his brother yawn sleepily, and, as if on cue, Mrs. Hatch appeared. "Begging your pardon, Master Liam, but I have taken the liberty of making up your room."

"Ah, Mrs. Hatch, you must be a mind reader. What would I do without you? I swear that if you were not so devoted to the memory of your late husband, I would just have to go ahead and marry you myself."

"And break poor Miss Felicity's heart? Get away with you now!" She flapped her apron at him before bidding them both a good night. After she had left, Rian posed a variation on the question his brother had asked of him earlier.

"So, when are *you* planning to return to Oakhaven, Liam?"

"I hadn't thought it would take more than a day or so to persuade you to leave with me, but in light of the circumstances, it only makes sense to extend my visit for a few days." A look that was part relief and part guilt crossed his face. "Felicity tells me the wedding preparations will be the death of her, but I suspect she and her mother have never been happier. I think a lot more will be accomplished without having me so close by."

"Are you proving yourself a distraction?"

"I didn't think so," Liam said in his own defense, "but I must be, for I have been accused of that very thing recently. More than once."

Now it was Rian's turn to smile sympathetically.

Chapter 16

Catherine felt as if she were on fire. She tried to swallow, but all that did was aggravate the rawness in her throat. She wanted to lick her lips, but her swollen mouth refused to open. Every muscle in her body felt bruised, and she winced at the pain searing through her, pain that alternated between agony so sharp it stole her breath, and a dull, throbbing ache that made her think she might never rise again. Even her hair felt as if it had been flayed.

What had happened to her?

From somewhere inside her head a voice explained that her body hurt because it was fighting to restore her health. She had a fever, which meant she was very sick. The knowledge was reassuring in an odd, disjointed way. Catherine knew about fevers. A fever came with illness, and with illness there was often pain. What she couldn't comprehend was why there was so much pain. Hesitantly she tried opening her eyes, but one refused to cooperate, remaining firmly shut as if some demonic seamstress had sewn her eyelids together. Panic threaded through her, even though the stinging throb that accompanied her effort clearly said her eye was injured in some way. Forcing her lips apart, she sucked down a greedy mouthful of air, then heard a sharp whistle as she exhaled. How could she be afraid when she sounded as if she was summoning a dog? Realizing that she might actually be doing more harm than good, Catherine sensibly gave up trying to force her eye open. As a reward her anxiety level decreased. Cautiously she opened her other eye, and focused on her surroundings.

The lone burning candle offered poor illumination, and as she tried to lift her head to better see, her entire body screamed in agony. She gasped as a wave of dizziness swept through her. Catherine ground her teeth together in an effort to dispel the discomfort, but a sizzling spasm running from temple to jaw declared her face had suffered the same punishment. Now instead of calling for a dog, she began to pant like one, fighting against the agony with short, openmouthed breaths.

With a supreme effort she managed to push herself up on one side before falling onto her back, shrieking as jagged bolts of fire ripped through her. Tears streamed down her face as she rolled onto her side, coming face to face with a young girl who stared back at her with a panic filled expression.

"Oh Lord!" Tilly exclaimed, putting her small hand on Catherine's brow and feeling the burn against her palm.

Flinching, Catherine pulled back, muttering weakly, "Who…are…you?"

"Please, Miss, don't get up! Lie back down and I'll get you some nice cool water."

Tilly wasn't sure exactly what Catherine was trying to say through her swollen lips, but there was no mistaking her intent. Placing her hands on Catherine's shoulders, the young housemaid attempted to push her charge back down onto the bed. Unfortunately, Tilly's charge was stronger than she, and it took only a moment before the slight housemaid was rudely knocked to the floor.

Struggling to her feet, Catherine loomed over the young girl. "Don't… touch…me," she wheezed, as her entire body trembled violently.

Recognizing the situation was beyond her control, Tilly scrambled away from the sick woman, not getting to her feet until she was certain she was safely out of reach. Hurrying out the door, she ran full tilt into Rian in the gloomy hallway. Awakened by the shrieks coming from the bedroom, he had scrambled into his breeches before coming to investigate. Tilly had never been so grateful to see him.

"What is it, girl?" he asked, taking hold of her shoulders while ignoring her wide-eyed stare at his state of undress.

"Oh sir, I need Mrs. Hatch." She pointed to the room behind her. "She's burning up with fever, and I can't settle her. I'm afeared she'll hurt herself." Yanking herself free of his hold, she ran down the hallway, disappearing in the dark shadows.

Catherine, weaving unsteadily, held onto the bedpost, watching the man who crossed the threshold and entered the room. She stared, frowning slightly at the sight of his bare torso although apparently quite impervious to her own nudity. Her one eye glared at him, glowing with a light that made her look wild and savage. All the bandages, save those still wrapped around her feet, now lay on the floor like discarded ribbons. Rian surmised a few had most likely come loose in her struggle with Tilly; the rest she must have pulled off herself. In any case, the physical exertion had reopened most of her wounds and his mouth formed a grim line at the sight of a trickle of blood sliding across her hip bone.

Catherine was held spellbound by the man across the room. His eyes, the warmest she had ever seen, mesmerized her. Deep brown flecked with gold and framed by thick, black lashes. There was kindness and strength reflected in his eyes, and a voice inside her head whispered that she was safe.

Trust him. He will not hurt you.

She could recall someone telling her that the eyes were a reflection of a person's soul, but she could not remember who might have spoken such words.

Trust him.

She wanted to, Good Lord how she wanted to, but then from a much darker place a different voice spoke. Loud and strident, it shouted inside her head, demanding to be heard.

He's a man, and it was a man who hurt you! Do not listen to him. He will only tell you silken lies. You must run; you must save yourself.

No, he will be your refuge, the first voice protested.

Silken lies whispered on a honeyed tongue! screamed the second.

The voices now took to quarreling, and Catherine found herself helpless to quiet them. For a moment she imagined the man across the room could hear them as well, because the expression on his face suddenly changed. The warmth in his eyes cooled and his mouth became stern. He was outraged, and Catherine knew she needed to tell him something, something important that he would understand; only she couldn't remember what it might be. And then the man moved toward her, and the moment was lost.

All the bed coverings were on the floor, and she watched as Rian approached, moving slowly as if afraid she might turn and run at any moment. His eyes never left her face, even when he carefully dropped to his haunches and reached for the sheet. She tracked his movement, turning her body to follow him and Rian found himself admiring her willpower. That she could stand at all was a miracle. Although seeing how tightly the skin was stretched over her knuckles as she gripped the bedpost, he knew the effort was costing her.

Doing his best to ignore the delicate curve of a breast as it peeked out from behind a tangled skein of her hair, Rian stretched his arms wide. In each hand he held a corner of the sheet, and he stepped forward with the intention of wrapping Catherine in it. She hissed at him, apparently not approving of his plan, and then startled him further by making strange, guttural noises. Rian hesitated. A fine sheen of sweat beaded her limbs, making her skin glisten, and her body, which had been trembling before, now shook more violently. He wondered how it was she had not yet fallen to the floor. Glancing at her still wrapped feet he concluded she most likely lacked the equilibrium needed to remove the bandages, and for that he was grateful. Especially as bright, crimson stains seeped through the strips of linen. A sure indication her feet were not yet ready to take the pressure of supporting her.

Rian was unable to stop himself from gazing at her. Matted with perspiration, her hair fell to her hips, and warmth suffused his face as he noticed the nest of slightly darker curls atop her thighs. As she tilted her head, the curtain of hair moved enough to hide the breast he had glimpsed, but in compensation it revealed the curve of her waist, the round flare of hips, and long shapely legs. She flexed slightly, surprising him with a display of muscle. More than he would have expected. This was a girl who had not spent her life in idle pursuits, but one who enjoyed the benefits of physical activity. And for some strange reason this pleased him.

She watched him. Her eye still glittered with that strange light, reminding him of a wild animal caught in a trap, and just as inherently dangerous. As if reading his thoughts, she curled her lip, bared her teeth and snarled at him. Rian did not need to be told that she was teetering on the edge of madness, or that equal measures of stealth and strength would be necessary to make sure she did not hurt herself.

He had managed to get as close to her as he dared, and feinted to one side in an effort to draw her off balance. His plan was to move in and quickly wrap the sheet about her, and his strategy almost worked. What he had not anticipated was the strength she drew from whatever dark place she was in. It was unexpected and powerful, and she used it to kick him in the balls. At least that's what would have happened had her stance been more secure, and her aim true. As it was, she managed to land a punishing blow that glanced off the inside of one heavily muscled thigh. Rian sucked in a breath while offering up a silent prayer of gratitude that he might still yet father a child one day.

Deciding to take advantage of his weight, he rushed her, and managed to get enough of the sheet wrapped about her body to pin her arms to her sides. The shriek of fury that issued from her nearly perforated his ear drums as she twisted and struggled within his embrace. She continued to kick out wildly, and Rian grunted when she caught him on the shin. It wasn't until she head-butted him, making him bite his tongue and suck in a sharp breath that he decided it was time to end her wild flailing before one of them really got hurt. Pulling her hard against him, he used enough force to unbalance her, but in doing so he also lost his own footing and fell back onto the bed, bringing the struggling girl down on top of him.

With both arms wrapped around her, Rian took the added precaution of throwing a leg over both of hers and pinning her against him.

"God damn it, woman, would you lie still? I'm trying to help you," he growled through clenched teeth and the taste of blood in his mouth.

At that moment Tilly burst through the open doorway, followed by the flawlessly turned out Mrs. Hatch who, in turn, had a tousle-headed Liam on her heels. All three of them now stared at Rian, and he realized that if the situation were not so dire, the picture he presented could easily be misconstrued. He lay half naked on his back with an obviously distraught female on top of him. A female who was obviously quite naked inside the sheet she almost wore.

He let out an exasperated sigh and wondered if he should explain that, up until a moment ago, their patient had been hell-bent on trying to ensure the continuation of the Connor line would fall to his brother alone. He doubted anyone would believe him, especially as she now lay meek and quiet in his arms with all trace of violence suspended.

As the moment of quiet lengthened, Rian could feel the feverish heat radiating from her body, and with a slight gesture of his head he motioned for Mrs. Hatch to come forward. Immediately the housekeeper took charge, going to the washstand and pouring water from the large pitcher into the basin before sending Tilly for more linen wraps and salve. Loosening his hold on the girl's arms, Rian began to ease himself out from under her, but as he shifted away, she managed to pull one arm free and grab his hand.

"No, don't leave me," she muttered hoarsely.

The firmness of her grip was something he had felt before, but at that time she had mistaken him for the person who had hurt her, and was begging him to stop. Now he could sense that she knew he was not the same person. Whoever she thought he was, her need for him seemed very real. Rian stared at her. The strange, almost feral light that had shone from her eye was gone, leaving the cornflower blue iris shimmering in a pool of unshed tears. Thick dark lashes glistened, and he watched as she silently pleaded with him. She swallowed, the movement of her throat making her grimace. A moment ago she had been positively violent in her effort to free herself from his hold, and now she was silently beseeching him to stay. Conflicted by this sudden change, Rian shook his head and looked to his brother for help. But the only response Liam had to offer was his own bewildered expression.

"She does seem a little quieter with you here, Master Rian," Mrs. Hatch murmured while dispensing a nod of encouragement.

"You wouldn't say that if you had seen her five minutes ago," he muttered sourly.

"Be that as it may, she is quieter now," the housekeeper continued, "and perhaps if you were to remain, she will lie still long enough for me to redress her wounds, and make her more comfortable."

It was a reasonable request and made good sense, so Rian perched himself awkwardly on the edge of the bed with his hand held fast in the girl's grip.

Tilly returned with the linen cloths and salve, and was then dispatched to brew a cup of Dr. MacGregor's special tea, guaranteed to calm a fractious body. Gently the older woman sponged the girl's face and wiped down her arms but her patient didn't seem to notice, keeping her gaze firmly fixed on Rian's face.

"I need you to lie down, child, so I can put some medicine on your back; it will help with the pain," Mrs. Hatch said softly, gently pressing her hand against her patient's shoulder. The girl remained rigid and uncooperative, and turned her head to stare at the matronly figure.

"You must let Mrs. Hatch help you," Rian said, grateful to see a flicker of recognition illuminate her face. Somewhere in the chaotic fragments of her mind, the housekeeper's presence registered.

Following her example, Rian put a hand on the girl's shoulder and pushed gently, surprised and pleased when she allowed herself to be lowered to the bed before automatically rolling onto her stomach. Her movement meant she had to release Rian's hand, and he swore he heard her whimper before she reclaimed it once more.

"Good God!"

Although Rian had described the girl's injuries to his brother, seeing them with his own eyes was another prospect entirely. Liam had been standing quietly, observing the interaction , completely unprepared for the sight of vicious welts and livid bruising that crisscrossed their patient's back. It produced a reaction in him similar to the one his brother had experienced at the sight. Unfortunately the unfamiliar male voice made her eye open wide with fear.

"I think, Master Liam, it would be best if you were to leave now," Mrs. Hatch told him. "I thank you for your concern, but as you can see, we are all quite safe, and in no danger." Her tone brooked no argument, and finding himself in sudden desperate need of a drink, Liam turned and left the room.

"I'll speak with him later," Rian said quietly.

"Aye, that might be best."

Cooing gently, Mrs. Hatch quickly applied the soothing ointment and, with Rian's help, once more bandaged the open wounds both on Catherine's back and her feet. Rian thought it likely the girl was in a state of shock. The pain, he knew, would come later.

Tilly returned with the tea, and Rian turned his head to grant some privacy as the patient was persuaded to sit up with her back resting against a mound of soft pillows. She still did not let go of his hand. After tucking the sheet around her for modesty, Mrs. Hatch quickly fashioned her long hair into a single, thick braid.

"When you feel up to it, I'll wash it again," she said kindly as she secured the end with a length of ribbon. Taking the cup and saucer from Tilly, she then dismissed the younger girl for the rest for the night. "Let's see if you can manage a sip or two."

Having kept his eyes averted while Mrs. Hatch attended to her patient, Rian now turned his head back, and gave what he hoped was an encouraging smile. The girl's expression did not change, but he felt her fingers flex as she squeezed his hand a little.

"I can sit with her now, Master Rian."

But moving from the bed proved to be impossible as she refused to let go of him, and any attempt to free himself only made the grip on his hand tighten. "I don't think she wants me to go just yet," he apologized.

The unnatural flush that colored her face was spreading, making its way down her neck and across her shoulders. He took the cup and persuaded her to take a sip. The honey sweetened brew soothed the rawness of her throat, and she greedily finished it for him.

"Can you tell me your name?" he asked, keeping his voice low so as not to frighten her.

"Catherine." It was an automatic response, delivered on a hoarse croak, but it was given without any hesitation. Rian and Mrs. Hatch exchanged glances.

"And your family name?" Rian kept the same, low tone. "Can you tell me that?"

Unconsciously he held his breath, watching the smooth forehead pucker in frustration as she tried to catch hold of something familiar and recognizable.

"Catherine…my name…is Catherine…" she repeated.

Her eyelid began to flutter, and she struggled to keep it open. There seemed to be something else she had to tell him, something important, but it was no use. The combination of the rising fever coupled with the calming brew was proving too much. The girl he now knew as Catherine sighed and closed her eye as her head fell against his shoulder.

"Mrs. Hatch?"

The housekeeper moved around the bed and placed her hand on Catherine's brow. "She's resting a little easier now, but the fever has yet to break. It will get worse before it gets better, but sleep is the best cure for her now." She looked at Rian. "Perhaps she will not notice if you were to slip away?"

He tried, but his movement made Catherine moan and clutch at him harder. "Perhaps not," he murmured.

"No," Mrs. Hatch agreed, "at least not just yet. In a little while perhaps."

Deciding to try again when Catherine had fallen into a deeper sleep, Rian resigned himself to remaining where he was. Trusting that her patient could not be in safer hands, Mrs. Hatch picked up the empty cup along with her tray of medicines and quietly left the room.

But Rian did not leave Catherine that night, or the one that came after. He remained as her sickness ran its course, sponging down hot, aching limbs with cool water, and holding her to him when chills shook her hard enough to make her teeth rattle. Dr. MacGregor came and left again. The Scot shook his head as his worst fears were manifested. He told Rian in his soft burr that he had done all he could. Catherine was now the architect of her own recovery. And despite the doctor's grim prognosis, Rian was pleased to discover the physician was a rarity amongst his profession. He refused to bleed his patient.

"Weakening an already compromised body is nae bloody use at all," he grumbled to Rian in explanation.

Mrs. Hatch and Tilly took turns, gliding in and out of the room like silent shadows, but Rian was the only one that Catherine would allow near her. He held her in his arms, rocking her gently as her dressings were changed. Poured cool water between her parched lips, and calmed her when Tilly needed to replace the soiled bedding. By chance he discovered she became less fretful when he sang to her, so he hummed songs from his childhood, and when he ran out of those his voice gently wrapped itself around some of the more polite shanties he had learned aboard ship.

But whenever he tried to leave her, Catherine would reach for him as if the physical contact was a lifeline she was afraid to release. If God was kind, he told himself, she would not remember clutching the back of his breeches every time he needed to use the chamber pot.

The hallucinations came as her fever entered its second day. At the height of her delirium, Catherine began to speak gibberish, her words garbled, and making sense only to herself. And with her incoherent speech came violence. Physical violence. The fierce aggressiveness that she displayed now was far worse than anything Rian had witnessed when he had first tried to wrap her in the bed sheet. Tearing off her bandages, she ripped and clawed at her own flesh before he was able to make her turn her rage outward and direct it at him. She came at him with a strength only those who believe they are in mortal danger possess. Caring nothing for himself, he used all his skill to make certain she did no harm to herself. Her fury became an entity unto itself as she fought against whatever monster had tortured her. And when finally she was spent, and fell exhausted into his arms, Rian knew that what she had endured had left an indelible mark on her.

At some point during the early hours of the morning, Mrs. Hatch softly stole into the room and found Catherine asleep. With one arm curled loosely around Rian's neck, and her head resting on his bare chest, she slumbered peacefully for the first time since her ordeal began. With her breaths coming in a deep, easy rhythm, Rian had finally let fatigue claim him. He slept with one arm around Catherine's waist, holding her to him.

The housekeeper smiled as the back of her hand on Catherine's forehead confirmed the fever's departure, but her good humor vanished when she saw the deep gash on the inside of Rian's free arm. A memento from long fingernails at the height of a particularly frenzied delusion.

"Shhhhh," Mrs. Hatch whispered, seeing him open his eyes as she cleaned and wrapped his arm. He gave her a grateful smile before slipping back into sleep. Liam may have been her obvious favorite, but he had long suspected the housekeeper kept a special place in her heart that belonged to him alone.

As quietly as she'd entered Mrs. Hatch left, but she was not surprised to find on her return a few hours later that Rian was gone. Catherine, sleeping peacefully, had finally relinquished her claim on him.

Chapter 17

While his brother had been wrestling with Catherine and her demons, Liam had not been idle. He made inquiries as promised, but could find no reports or rumors of anyone searching for a young woman fitting Catherine's description. And that he found very unsettling.

"It's the damndest thing, Rian, but you would have supposed that *someone, somewhere* would know she was missing. Every avenue I have pursued has resulted in a dead end. I simply cannot find a living soul who knows a thing about her."

"Or one who will admit to it," Rian observed quietly. He was now more certain than ever that anyone searching for Catherine would be the person responsible for her abuse.

A week had passed since he had carried her into the house. Dr. MacGregor had been seriously concerned at the violence she had shown as a result of her feverish episode, and had prescribed a course of treatment that kept his patient sedated for the greater part of each day. His intent was to make sure she got enough rest so her body could heal itself, and, from all accounts, his method was having the desired effect. Catherine was recovering so well that Dr. MacGregor had given orders for her to be weaned off the sleeping draughts. However, the physician was not the only one concerned over Catherine's behavior during her illness. Until he knew how much she might remember about all that had passed between them, Rian thought it best to keep his distance. She would, no doubt, be mortified to discover she had spent so much time in the arms of a man she had no connection to. So he left her care in the more than capable hands of Mrs. Hatch, Tilly, and Dr. MacGregor.

Now as he looked across the dining table at his brother, he could sympathize with Liam's frustration. "Trouble yourself no further with the matter," he instructed, pausing to refill his wine glass as they ate supper.

Liam merely grunted. This was a mystery and he was not overly fond of mysteries. Still, even if his inquiries had brought forth results, Catherine was in no condition to be moved. Dr. MacGregor had been most forceful in his instructions regarding her care.

"We shall just have to wait until Catherine can solve the riddle of her own past," Rian said, thanking his brother for what had turned out to be an exercise in futility. "And you have other things you had best be thinking about this close to your wedding day."

Liam opened his mouth to speak, but whatever he was going to say was disrupted by Tilly, who came bursting into the room.

"Sir!" she exclaimed, looking at Rian. "Mrs. Hatch said to come fetch you right quick. She's awake, and asking for you!"

Before Liam had time to react, his brother was already out of his seat and taking the stairs two at a time. Seeing Mrs. Hatch standing outside the master suite, Rian calmed himself. "Has she said anything?" he asked.

"Only asked to see the person who brought her here," she replied, placing her hand on his still bandaged arm. "But you must not tire her, Master Rian. She's still very poorly."

"Of course, I understand." He paused a moment before asking, "Does she remember anything?" They both knew he was referring to the events of a few days ago, not what had occurred prior to Catherine's arrival.

"She hasn't said, but I suspect you will know soon enough." Offering him a motherly smile, the housekeeper opened the door.

The first thing Rian noticed was how pale Catherine looked as she sat propped up against the pillows. It was a healthy paleness, if such a thing was not a contradiction. The last time he had seen her, most of her body had been flushed with fever, and it was something of a shock not to see the high color staining her skin. But he was relieved to note that the savagery which had possessed her at their last meeting was no longer present. Narrowing his eyes, he continued his perusal of her.

The swelling about her mouth was considerably reduced. The once-purple bruises mottling her skin had turned to varying shades of yellow and green which, unfortunately, did little to improve the pallor of her face. As he had suspected, the swelling of her eye had lasted only a few days, and he was pleased to see it now opened quite naturally. Dr. MacGregor had told him that, as far as he could discern, there appeared to be no permanent damage to either the eye or the rest of his patient's face. Good news indeed.

He waited for the slightest sign of discomfort, prepared to excuse himself, but Catherine gave no indication she was embarrassed to see him. If anything her brows pulled together in a manner he could only describe as quizzical curiosity. Deciding she had no recollection of what had happened during her fever, he crossed the room and seated himself in the chair that had been placed by the side of her bed.

Her eyes were the most incredible shade of blue he had ever seen. The same iridescent color that had amazed him the first time he looked into them. She raised her hand and fussed with the neckline of the nightgown she wore, as if wanting to draw his attention to it. A smile tugged at the corner of his mouth. He recalled all too clearly how she had felt in his arms wearing absolutely nothing at all. No matter how she was dressed, nothing would ever erase that from his mind. Perhaps it was a good thing that only one of them had retained the memory, although he thought he saw a glimmer of apprehension cross her face, but it was gone so quickly he couldn't be sure if it had been real or his imagination.

Giving what he hoped was a welcoming smile, Rian asked, "How are you feeling?"

She said nothing, her frown intensifying as she searched his face. What she was hoping to find, he could not say. Her gaze was penetrating, but revealed no flicker of recognition. Rian felt himself relax. It would seem a benevolent God had clouded her memory of the past few days. With a barely audible sigh she dropped her eyes, leaving Rian with the feeling he had somehow disappointed her. He was not the person she had been hoping to see.

She gave a furtive glance at some spot behind him, over his shoulder. Catherine might not have been embarrassed, but that didn't necessarily mean she was comfortable in his presence. Getting to his feet, Rian fetched another chair and placed it on the other side of the bed. "Mrs. Hatch, would you be so kind as to join us? I think your patient would be more at ease if you were close by." He waited until the housekeeper had settled herself before continuing. "I understand you asked to see me."

Catherine swallowed nervously before answering him. "Yes...I am told"—her eyes flicked to the housekeeper—"that I owe you my life, and I wanted to thank you. I am in your debt, sir."

Her voice was low and husky, and it sent a hum through Rian's veins that he had not felt in a very long time. It was the same feeling that had surged through him when she'd grasped his hand and asked for his help. He was surprised to find the sensation repeating itself, becoming stronger now than when he'd first experienced it. Seeing that the young woman before him was waiting for some type of acknowledgment, he pushed the feeling aside.

"There is no debt owed," he said, brushing off his part in her rescue, "but can you tell me what happened to you?"

"What happened?" She sounded hesitant, unsure, and the tips of her fingers involuntarily brushed the corner of her mouth.

"You were injured, quite badly." Rian was aware of how difficult this conversation was going to be, and he kept his tone gentle. "Do you recall how you were hurt, or anyone who would wish you harm?"

Catherine shook her head. "No…I cannot."

Rian glanced at the housekeeper, noting her frown of concern.

"Then can you tell us"—he gestured to himself and Mrs. Hatch—"what you do remember?" Although there was a chance the memory could be upsetting, Rian thought it was a risk they had to take. "Anything at all," he added.

Looking lost and vulnerable in the big bed, Catherine frowned. Her slender fingers plucked at a loose thread in the cover and she was silent for so long that Rian wasn't sure if she understood what he was asking. Perhaps English was not her native tongue, although he had not detected an accent of any kind in the few sentences she had uttered.

From across the bed, Mrs. Hatch reached for Catherine's hand, and began to pat the back. "There, there lass, you take your time," she said, encouragingly.

Her eyes downcast, Catherine did not look at either of them. Instead she seemed to want to focus on the loose thread. Rian was about to rephrase his question when she spoke.

"I cannot remember…anything." Her voice was a tremulous whisper, and her answer, while disappointing, was not unexpected.

"'Tis of no great importance," Rian said, telling himself he was guilty of expecting too much, too soon. "I'm sure you'll feel better after you have rested some more, and if you remember anything you can always tell Mrs. Hatch if you prefer."

"You don't understand," she said, a raspy huskiness filling the space between them. "I don't remember anything…*anything at all*."

An incredulous look appeared on Rian's face as the full impact of her words registered.

"Nothing? Absolutely nothing?" he repeated, dumbfounded.

She shook her head slowly and wiped at the tears that now spilled down her cheeks.

"What about your name, lass?" Mrs. Hatch asked. "Do you know your name?"

Rian held his breath, waiting to see if she could repeat what she had told them before. He could almost see the fog that clouded her mind, and her struggle to find a way through it.

"Catherine!" she burst out with obvious relief. "My name is Catherine." A look of wonder filled her face, and this time she gave a small laugh as she wiped at her tears.

After giving Mrs. Hatch a hopeful glance, Rian turned back to the girl in the bed. "It's a very nice name. Tell me, do you also recall your family name?"

She tried, but sinking back in the pillows, she shook her head. "I don't know." Her hand curled into a fist, and she beat it weakly on the counterpane. "I should know it, but I cannot remember."

Concerned by her growing agitation, Rian instructed, "Don't vex yourself, Catherine. It will all come back to you soon enough. You just need to be patient."

Wanting to offer a small measure of comfort, he placed his hand on top of hers, strong fingers covering her small fist. It was meant to reassure her that all would be well, but she snatched her hand away as if his fingers were a hot iron that burned her skin.

Rian's eyes narrowed and he tried to read beyond the panic that was clearly etched on her face. He told himself he had made a mistake. He had misread the expression in her eyes, and he chastised himself for seeing something that had not been there. It was not like him to make such an error, especially not where women were concerned. But he could not deny the message Catherine's reaction had just sent. His touch repelled her. A strange dilemma when he considered how, a few nights ago, she clung to him as if her very life depended on his touch. But then delirium had her firmly in its grip, and she could not be held responsible for actions she could no longer remember.

"My apologies," he said, quickly withdrawing his hand. "I did not mean to distress you."

Catherine shook her head, puzzlement replacing the look of panic. "Indeed, I know you did not," she told him, "and I do not know why I behaved in such a rude way. I apologize for my ill manners." Her confusion deepened. "Is it possible that we know each other?"

"Why, do I seem familiar to you?"

"I can't say." She was clearly frustrated. "But I feel a certain familiarity, as if I know you, or at least I ought to, but…who are you?"

The bewilderment he had seen in her face only moments before disappeared, and he found himself once again held fast in her steady, unwavering gaze. A rush of feeling came over him. Not the protective urge he had felt before, although that was still very much present; this was something else. A yearning he thought suppressed long ago had awakened.

"My name is Rian Connor."

Catherine repeated his name, letting the syllables dance on her tongue as if hoping the act of saying it aloud would be a key to a door she could unlock. Rian found he very much liked the way it sounded in her voice.

"Are we married?"

The question was asked openly, with no deceit or guile, and it startled both Rian and Mrs. Hatch. He swore under his breath, and the sudden rush of color to the housekeeper's cheeks told him his profanity had not escaped her ears.

"Bless you, child," she said, coming to Rian's rescue, "we may not know who you are ourselves, but I can assure you, you are not wed to Master Rian." She patted Catherine's hand, which, Rian noticed, was not pulled away. "You wear no ring, but do you think you are married?" Mrs. Hatch asked.

"I-I d-don't know," Catherine stammered. "I have nothing to base the feeling on, but no, I don't think I am married."

"Then why ask such a question?" Rian watched in fascination as a dark pink flush rose from below the neck of the nightgown to color her face.

"It was the only explanation that seemed possible," she said, looking him in the eye.

"Explanation for what?"

"The intimacy I feel between us."

"Oh my!" Mrs. Hatch gasped as her face turned a shade similar to Catherine's.

Looking decidedly worried, Catherine hurried to explain. "What I mean to say is I feel as if we are accustomed to one another, but in a private way." The huskiness of her voice sent a delicious shiver down Rian's spine, something he knew he would like to feel again, only under very different circumstances. "But surely I would remember such a detail, would I not? I mean had we been married and enjoyed the intimacy of a husband and wife…" Her voice trailed off and though her tone did not change, the flush on her cheek deepened. Rian found it very becoming. "*Do* we know each other, Mr. Connor?"

Afraid that he might let another profanity slip, Rian broke eye contact with her. It was a few moments before he could speak without danger of upsetting his housekeeper. "We do share a history," he acknowledged, "but it is very recent in nature and, although what occurred between us could be described as intimate by some, it would not be the word I would use."

"And what word would that be?" Catherine asked him.

"Exhausting," Rian replied, bluntly.

"Oh…I see."

Her face fell and she looked crushed, and mentally Rian kicked himself for his poor word choice. He had disappointed her again, and he did not know why that weighed on him, but it did. He braced himself for more questions, wondering how much detail he should offer regarding both her actions and his during her state of delirium. Catherine, however, had apparently decided not to pursue the matter any further, but the smile she gave took a great deal of effort to produce.

"I am truly grateful to you, Mr. Connor, for the kindness you have shown me. I don't know how I will ever be able to thank you." Her words were polite, and exactly what was expected from a young woman of breeding. A wall of good manners was something she could hide behind. And she was not the only one who could do so.

"You have a long way to go before you are truly well, but once you are, it will be all the thanks necessary," Rian told her.

He had embarrassed her after all, but she had raised the question of intimacy not he. Did she remember being feverish? Perhaps she did, and that was why she was now shutting him out. Should he try to explain what had happened between them? What would he say? He watched as Catherine pursed her lips.

"I think Miss Catherine needs her rest now," Mrs. Hatch said, bringing their meeting to a close. Rian was amazed at how easily his housekeeper now referred to her charge. As if the girl in the bed were already family.

He nodded and got to his feet, giving Catherine a respectful bow. At the door, however, he paused and looked back at her. She was leaning forward, supported by the housekeeper's arm as Mrs. Hatch plumped the pillows behind her. Feeling the weight of his gaze, Catherine raised her eyes to meet his, and the look she gave him said there was no need for him to worry over what to tell her regarding her feverish episode. She might not recall the details, but she remembered enough to know how she felt. Especially about him.

Chapter 18

Alone once more, Catherine allowed herself to give in to the fear that had been slowly building. It overwhelmed her, reducing her to a sobbing, frightened child. This time she did not try to hide her tears, but she did not want anyone to know, least of all the kind woman who was taking care of her, just how terrified she truly was. Her mind was a fog of shadowy images. One by one they slipped away, leaving behind nothing but a gaping void, and the echo of mocking laughter.

Her world had become this room and the only four people she now knew. Mrs. Hatch, the young housemaid Tilly, Dr. MacGregor, and Rian Connor. But according to all their accounts, she had known them only a matter of days. So who was she? Burying her face in the pillow and using it to blot her tears, Catherine made herself examine the few things she was certain of.

She placed Mrs. Hatch, Tilly, and the kindly doctor in one group, instinctively sensing that everything they told her was true. She had not known them before being brought to this room, and though she was certain she had never been in this house before, a vague feeling told her she knew what it was to sleep in such a grand bed with fine linens and embroidered covers. If they had asked her, Catherine was sure she could give a rudimentary outline of the responsibilities of the mistress of such a house. Though how she came by such knowledge was a mystery. But know it she did.

Her thoughts now turned to the other person in her equation, her benefactor, Rian Connor. She kept him separate because her response to him was quite different.

When he took the seat at her bedside she knew he spoke to her because she saw his lips move, but all she could hear was the pounding beat of her own heart filling her ears. Her rib cage constricted, making it hard to breathe, and from somewhere deep inside her a throbbing ache started to rise. It was a sensation that was both familiar and yet completely unknown. A sweet pain that flowed through her limbs, carrying with it an unexpected rush that intuition told her was desire. And then when he had touched her hand, it was as if the warmth of his skin against hers had jolted something free inside her. Terrified by this sudden, uncontrollable swell of passion racing through her, Catherine had snatched her hand away.

Now she was filled with shame at her reaction. How was it possible to provoke such a strong emotion simply by skin brushing skin? Catherine didn't know, but the sudden flare she saw in Rian's eyes as his hand closed over hers told her he was not unaffected. She wanted to tell him about the inexplicable craving she was feeling. Wanted to ask him if the sudden light in his eyes, the barely noticeable heightened color in his face, and the rush of breath through parted lips meant he felt the same. But the sudden change in his expression told her she was mistaken. He felt no affection toward her.

The man had saved her life. The last thing he wanted to hear was how the mere brush of his fingers across her hand had unleashed a wild longing in her. Created a hunger that rose so quickly and with such force, it unsettled her. Unsure of what to do, she had reacted in the only way she knew how. Her only explanation for such behavior was that shock had caused her to overreact. Her attraction to the man with the dark, penetrating gaze could not be denied, which was unfortunate for her. And then she had made things worse by asking the most inappropriate of questions. How could she think they were married? Rian certainly didn't behave as she imagined a husband would. He uttered no endearments, no words of relief at her recovery, and displayed no sign of affection or tenderness toward her. And yet that feeling of intimacy had refused to let go of her. So she had asked the question, unsure whether she would be relieved or horrified if he had told her yes.

In the end it mattered not. Rian had firmly denied any prior acquaintance between them, brushing aside her feelings by telling her the encounter between them was recent and had been exhausting. Exhausting! What on earth could have happened to produce such indifference on his part? It had taken all her willpower to hide the crushing blow his comment had created. If only she could recall the circumstances, she might agree with his point of view, although from the way her body was reacting, Catherine doubted it. Even now, lying back against the pillows, she could feel a heat in the pit of her belly that would not be denied, and a throbbing ache rising as she brought the image of his face to mind. The tilt of his chin, the thickness of his lashes, the curve of his mouth all made her pulse quicken. Unable to banish Rian's face from her mind, Catherine closed her eyes and let her thoughts drift, trusting they would help her make sense of what she had been through.

At the height of her fever, when her body had been nothing but a battleground, instinct had made her fight for her own survival. In her delirium she saw unknown hands reaching for her from every direction, trying to drag her down into the bottomless pit they inhabited. But she fought against them, crying out for help in her hour of desperation. She could feel her strength waning, draining to its lowest ebb, so she made one last, frantic lunge back toward sanity, reaching for something, for someone, for anyone, and hardly daring to believe it when her cries had been answered.

Alone in the wasteland of her nightmare, when she thought all was lost, Catherine had been picked up and swept away by a male presence that came out of the darkness to give her the strength she needed. She let him calm her fears and wrapped herself in his protection. There was safety in his arms. No harm would come to her now, so she gave herself up to him. Her strength depleted, she had yielded her very essence, offering herself to him, drawing on his strength and taking it for her own. Shamelessly she pressed herself against him, not caring who he was or what he might ask of her. Her only desire was to take him with her as she sank into oblivion.

When Catherine finally opened her eyes again, it was to find herself alone in the big bed. No strong arms comforted her, no warm body held her close, and she wept with the realization her savior had been a delusion. A product of her feverish imaginings enhanced by the potions prescribed by the caring physician. And as her reason returned, she told herself that none of it, least of all the man she had clung to, had been real.

And then she had met Rian Connor.

She was certain there was more to the connection they shared than he had described. How could he not sense the emotional maelstrom he had unleashed in her? This strange, inexplicable attraction she felt for him was too strong to be her burden alone. Rian Connor may have saved her life, but was that all he had done?

Sighing, Catherine felt the start of a headache thrumming at her temples. Her head was swimming with questions. Too many to be dealt with at the present, so she pushed them to one side, locked them in a corner of her mind to be examined and answered later. The headache was telling her she was overtired and needed to rest, but as she drifted off to sleep one thought kept echoing in her mind.

Whatever had happened between her and Rian Connor, it had been strong enough to set her heart racing, and light a fire within her. And whether he felt the same toward her or not, Rian was the one with the answers. Answers she was determined to get, even if it meant knocking him down and forcing him to tell her.

Exhaustion be damned!

Chapter 19

Another late night with the clock chiming midnight, and Liam and Rian sat before a dying fire in the library talking in low murmurs. The evening had been spent reacquainting themselves with the missing portions of one another's lives as only siblings with absolute trust in each other can do. Still, it had not been easy. The conversation had been peppered with emotions ranging from angry, painful outbursts to regret and sorrow for what had been lost. Each of them trying to understand how their separation had affected the other's life.

For Rian it was a chance to admit that, even if the bitter disagreement with their father had not occurred, he still would have felt compelled to leave home. There was a part of him that thirsted to see what lay beyond the boundaries of Oakhaven. It was a need that would not be ignored.

"And did any of it disappoint you?" Liam asked.

"The sights I saw no, the people..." Rian gave a shrug. "Men are men, no matter what land they call home or what language they speak. All are capable of great kindness, as well as the very worst behavior imaginable."

"And will you resume your wanderings when you decide life at Oakhaven is too tedious to contemplate?"

Rian gave his brother a searching look, wondering if there was a very different question he wanted to ask. "Perhaps I will find a reason to keep me here."

"Perhaps you will," Liam murmured, "but tell me, why did you choose the Americas as a place to settle?"

Listening to his brother recall the opportunities granted to him, Liam could tell Rian's love for his adopted homeland was genuine. But sometimes good fortune came at a high price. Liam couldn't help wonder if his brother would have considered returning to England had his wife still lived. The details of Sophie's death were something Rian had never shared, and hesitantly Liam now asked what had happened.

In a low voice, Rian recalled the happiness his bride had brought to his life, before she was lost to him and he succumbed to grief and despair. When finally he was able to move on, Rian realized that, although his grief was spent, his guilt remained. A burden he would carry with him always. He did not elaborate on the circumstances of his wife's death, and Liam knew better than to press him for details. It was clear to see the impact was deep. If his brother wanted to tell him, then he would do so in his own good time, and Liam would willingly listen.

"And what now, Rian?" Liam asked, stoking the dying embers of the fire.

"Now, I am come home. If you can find it in your heart to forgive me for ever leaving. It was selfish of me."

"No, it was self-preservation. You can blame wanderlust, but we both know the truth. I saw how things were between you and Father. If you had never raised your voice to each other, he still would have found a way to push you out the door."

"You think so?"

"I know so. I was the one left behind, remember? He lasted only a year after Mama died."

"Ah, Liam, man!" Rian ran his fingers through his dark hair. "Why did you not tell me sooner?"

"Because you had to come back when you were ready, and not before."

Looking at his brother with a new level of respect, Rian asked, "So how bad was it?"

If the loss of their mother had been hard on Liam, the loss of their father was even harder, though for completely different reasons. Without the guiding hand of his older brother, Liam was forced to mature overnight. Any resentment he felt about Rian's absence was described in short, clipped sentences. It was as close as the younger Connor would come to a display of anger or bitterness.

Staggering under the weight of his new responsibilities, Liam had thought he would fail miserably. But slowly, with each passing season, he managed to find his balance. Inexperience forced him to ask questions, seeking advice from whatever quarter would provide it, and in doing so, he had earned the respect of his tenants and the indulgent bemusement of his peers. Then, when he was certain he knew exactly where his life was going, he found out just what else he was missing.

That he had been desperately lonely after Rian's departure was something Liam had never shared with his brother until this moment. It was this isolation that made him purchase the city townhouse on a whim. Here he could distract himself as the need arose with the various pleasures offered in the capital. But the enjoyment was hollow, and the gratification fleeting, and he never stayed at the townhouse for any length of time.

He couldn't say what made him accept an invitation to attend the summer ball given by the Pelham family at the neighboring estate. Over the years Liam had received many such invitations from various families in the county, but only a few homes had been graced by his presence. This was the first one he had accepted in a long time. Perhaps it was the proximity of the Pelham land to his own, and he was just being neighborly, or perhaps he couldn't be bothered to find a reason not to go. Either way, in retrospect, it was a defining moment.

Standing on the marbled terrace, Liam had found himself staring morosely at a sea of color in Emily Pelham's beautiful manicured gardens. Unfortunately the overall splendor did little to lift his misery, and he wondered, again, what madness had possessed him to accept this invitation. It was proving to be a terrible mistake. The careful façade he wore to conceal his awkwardness around the opposite sex was being severely tested, and he could feel his anxiety growing with every new face presented to him. Which explained his escape to the secluded area of the terrace. Deciding that no one would miss him, and wanting to return to the familiar comfort of his own home, he started down the broad terrace steps. If he was lucky he would reach the stables without anyone questioning his destination.

He had reached the bottom step when a fluttering motion in the oncoming twilight caught his eye. Something pale moved in and out of the lush greenery, and as he narrowed his eyes he saw a young woman moving through the shrubbery in a manner that could only be described as furtive. She gave the appearance of someone who, like himself, was trying to avoid detection. Not realizing she was being observed, the young woman turned her head and gave Liam a perfect view of her face. He was surprised to find himself staring at Felicity Pelham, his neighbor's extremely eligible daughter. As he continued to watch, she took a step forward and was immediately pulled back as the hem of her dress snagged on the boxwood shrubbery. Tugging on the delicate material she uttered a most unladylike word, and succeeded, albeit unknowingly, in bringing a smile to Liam's face.

"Allow me," he said, going to her aid and freeing the silk from the clutches of the vegetation that seemed determined to keep the host's daughter to itself.

Felicity took a few steps back, shaking out the pleat of her ball gown before looking up at her rescuer. "Oh…it's you." Recognizing Liam, she gave him a shy smile. "The boy who rescued me from the duck pond."

Surprised that she would remember the incident, he returned her smile. "And now I see you've progressed to predatory hedges," he observed. "What were you doing? Running away?"

With refreshing candor, Felicity admitted that was exactly what she was doing. Like him, she was trying to avoid more introductions to the opposite sex. It was no secret that she was promised a dowry generous enough to tempt a great many suitors, and any son she bore would inherit Pelham. All of which made her feel like she was a prize heifer on display at the county fair. She envied Liam his ability to just leave, and told him so. They spoke only briefly, no more than a few sentences, but it was enough for Liam to know he was hopelessly, wonderfully, and perfectly in love. It came as a great relief when, a few days later, Felicity's father gave permission for him to formally court his daughter. And no one was surprised when he later gave him her hand in marriage.

The evening was a therapeutic purging for the brothers, but now their focus returned to the subject of the young woman recovering in the master suite.

"Do you think her memory will be fully restored?" Liam asked.

Rian shook his head before replying. "I honestly don't know. Dr. MacGregor says he has seen episodes like this before. The body sustains a horrible ordeal, and the mind, unable to deal with the reality, simply shuts it out. Sometimes a person remembers, and sometimes they do not." He sighed and steepled his fingers beneath his chin. "It is possible that Catherine may never regain the memory of what happened to her, but that doesn't mean she will not recall more pleasant memories of her past."

"What are you going to do, Rian, if her memory doesn't come back?" Poker in hand, Liam continued to prod the dying fire, attempting to coax it back to life. His efforts did nothing but stir the embers, making them glow brightly.

"Do?" Rian seemed baffled by the question.

"Yes, what are you going to *do* with her?" Liam put the poker back in the stand. "You know absolutely nothing about the girl, or her situation. Whether or not she has a family, is an orphan, or running to escape the gallows. Are you really going to take full responsibility for her?"

"Always the cautious one, eh, Liam?" The remark was spoken with affection and a mutual respect that accepted the differences between the two of them.

Liam already knew the answer to his question, had known it from the first night he'd arrived, but he wanted to hear his brother speak the words.

"You're correct, as always," Rian continued. "I know nothing about her, but I think we can agree there are some facts we can safely assume."

"And those would be what?"

"Well, as Mrs. Hatch already pointed out, Catherine is clearly not a working girl"—he held up a hand anticipating his brother's interruption—"and I don't even want to know where or how our housekeeper obtained her knowledge about the habits of prostitutes." Effectively silenced, Liam closed his mouth so Rian could continue. "Also, Catherine's manner of speech would suggest she has received more than a rudimentary education. The cloak she was wearing is of fine quality, and I have no reason to think it is not her own, and Mrs. Hatch told me that, though her hands bear some calluses, they are not from sustained manual labor." He drummed his fingers on the leather arm of the chair. "I think it is safe to say that whoever she is, Catherine was not raised with the expectation of having to earn her keep as anything other than the wife of a man of some means."

Finding nothing to dispute, Liam grunted in agreement.

"As for my being prepared to accept responsibility for her"—Rian spread his hands before him—"I prevented her from throwing herself into the river, Liam, so how could I do anything else? It is not an obligation that I would task you with, even though I know you would take it upon yourself were I to make such a request. You are about to be wed, and it would be most improper, no matter how understanding Felicity is." He smiled at his brother, lightening the mood a little. "Until she can tell us who she is, who her people are, and who hurt her, Catherine will remain my responsibility."

"For how long?"

"As long as she needs me to be."

Liam gave his older brother a puzzled look. There was something in Rian's voice, a low tremor behind the words that made him wonder if his sibling felt something more than basic compassion for the girl he had rescued. "And what does Isabel think of your rescuing a damsel in distress?" he asked quietly.

Rian looked at him in surprise. "Isabel? Why should she think anything?"

Liam started to speak, and then paused, narrowing his eyes. "She doesn't know about her does she?"

"I've not mentioned Catherine to anyone outside this house, and that includes Isabel."

Liam understood his brother's reasons for secrecy, but he was surprised he would include Isabel in the exclusion. "But...why ever not?" he asked.

"Isabel is not my wife, Liam. I owe her nothing in that regard, and besides, she's been visiting at Charlotte Maitling's country estate."

Liam hesitated a moment before blurting out, "You do know there's a rumor that Isabel would not be opposed to being married again, provided it was to you."

Rian sighed. "Is that gossip still being passed around?"

"So it is a falsehood."

"I'm surprised at you, paying attention to such hearsay," Rian rebuked gently.

"Ordinarily I would not," Liam admitted, "but when it involves my brother and matrimony I think it would be remiss of me not to listen to what is being said."

Rian snorted in disgust. If society was to be believed, he had proposed to at least a half-dozen eligible young women in the past week alone. But the fact that his brother, residing over a hundred miles away from the nearest fashionable salon, was aware of such a rumor told Rian this was more than nonsensical gossip mongering. Something had given this particular fantasy some teeth.

"I promise you, Liam, 'tis a falsehood. I am most definitely not about to take a wife."

"Perhaps I am not the one who needs to be told that."

Rian looked at the troubled expression on his brother's face. "You think Isabel is the source of the rumor?"

"I did not say that," the younger Connor quickly amended, "but it's my understanding she does not deny it, and has, on occasion, added her own embellishment."

Though he was aware of Isabel's thoughts on the subject of marriage, Rian had never imagined her as the originator of this lie. Did she think that by planting such a story she would force his hand? A foolish strategy for such an intelligent woman.

"From what I know of Isabel," Liam added glumly, "once her mind is set on a thing, she will move heaven and earth to make it a certainty."

"Would it surprise you to know I have considered the idea of a union between us ?"

A strained silence filled the room before Liam said, "Yes, actually it does."

"You do not think we would be a good match?"

"May I be candid?" Liam asked. At Rian's nod, he continued, "She's not the right woman for you."

"Really?" Rian raised an eyebrow. "What makes you think that?"

"I'm not sure I can put it into words." Liam gave his brother a hard look, and Rian noticed he wasn't the only one with lines on his face. "I will be the first to admit that she is beautiful and charming, and of course there is her wealth, though I know that is no lure for you, but there is something in her character that makes me uneasy. The idea of you taking her to wife…I admit, it does not sit well." The smile he gave looked more like a grimace. "I apologize. When I am tired I speak nonsense. If you tell me that Isabel is to be my sister-in-law, then I will welcome her to the family, and ask you to forgive and forget my foolishness."

"Forgiveness is unnecessary, Liam, and your concerns are never foolish. Put your mind at rest. I considered the possibility of marriage, and discarded it."

"And Isabel knows this?" Liam asked cautiously.

"We have not discussed the matter," Rian answered, "but I have never given her any indication our relationship would go beyond what it currently is."

"Perhaps she does not realize that," Liam told him. "When was the last time you saw her?"

"Not since…" Rian gestured to the ceiling, indicating the master suite situated directly above them.

"Good Lord, that's been almost two weeks! Have you sent no word?"

"Calm yourself, little brother. As I said, Isabel has been in the country with Lady Maitling, and was due to return—what is the date?" He wrinkled his brow as Liam told him. "Ah, then she has only been back a few days."

"A few days with no word from you? I am surprised that she is not even now beating a path to our front door."

Rian had the grace to look a little sheepish. "To be perfectly honest, my attention has been occupied elsewhere of late."

"Oh, for heaven's sake, man!" Liam chided, shaking his head in exasperation. "What do you suppose she will make of your absence, to say nothing of your silence?"

Rian responded with a nonchalant shrug, amused by his brother's agitation over this apparent social blunder.

"Well, big brother, you had best think of something to tell her. I cannot imagine the formidable Lady Howard permitting you to go much longer without an explanation for what it is that keeps you from her bed!"

"Liam, Isabel knew you were planning to visit, and has probably been told you are already here. Perhaps she does not wish to intrude on our time together."

Now it was Liam's turn to snort, and he muttered something under his breath before suddenly asking, "Are you looking to end your affair with her? Is that why you've kept your distance?"

"Do you really dislike her so much?"

Liam dropped his eyes, unsure if he had gone too far with his condemnation of Isabel. It seemed prudent to hold his tongue.

"If rumors of marriage have reached even your ears," Rian said with a sigh, "then I fear my involvement with Isabel has become more complicated than I would wish. Perhaps you are right, and I should remind her the only future I can offer is one of friendship." He met his brother's concern with a wolfish smile. "A friendship with some admittedly delightful advantages."

The chiming of the clock reminded both men of the lateness of the hour.

"I must be away early in the morning," Liam said. "I will give your apologies to Felicity for not returning with me." He got to his feet. "Why not send Catherine to Oakhaven as soon as she can travel? The change of scenery could be very beneficial, and I have a feeling being away from the city may aid in her recovery."

"Why is that?" Rian asked curiously. "Do you know something that I don't, little brother?"

"I'm not sure, but Mrs. Hatch tells me that city life holds no appeal for Catherine. She shows no more than a passing interest in talk of theater or museums or fine dining, but mention wheat yields and her face lights up."

"Now I know you are jesting with me!"

"That's exactly what I told Mrs. Hatch, but she swears it is the truth," Liam declared, placing his hand over his heart. "Trust me, Rian; our housekeeper believes that Catherine is a country girl. Send her to Oakhaven, and we will see. Besides she will not be without companionship. Felicity will welcome her, and she is very gentle as you know."

"You will be newlyweds. It would be indelicate of me to impose on the privacy of a new bride. Felicity would never forgive me."

Though not an expert in all the subtle intricacies of marital bliss, Rian was still fairly confident that the best beginning for any newly married couple was the time they spent alone together before resuming their roles at the family seat.

"I think you have been gone too long, brother," Liam teased. "Oakhaven has more than enough rooms to guarantee the privacy of several newlywed couples. All at the same time."

Rian grinned. "Well, in that case, perhaps sending Catherine to the country would be an excellent idea."

Chapter 20

Rian paced in front of the fireplace in Isabel's parlor. It was late afternoon, but Lady Howard had not yet risen. Rian had made the suggestion, somewhat tersely, that perhaps she could be woken and told he was waiting. Was Isabel still abed? That he didn't doubt, but sleeping? He made a rude noise to the empty room. He was being punished, and was secure enough to admit he deserved it. He had promised Liam he would call on Isabel the next day, but his brother had been gone a week and he was only now making good on his promise. Still, Liam could not chastise him for his unintentional oversight. Prearranged meetings with bankers and lawyers and men of business had commanded his time as he dealt with the management of his wealth. As a woman of independent means, he'd hoped Isabel would understand.

It would seem not.

At least his other female concern was not finding fault with him. Catherine was making remarkable progress, so much so that Dr. MacGregor had decided further visits on his part were no longer necessary. He had sounded positively mournful when he informed Rian of his decision, but the dour faced Scot was quick to point out that his attitude was not a reflection on his patient, but more the fact that he would miss the bountiful table he was always invited to share. Rian laughed. He had taken a liking to the physician and made a mental note to invite him to dine at least once a week whenever he was in town.

Now he decided he would not help his cause with bad humor. Especially not when he had no one to blame but himself. He should have called on Isabel as soon as she returned from the country with Charlotte Maitling. He had sent flowers with his apologies, and received a carefully worded note in return. Isabel told him to call when his guest no longer occupied his time. The reference could have meant his brother, but Rian suspected this was Isabel's way of telling him she knew about Catherine. He wasn't surprised. Obviously someone had talked. Secrets and servants were never a good mix.

Sitting in one of the large, walnut wing chairs by the fireplace, he waited for Isabel to grace him with her presence. She would appear when she was good and ready, and not a moment before. He took a deep breath and let it out slowly. There was nothing he could do to hurry the process so he looked about him, admiring the subtle blending of blues and browns that were the dominant colors of the room. It had a strong, masculine feel, and he wondered if this was why he felt so comfortable. Isabel was very clever to have furnished it specifically with gender in mind, but then she was very intuitive about the opposite sex.

"Rian darling, I am so sorry to have kept you waiting."

At the sound of her voice he got to his feet, and watched as she came toward him. Looking sleep mussed, she was busy tying the sash on her robe, and he thought perhaps he might have been wrong and she really had been sleeping. Then he wondered who was keeping her from her bed until the dawn hours. A thought he quickly pushed away. He had no right to reproach Isabel if she sought another's company. Standing on tiptoe, she kissed him. The scant pressure of her lips was notice she had not yet forgiven him for his neglectful behavior. "I apologize for not being dressed," she said, "but I suspect I might still be wearing too much to suit you."

She punctuated the confidence she had in her own sexual allure with a throaty laugh, something that, at any other time, would have immediately set his libido racing. But not today. Instead he thought her laugh sounded brittle, and her attitude an irritant that scraped on his nerves. Although he could acknowledge the physical pull that drew him to her—it was just as strong as ever—now he also saw what was missing. Whatever flame burned between them, it no longer glowed quite as brightly. At least not for him.

"Isabel, there's something we need to talk about."

"My goodness, you're being so serious."

Rian watched her face intently, searching for any sign that she already knew what he wanted to say. Though her expression revealed nothing, something in her tone made him think perhaps she had not been quite as asleep as he had been told. He became thoughtful, watching as she walked away and seated herself on the large sofa. She patted the cushion beside her. An invitation he declined by remaining on his feet with his back toward the fire. Isabel shrugged and tilted her head before speaking.

"Hmmm, let me see if I can guess what might be on your mind." Her expression turned petulant, and sarcasm coated her words as she continued. "The man I believed to be an ardent admirer of mine has chosen to ignore me since my return from the country. Ignore me to the point that I am left to wonder what might have transpired in the seven days we were apart, as well as the ensuing days that have passed since then." She paused and gave him a smile that was more predatory than pretty. "Now in all fairness, I did receive a large bouquet with an apology attached, but no other communication to explain such mystifying behavior. No letter or card, not even a scribbled note in his hand, so I ask you…what on earth could you possibly have to say to me?"

The realization that he had woefully underestimated the depth of Isabel's anger dawned on him. Whether real or imagined, whether deliberate or accidental, it made no difference. More than Isabel's feelings had been hurt by Rian's apparent disregard. Her pride had been crushed and she felt humiliated. Accepting every ounce of disdain that laced her words, he made no excuse for his neglectful behavior.

He guessed that Isabel had noted the cooling of his affection toward her the moment she walked into the room. He ran his fingers through his thick hair in frustration.

A small wrinkle marred her normally smooth brow. "Good God, Rian, if it's this bad, then we're both going to need a drink."

She rose from her seat and went to the table where some wine and glasses had been placed. After pouring them both a drink, she came toward him, her robe opening with each step, displaying her shapely legs. Rian took a generous swallow as Isabel resumed her seat. Crossing her legs exposed her from mid thigh all the way down to small, delicate feet encased in high heeled red satin slippers.

"I think you were about to apologize," she prompted.

A second swallow emptied the glass, and Rian came straight to the point. "I do offer my sincere apologies, Isabel, and I want you to know how much I have enjoyed our time together, but the time has come to end our relationship. It is for the best."

For the next few moments the only sound heard in the room was the brave ticktock of the ornate porcelain clock on the mantel. Rian watched Isabel closely, but her only reaction was to flare her nostrils slightly before asking, "Best for whom? No, don't bother saying anything for I already know what your answer will be." She paused and smiled. "Why don't you want to see me anymore?"

"I intend to return to Oakhaven after the wedding, and I am uncertain regarding my future plans."

"I see." She dipped her forefinger over the rim of her glass into the wine and then put it between her lips, slowly sucking on it while at the same time giving the appearance of being lost in thought. "Forgive me, Rian," she said with a querying look, "but I'm trying to recall when I asked to be included in your future plans. The moment escapes me. Do you remember it?"

She was clever, he'd give her that. "In truth, you never have," he admitted.

"Did I ever embarrass you either publicly or in private?"

"What? No, of course not!"

"Am I to assume I am now a bore?" Rian shook his head. Isabel could never be considered a bore. "Then it must be my appearance. Is it my hook nose, pointy chin and hairy warts that you now take objection to?"

"Isabel..." he growled, starting to lose patience with this game she was playing.

She softened her tone. "But you no longer care for me?"

"Of course I still care for you. I just think it would be better for us to part now."

Tilting her head, Isabel stared at him as though she was carefully weighing his words, and then she laughed. "I'm sorry, Rian, but you're making absolutely no sense. Perhaps if you were to explain it once more?"

He watched as she dipped the tip of her finger into her wine glass once more and this time there was no mistaking her intent when she put her finger in her mouth. He had been prepared to deal with an angry, spitting Isabel and found he was thrown off stride by the calm, reasonable woman sitting before him.

And God, she looks gorgeous.

The silky fabric of her robe molded itself perfectly to the contours of her body, a body he knew only too well, and she teased him by remaining perfectly still, allowing him to feast his eyes. The physical attraction flared stronger than it had ever before, almost as if his body was aware this was the last chance he would have to bed her. He could feel the lust rising as he caught the scent of her perfume. It was a tantalizing fragrance. Just like the woman who wore it.

With an effort he turned away and stood before the large picture window. Paying no attention to the view beyond the glass, he tried to decide how to proceed.

Isabel toyed with her glass as she waited for him to speak.

"The country has its own unique charms, but I fear such provincial delights would quickly bore a woman of your intellect," Rian said, turning to face her. Though lame, the excuse did hold the ring of truth.

She eyed him quizzically. "Shouldn't I be allowed to decide that for myself? Even I might find the peace and quiet of country living quite intoxicating…given the right inducement."

"It really wouldn't be fair."

The icy bite of her words belied the dazzling smile she gave him. "Your *concern* is most thoughtful." Dropping her eyes, Isabel became engrossed with the pattern on the toe of her slipper. It seemed like an eternity passed before she finally looked up."How is the health of your guest?"

Rian was surprised she had waited this long before raising the subject. Still, unsure of how much Isabel knew, he feigned ignorance. "Liam was in excellent health the last time I saw him."

Isabel narrowed her eyes and a vertical line appeared between her brows. "Now you're being insulting," she snapped. "Let me offer you a piece of advice, Rian. If you want to know what is happening above stairs then always seek your information below them."

"I'll keep that in mind."

"So, no more games. Tell me about the girl."

"There's really nothing to tell." He balked.

"Then it won't take you long, will it?"

Rian felt deflated, only he wasn't sure why. Given their history, Isabel wasn't being unreasonable in wanting to know about Catherine, but he was reluctant to share any information with her. On the face of it his disinclination was quite juvenile, but he couldn't help himself, and so he gave only give the briefest account. It was disconcerting not knowing what facts Isabel possessed.

"It was very Christian of you to come to her rescue," she said after hearing his version of events.

He shrugged. "It was the right thing to do."

"So you are quite determined to return to the country after your brother's wedding?"

He frowned. Was she done interrogating him about Catherine? He didn't think so for one minute, but decided to go along with whatever game she was playing until her true intentions were revealed. "Yes, for a while anyway," he told her.

She flexed her foot back and forth, making the jeweled slipper dance. "And you don't think I would enjoy being at Oakhaven?"

Wanting to prove to himself the hold she had over him had truly diminished, Rian sat down next to her. "For a brief visit yes," he admitted, "but I think in a matter of days you would wish to return here." He made a point of looking about the room with its expensive, tasteful furnishings. "This is where you belong, Isabel, and believe me when I say it is not my intention to hurt you." He took her hand and brushed his lips across her knuckles.

She raised a brow and gave him an amused look. "So I am to believe the only reason for this change in affection is your wish to sequester yourself away in the country? Is that it?" Rian refused to rise to the bait. "And you are certain there is no other rationale to account for it?"

Though not fooled by the expression of innocence she wore, Rian also wasn't completely certain he understood just what she was asking him. The last thing he wanted to do was say the wrong thing and upset her further, so he decided to play it safe. "I have no other reason," he told her.

"Liar."

This time her smile was warm and genuine, and, believing she was teasing him, and because he liked her, he smiled back. "Isabel, we have shared a wonderful time together, a time that I will always treasure and you know I will keep you fondly in my affections, but—"

She pressed her fingers to his mouth, silencing him as her voice became a husky whisper that inflamed the heat already pooled in his groin. "Rian, we are both adults and you made me no promises. No matter what others might say."

He started.

Isabel was acknowledging, and dismissing, the marriage rumor. She leaned toward him, and the lust that flared was his body's undoing. Isabel's eyes turned a brilliant green. "May I count on you to still escort me to your brother's wedding?"

How was it women could jump from one subject to another, and then back again with such ease? It was no wonder that most men found themselves saying the wrong thing.

"Of course," he told her.

"Good, then no more talk of your leaving the city. At least not today." She smiled prettily at him. "Now, I know that you will be standing up with your brother, and have duties as his best man that require your attention. Is that not so?" She leaned forward, just far enough to offer an enticing glimpse of her breasts as her robe gaped open.

Rian nodded in response to her question, his eyes automatically straying to the creamy alabaster skin as his groin became an inferno. This close, her fragrance was subtle yet completely overpowering, inflaming his desire. She shifted slightly and her hand brushed against his thigh. It felt like liquid lightning, and Rian bit the inside of his cheek to stop himself from groaning out loud.

"Well in that case," she continued, "you will be far too busy to pay me any attention, so why don't we just agree to divert ourselves with other amusements until the day of the wedding?"

"You don't want to see me until Liam's wedding?" The question slipped out before he had a chance to think how it sounded. "Of course I want to see you, darling." She gave a throaty purr that sent his libido racing, even though she seemed oblivious to the erection straining against the front of his trousers, blissfully unaware of the effect she was having on him. "I am simply saying I understand that you are going to be busy, and the last thing I want is to become a burden." The round firmness of her breast pushed against his arm, and he nodded. Isabel was being perfectly logical. He needed to get up and move. Readjust his clothing at the very least. "But you don't have to attend to any of those duties at this immediate moment…do you?" she whispered.

"What? No, not yet."

He watched as she ran the tip of her tongue across her lips and turned predatory. "Then we have time."

"Time for what?"

Leaning forward, Isabel kissed him on the mouth, reminding Rian of how wonderful she tasted. Her tongue teased him, while her teeth gently scraped his lower lip. She grasped his hand and slipped it inside the opening of her robe, filling his palm with the lush fullness of her breast. He automatically curled his fingers, feeling the stiff peak of her nipple rub against his skin. More than ready for him, Isabel moaned softly in his mouth as her tongue stroked his own. She dropped a hand and pressed it against his groin, promising to deliver the relief he needed.

Rian's lust roared through him, and he groaned. Isabel pulled her mouth from his and stood up. A slight movement and the robe slipped from her shoulders and fell to the floor, leaving her gloriously naked save for the high-heeled slippers on her feet. Reaching for his hand, Isabel placed it back on her breast, a seductive smile lifting her lips as she gave a husky sigh. It was a sound that was filled with need and wanting, and she was rewarded when Rian, no longer able to deny his own hunger, pulled her down onto the couch and lost himself in the silky perfume of her skin.

Chapter 21

Rian rubbed a finger across his chin as he stared out the carriage window, seeing nothing of the scenery beyond. It had not been his intention to enjoy Isabel's bed, or her couch as it turned out, but he also accepted that he had done little to prevent it from happening. Did that make him dishonorable? Any other woman would probably think so, but then any other woman would not have received him wearing practically nothing. He sighed. He was as susceptible as any man when it came to a beautiful, desirable woman, and there was little to be gained by berating himself over his physical reaction to the alluring presence of a skilled temptress.

He had been seduced by the perfume of her skin, the soft velvet feel as she moved beneath him, the silky whisper of her hair across his body. Allowing Isabel to arouse every sensuous fiber in him, he had answered her siren's call like a drunk needing to slake his never-ending thirst. His mind had warned him beforehand that she might try to seduce him as a way to make him reconsider his decision. He told himself he could withstand whatever temptation was put in his way. Too bad he hadn't checked to make sure his cock was also in agreement.

He couldn't decide if he was more angry or disappointed in himself, although, in truth, why he should feel either was a puzzlement. He was a grown man with a grown man's appetites. Isabel's choice of wardrobe made it clear what she wanted, and she had both acknowledged, and then dismissed, the marriage rumor. Even if her dismissal had struck him as a little too quick, her regard too casual.

But, as he moved them both closer to their climax, he had been filled with a sensation that he had not recognized at first. It was not until he was about to satisfy the wave of his own hunger that he was able to put a name to the feeling that pulled and nagged at the edge of his mind.

Guilt.

And as he came crashing down, his breathing ragged, all he could think of was that somehow he was betraying Catherine. And this he didn't understand at all. Wanting to end his relationship with Isabel had nothing to do with Catherine...did it?

The beautiful woman who had used him to fight against her inner demons had been a sight to behold. Completely vulnerable at the height of her fever, she had clung to him, needing his strength to keep her safe. Never had any woman so completely offered herself to him, body and soul, while asking for nothing in return. Was it any wonder she had unwittingly released in him sensations he had thought buried long ago?

The attraction he felt was not for the frightened girl who pulled away from him, but for the woman hiding inside her. The one who would not shy away from his touch, but would welcome it. The woman he hoped to meet again, very soon. In the meantime he would gain nothing by showing his feelings, and until he had a sense that Catherine would welcome his company, there was no reason to see her. He could find enough distractions to keep him occupied during the day, but the nights were not so easy.

Tossing and turning in his bed he found his sleep broken by images of a blue-eyed beauty who called to him. Like a hungry animal, she prowled through the jungle of his dreams, becoming a thirst that needed to be quenched, a hunger to be fed, and making his own needs rise in response. Rian found the only way to appease the fire that flamed within him was to sit by Catherine's bedside and keep watch over her while she slept.

Now he leaned back against the padded carriage seat and closed his eyes. What had happened with Isabel was regrettable, but could not be taken back. He would, as promised, escort her to his brother's wedding, and then return to Oakhaven and not see her again. His departure from the city would allow her to give whatever pretext she chose to explain the demise of their relationship. He had made a mistake in making love to Isabel, and he cursed his own foolish male susceptibility for it.

* * * *

Seated at her dressing table, Isabel began to restore order to her hair. Brushing the dark locks, she replayed the encounter with Rian once more in her mind, recalling every word, every gesture, and every nuance. It all unfolded into a scenario that did not please her. Even though Rian had made love to her with as much skill as ever, something was different this time. She could feel it the moment he took her in his arms.

In the past their lovemaking had always been filled with a sense of abandon and spontaneity that exhilarated her, but this time Rian had been careful, restrained even. It was as if only his body had been aroused while his mind had been...elsewhere. She slammed down the silver-backed hairbrush as the truth hit her.

How dare he! While he'd been making love to her, *he'd been thinking of someone else!*

Suddenly she began to laugh, but it was a vicious, ugly sound. Though he hadn't said it, Rian was looking to replace her, and it didn't take a genius to figure out who aspired to slip between his sheets and curl herself around his magnificent body. The dockside whore he had rescued had managed to cleverly drive a wedge between them. One strong enough to make Rian believe he had feelings for the strumpet.

Isabel stared at her reflection in the mirror before picking up the brush and resuming her task. She knew Rian well enough to know he had not yet taken the girl to his bed. If he had, nothing she did could have induced him to make love to her. The face that looked back at her became thoughtful and calculating. If Rian had coupled with her once, then he would do so again. She knew how to arouse him, how to make him want her. As for the whore, well, she had no idea whom she was dealing with...but she would soon find out.

Putting down the hairbrush a little more gently this time, Isabel moved to her writing desk. Quill in hand, she scribbled a hasty note. She had to act quickly, unable to afford the luxury of wasting any more time. Her rival had been under Rian's roof for too long already. Her plan was not complicated. She needed to find out all she could about the other woman, exploit her weaknesses, and then dispose of her. It was a method that had always served Isabel well.

Folding the sheet of parchment, she melted wax and affixed her seal to the note. She was not the type of woman who would meekly accept being replaced, and if Rian thought for one minute that he had seen the last of her, either in or out of his bed, he would soon discover that he was gravely mistaken. She would not give him up so readily. This temporary madness of his would pass. It had to because she had quite set her heart on becoming the future Mrs. Rian Connor. And Isabel always got what she wanted.

* * * *

John Fletcher made his living by listening. He was constantly surprised at how such a simple task was so difficult for most of the human race to master. No one ever really listened to what was being said which, on reflection, was a good thing or else he might not have been able to achieve the success he had in life. A quiet, nondescript man, he exuded an air of confidence that inspired complete strangers to reveal their innermost thoughts to him. And with this unique talent, he became the repository of a great many details about a great many things. He was a gatherer of knowledge. A keeper of secrets.

His sharp mind, coupled with a talent for knowing the optimum moment to use the information he gathered, earned him a reputation as a man who could get things done. It also took him from the slums of his birth to the finest salons and drawing rooms of the aristocracy. Recognizing that discretion was the most valuable weapon in his arsenal, he became so accomplished that it was rumored some members of the Royal Family had availed themselves of his talents. It was a rumor John Fletcher wisely chose to neither confirm nor deny.

His first brush against the fringes of respectable society came when his name was whispered in the ear of Lord Howard's first wife. Unbeknownst to her husband, she had foolishly used a family heirloom as collateral to cover a gambling debt. With the obligation satisfied, she found retrieving the diamond necklace had proved unexpectedly difficult. A single meeting between John and her ladyship was all that was needed before the brilliant gems found their way back to their rightful owner. Lady Howard never asked what means of persuasion had been used to recover her property, suspecting that even if she had, John would not have told her.

It soon became apparent that foolish choices were made just as easily by the rich as the poor, and John seized the opportunity to make himself useful in a wide variety of ways. Lady Howard discreetly circulated his name amongst her friends, becoming his unofficial patron, and he was genuinely sorry when she died.

It did not take him long to see that Lord Howard would not last six months without a wife, much less the year that society demanded. He became instrumental in making sure his lordship, seeking a diversion from his grief, was introduced to a dark haired young beauty who was more than willing to offer comfort to the grieving widower. Desire quickly turned into infatuation and marriage was quickly proposed, which the young woman eagerly accepted.

Like others before him John was under the spell of the young, vivacious Isabel Blackwood, but his fascination with her walked an entirely different path. In most men Isabel whetted the carnal appetites, but John's interest was on a different level and he had no physical desire for her. Though he liked women well enough to bed them if that was a necessary requirement to obtain his goal, in general he felt quite ambivalent toward the fairer sex. Beyond Isabel's sexual flirtations was a determination to rise above the accident of her birth at all costs, and he was filled with an admiration for her cunning instinct for survival. It was much like his own, and John wondered if she knew the common link they shared. The rich were not the only ones with secrets to keep.

Lord Howard was so besotted with his young bride-to-be that he was willing to overlook the issue of her parentage, but a past indiscretion could not be ignored. Should certain facts become common knowledge after they wed, Lord Howard would have no option but to divorce his young bride. John proved his usefulness by persuading the indiscretion to pledge himself to service in His Majesty's Navy. The aid of a press gang helped the foolish youth cement his decision. Grateful to have her problem solved, Isabel tried to thank John by inviting him to her bedroom, but he had politely suggested they enter into a more mutually beneficial arrangement. One where any services he might provide for her were rewarded with coin of the realm. Over the years it had become a most satisfactory agreement.

Now, as he scanned Isabel's hastily scribbled note, a look of concern crossed his face. This was out of the normal scope of their business dealings. Isabel was adept at using financial ruin as a way of attaining her objectives, and he was just as good at furnishing her with the details she required. But this time her request was different. It was personal.

He sat in his modest suite of rooms and came to a decision. He would not entrust this matter to anyone else. The present Lady Howard, like her predecessor, whispered his name into many ears, helping him to build on his success. John knew as little about Rian Connor as anyone, but he was confident that it would only be a matter of time before a maid could be persuaded to disclose the secrets of her master's house to him. He could be patient, and he would persuade Isabel to follow his lead, for they both had a personal stake in her future.

Chapter 22

Felicity Pelham was blessed with what was called a quiet beauty. While not plain, she did not possess the type of prettiness that would warrant a second glance. Able to blend into the background at any gathering, she was frequently overlooked, something she took advantage of as often as she could. As an only child she had been raised to be a loving and dutiful daughter, and it never crossed her mind to question the influence her parents had over her life. She deferred to their judgment in all important matters, and never more so than on the subject of a suitable husband. It had been a wonderful shock to discover her father thought Liam Connor would be an excellent choice.

Lured by the promise of a generous dowry, along with even more wealth attached to the Pelham name, many suitors had asked for Felicity's hand. All had been rejected. Charles Pelham loved his daughter and prided himself on being perceptive enough to notice if a young man caught her interest. None did until Liam Connor. A blind man would have seen the flush on her cheeks and the sparkle in her eyes whenever his name was mentioned. It was a sparkle he had first noticed when Felicity had been barely more than a child. And so he had taken it upon himself, as a loving father, to take a more active interest in the young man who had turned his daughter's head.

There was a certain quality about the younger of the two Connor boys. A quality that spoke of a serious bent of mind. One similar to his daughter's. No one could tell Charles why, at close to thirty, Liam had yet to take a wife, but suspecting it would please his daughter, he agreed to the courtship. Other than his own choice of wife, and fathering Felicity, Charles Pelham soon came to realize it was one of the best decisions he had ever made. So when Liam asked for Felicity's hand, he was delighted to give it.

News of the Pelham-Connor engagement spread quickly, and the more vicious tongues lost no time wagging. Before long it was generally concluded that the marriage was nothing more than a business venture. The merger of land and money. The gossips would have been most put out if they had only known how single-minded Liam had been in the pursuit of his bride. He would have taken Felicity with no dowry, and no prospects.

But he had been delighted to discover his fiancée possessed a fine brain, and with the proper encouragement, she could converse quite animatedly on a wide variety of subjects. Indeed, when engrossed in a subject she was knowledgeable about, Felicity's confidence grew, making the quiet beauty very loud indeed. In his heart Liam knew he wanted to share his life with no other.

To Felicity, Liam was the answer to a prayer she had only had the courage to whisper to herself in the dark. She had been ridiculously happy to know he still remembered the timid girl who spent one glorious summer tagging along with him and his brother as they roamed the countryside. Rian, being the eldest, gave permission for her to join them, but it was Liam who took care of her. Offering his hand when she needed help climbing over a stile, carrying her piggyback across a stream so her boots wouldn't get wet. And it was Liam who gently wiped away her tears and comforted her when she fell and skinned her knees. Was it any surprise she had fallen in love with him?

Emily Pelham, away visiting a sick relative, had been horrified on her return to discover just how and, more to the point, with whom her daughter had been spending her days. Declaring both Connor boys to be totally unsuitable as playmates, she had put an immediate end to the friendship. Sometimes Felicity wished they all could have known each other better growing up, but her mother had spoken and no one was going to defy her wishes.

Through the years, Felicity comforted herself with her daydreams. Sitting unnoticed in the kitchen, she would perk up when a conversation mentioned the latest mischief involving the Connor boys. Usually Rian was the subject of the conversation, but every now and then Liam's name would be thrown into the mix. It was generally agreed that Liam was the more sensible of the brothers. Rian reminded Felicity of a thunderstorm. Unpredictable and wildly exhilarating but far too exhausting for the likes of her. Liam was the calm that came after the storm. Still, it was said about the village that when riled, usually in defense of his sibling, Liam's temper was quick to rise, and only a fool would underestimate him. Temper or not, Felicity knew her heart would belong to no other.

Now, with her wedding barely two weeks away, she was experiencing an overwhelming case of premarital nerves. Her parents may have chosen to live most of the year at their country estate, but the Pelham name still wielded respect in the upper echelons of society. Because of this, the wedding of their only child had become one of the season's high points. Felicity had resigned herself long ago to having a large crowd in attendance. If left to her, she and Liam would have exchanged vows in the family chapel with only her parents and Rian to stand witness. She certainly didn't need all this pomp, but she accepted that her parents, by virtue of who they were, had to put on such a display. She was just thankful that Liam seemed perfectly happy to let his prospective mother-in-law have her way. He viewed the elaborate planning with all the bemusement typical of a groom.

This did not mean, however, that Liam was insensitive to the heightened anxiety his fiancée was experiencing at the prospect of becoming the center of attention. Taking her to one side, he promised that he would not leave her alone for a single moment on their wedding day and with this reassurance, Felicity felt she could face anything. To prove her newfound confidence, she did not hesitate when Liam told her he wanted to spend a few days with his brother.

"See if you can persuade him to return with you," she told him with an easy laugh.

"That may all depend on how strong a hold Lady Howard has on him," Liam responded with a troubled frown, relieved he did not have to conceal his opinion from Felicity.

"So, you believe there is truth in the rumors concerning the two of them?"

"That, my love, I cannot say, but this will be my chance to find out." He smiled as Felicity took his hand in hers, concern on her face.

"All the more reason to bring him back with you then," she repeated firmly.

"What a godsend you are," Liam murmured, brushing the back of his hand lightly across her cheek.

Felicity cast her eyes downward, but did nothing to hide the smile that lifted her lips. Gently Liam placed a finger beneath her chin and raised her face to his and then, with the utmost tenderness, he kissed her fully on the mouth. It was the first time he had ever kissed her like this, and her entire body tingled in response. At his silent urging she parted her lips, dazed to feel the warmth of his breath in her mouth. Her inexperience was evident, and Liam was cautious with his exploration. Gliding lightly across her teeth and the inside of her lower lip, he gently invaded her mouth. And while he playfully danced with her tongue, loving the taste of her, he subtly let his bride-to-be feel the force of his need as he held her to him. His reward was to note her reluctance to release him when he ended the kiss. While moments alone were not unusual for a betrothed couple, Liam did not want to do anything that might make his future mother-in-law regret such lenience.

"I doubt we shall be alone like this again before I make you my wife," Liam said, refusing to apologize for taking advantage of the unexpected moment.

Still caught in the passion of his kiss, Felicity gazed up at him with shining eyes. Liam kissed her again, but this time it was a more chaste press of his lips to her forehead. Once he was gone, Felicity hugged herself tightly and wondered how it was possible for one person to be so supremely happy.

Now, in the middle of a last fitting for her wedding gown, she received a note from Liam requesting to speak with her privately. As quickly as she could, Felicity scrambled out of the yards of pale blue material and changed into her day dress. She was still tucking away a few stray wisps of hair when she entered the morning room and found her future husband waiting for her. Over tea he told her about Catherine, glossing over the extent of her physical injuries and his own speculations on how she had come by them.

"I have asked Rian to bring the girl to Oakhaven," he said speaking earnestly, "and I hope that you will find it in your heart to befriend her."

"Oh Liam!" Felicity exclaimed. "Can you imagine how horrible it must be for her to have no memory of who she is, or where she comes from? Poor girl must be scared to death. Of course she must stay with us, and Oakhaven will be perfect."

Liam smiled and moved so he now sat next to her. Taking her hand in both of his, he turned it over and tenderly kissed her palm, making Felicity blush furiously. "You're a wonderful woman, Felicity Pelham, and I have no idea what I have done to deserve you," he remarked softly, before a look of concern crossed his face.

"What troubles you, my love?" She was still hesitant about addressing him so informally, and she used the endearment shyly.

"I think this girl is having the most profound effect on my brother, more than he cares to admit."

"Perhaps he sees some special quality in her," Felicity observed. Liam gave a thoughtful hum. "In any case," she continued, "one more guest at our wedding will make little difference ."

Liam shook his head slowly. "Oh, my love, I doubt her injuries will permit her to attend, and I cannot imagine she would be comfortable amongst so many new faces."

Felicity's face fell as she realized the foolishness of her suggestion.

"I know you only meant well," Liam told her. "Your heart was in the right place."

She looked so forlorn however, that Liam decided to spend the next hour or so restoring her good humor by asking about the latest additions to their guest list, and regaling her with tales about the new names. Most of the stories were humorous, a few slightly risqué, but none were told with malicious intent. He simply wanted to put Felicity at ease. He treasured these moments with her. In her presence, he never felt the need to be anything other than himself, and he looked forward to the quiet pools of solitude she offered in response to the sometimes turbulent events of his life. Being accountable for an estate as large as Oakhaven created its own set of demands, and it was a responsibility he took seriously.

He sighed, relishing the moment of absolute contentment. Felicity was the rock to which he would anchor himself for the rest of his days. He wondered if she would ever truly know how much he would depend on her.

Chapter 23

A week had passed since Rian's ill-fated meeting with Isabel. He had long since stopped scolding himself for his actions. It was a waste of time for one thing, and constantly revisiting the moment would not change what had happened. Whether she knew it or not, Isabel's decision not to see him before the wedding was exactly what he needed. Though he could admit to missing her friendship, he found the separation liberating. And he already knew there would be no invitation issued for Isabel to visit Oakhaven.

His emerging feelings for Catherine, emotions he thought never to experience again, needed to be examined without any distraction. He still did not know if they were substantial enough to pursue, or merely his response to a woman in distress. If all he had to go on was the way she had reacted to his touch when last they met, a sensible man would believe he had his answer. But Rian knew there was so much more to Catherine.

All the same, he was taken completely off guard to hear her light, feminine voice utter a string of profanity. He thought at first he was hearing things, but when the vulgarity was repeated, he realized Catherine had no idea just how far her voice carried. Curious, he approached the master suite and seeing she had her back to him, Rian leaned against the open doorway waiting to see if he could discern what had prompted the string of profanity.

She was standing next to the bed, holding onto the carved wooden post with a grip strong enough to turn her knuckles white. It was the first time he had seen her in the daytime since their previous meeting, and although he was kept informed as to her progress, it was gratifying to see the improvement with his own eyes. He recognized the dress Catherine was wearing as one of those he'd had made for her. Although calling it a dress was being generous. More of a shapeless sack, it was fashioned from a lightweight fabric and intentionally constructed to be loose fitting so as not to chafe her back or legs. Rian was able to see her feet poking out from below the hem of the roomy garment. Now that Catherine no longer needed the bandages, Mrs. Hatch had found some soft slippers for her to wear. Her hair hung down her back in a single pale braid that was as thick as his forearm, and he smiled as the ribbon tied about the end danced in the hollow of her back.

The breath caught in his throat when she suddenly let go of the bedpost and took a step forward, swaying perilously as she did so. The air was instantly filled with more salty words. Rian raised a hand to cover his mouth, curious to know who might have taught her this particular phrase. Even the most generously endowed man on the planet could not abuse himself in the manner she was suggesting. Taking a second step, Catherine repeated the first curse he'd heard, which told him these were the only two phrases she knew. Or perhaps the only two she remembered. He couldn't imagine what explanation he would give Mrs. Hatch if it turned out Catherine was no stranger to vulgar language.

But the thought did not stop him from grinning as he imagined Catherine cursing her way across the room. Apparently her feet still pained her, but she seemed determined to make use of them. Another step and then another, only this time the sharp intake of breath did not allow for words of any kind to be spoken. Filled with admiration for her strength of will, Rian looked on as she forced herself to keep moving.

Catherine had now reached the middle of the room, and stopped to catch her breath. She was in a sort of no-man's-land. Too far away from the bed and the support of the bedpost to return, but not yet close enough to the chaise which was her next anchor. Before he could offer any assistance, he found she was suddenly staring at him from over her shoulder. Eyes the color of cornflowers were filled with unexpected warmth and her smile proclaimed genuine pleasure at seeing him. Indeed, she gave no sign of suffering any anxiety knowing he'd been observing her.

"Hello, Catherine." It was all he could think of to say.

"Mr. Connor."

Her voice held a breathy tone that he decided was more a result of her exertions than caused by his presence. But he couldn't deny he liked the way she said his name. It was a shame she hadn't called him Rian.

"I'm getting stronger," she stated.

"So I'm told."

At that moment her legs decided to prove her wrong, and it took Rian no more than three strides to reach her. Gathering her in his arms, he caught her as her knees buckled. Disappointment filled him as he felt her stiffen in his embrace. Catherine might be all sunny smiles and friendliness, but her body was telling him something different, and although she wasn't trying to throw herself out of his arms, Rian could tell she wasn't comfortable being in such proximity. Carefully he rose to his full height and resettled her in his arms. She wasn't heavy, but catching her as he had made his hold on her somewhat awkward, and he didn't want to risk dropping her. The scent of her hair filled his nostrils, and the heady thrill of pleasure that jolted through him was a firm declaration of his attraction to her. Unlike the magnetism that had drawn him to Isabel, Rian sensed this had the potential to be something more. A feeling that ran deeper and stronger.

Catherine glanced up at him from beneath her lashes, and something in his belly caught fire. Rian felt as if he could whisper every foolish dream he had ever had to her, and she would keep them all safe. And this time there was more than a protective need stirring deep within him.

"Perhaps not quite as strong as you thought," he observed, seeing her cheeks turn a delightful shade of pink.

The absence of both corset and petticoats emphasized the feel of her body, and Rian couldn't recall the last time holding a woman had felt so right. Unable to help himself, he pulled Catherine closer only to be chastened by the quick compression of her lips. "Am I hurting you?" he asked.

Her reply was delivered in a curious squeak as she placed the flat of her hand against his chest, and pushed. "One of your buttons is poking me," she told him, referring to the fastenings on his waistcoat.

He didn't know what to think as she repositioned herself with a wriggle, and then put her arms around his neck as he continued across the room. "What were you trying to do?" he asked.

"I would have thought that was obvious. I was walking."

"And has Dr. MacGregor given his permission for such activity?" The physician, being in the neighborhood, had paid a visit earlier that morning.

Rian deposited her gently on the cushioned seat of the chaise. It might have been his imagination, or a case of wishful thinking, but he could have sworn Catherine hesitated as she pulled her arms from around his neck.

"Well, he didn't tell me *not to,*" she answered in her own defense, refusing to look up at him. "And besides, I *am* getting stronger every day."

"That may be," he told her, "but your balance still needs practice."

"I would have been perfectly fine if you hadn't distracted me."

"I saved you from falling over."

"I only fell because you were looking at me," she told him, mulishly.

He stared at her in disbelief. How had this become his fault? He took a breath and decided to try a different approach. "Were you planning on taking a few turns about the room, or did you have a specific destination in mind?"

Catherine pointed over his shoulder. "I was trying to get to the window."

"Whatever for?" The words slipped out before Rian had a chance to stop them, and he didn't need to see the look on Catherine's face to tell him he was an idiot.

"Because I'm tired of staring at bed curtains," she said, speaking with an exaggerated patience normally used to address a child. A very young child.

Rian immediately felt contrite. Obviously Catherine was not used to being inactive. The feel of her lithe build told him she was no stranger to physical activity, and he could sympathize with her frustration at being confined to the bed and this room. Testing the limits of her physical capabilities had been the reason for her impromptu stroll toward the window. Unfortunately, overexertion could also keep her bedridden longer than was necessary.

"Do you like to read? There is a library downstairs. I could see if there's anything that might help occupy your time."

"I don't know," Catherine said, wrinkling her forehead. At least she was looking at him.

"You don't know about what?"

"Reading."

"You don't know if you can read?" Rian frowned. It never occurred to him that perhaps she couldn't.

Her laugh sounded like a bubbling spring. "No, I'm certain I know how to read." She paused, looking at him with an expression that made his own pulse quicken.

"What is it? Have you remembered something?"

Catherine shook her head. "Not exactly, it's more like an impression." Opening her hands as if something rested in her palms, she stared at them. "I can sense holding a book in my hands," she rubbed the pad of her thumb across the tips of her fingers, "feel the texture of the pages," she continued.

"Can you recall the name of any book or an author perhaps?"

She pulled on her lower lip with her teeth, and Rian's quickening pulse was now intensified by a sudden heat spiking in his groin.

"No…I…don't know."

"Then I'll bring you a selection." His voice had turned unexpectedly husky. "Perhaps you will find something familiar, or possibly something new."

"They might be one and the same," Catherine observed.

"A possibility, but a slender one I think."

Taken aback by both the tone of his voice and the kindness of his gesture, Catherine thanked him. She was ashamed by how snappish she had been. It really *wasn't* his fault she had almost fallen. Her knees would still have probably buckled even if there was nothing wrong with her feet to begin with; he had that effect on her. But, in retrospect, maybe she ought not to have been walking unassisted.

"I really *am* getting stronger," she repeated firmly, looking up at him and daring him to contradict her.

Rian found himself suddenly drowning in a pool of azure blue. His mouth was dry and he could feel his pulse racing. He wondered how long his heart could maintain its sudden frenetic pace before simply exploding inside his chest. But as he pondered such a fate, a voice in his head whispered, *there are far worse ways for a man to die.*

* * * *

Mrs. Hatch had assured her that Rian didn't always look so austere, but the manner of her injuries, as well as her memory setback, concerned him deeply. Deciding it wasn't good for a person to be so serious so much of the time, Catherine was certain that with a little effort she could coax a smile from him. But when he asked about her walking and the doctor's lack of instructions, his tone said he was cross with her. It suddenly occurred to her that he might think she was deliberately jeopardizing her health in order to prolong her recovery, and so remain under his care. Determined to quell such a notion, she repeated her earlier declaration regarding her progress, and followed it by asking who was keeping him informed.

"Pardon?"

"I asked how you knew," Catherine repeated.

"How I knew what?"

Apparently occupied with other matters Rian had not been listening to her, which was both rude and frustrating. "That I was getting stronger," she said, doing her best to stay calm. "You said you were being told. By whom?"

He looked down at her, and Catherine could see from his expression that receiving reports about her health was supposed to be a secret. Did he think she was a complete nincompoop, unable to work out for herself his source of information? She was asking merely for confirmation. She sighed. "Mrs. Hatch or Tilly?"

"Both," he admitted.

She nodded and dropped her eyes. Of course they would keep him informed, as was his right. Once she was well enough, he would be able to relinquish all responsibility for her. Why did the thought of never seeing Rian Connor again make her feel apprehensive?

Catherine suddenly raised her head and looked at him in alarm. Her eyes opened wide enough to make Rian ask, "What's wrong? Are you hurt somewhere? Can I help you?"

He reached down as if he was going to pick her up again, but without thinking, Catherine slapped his hands away.

A notion had struck her, one so awful she pulled a small pillow onto her lap and began plucking imaginary threads from it. Nervously she cleared her throat.

"How long were you standing there…in the doorway?" she asked in a horrified voice.

Rian frowned, wondering where her train of thought was headed before he realized exactly what she was asking. He may have been leaning against the doorframe *watching* her, but he'd also been *listening* to her. A fact Catherine had apparently failed to grasp until this exact moment. It took all he had to keep his countenance one of serious reflection.

"For a little while," he replied. "Why do you ask?"

The air of innocence he affected was rewarded by the gasp that escaped her. He watched in fascination as the pink glow on her cheeks deepened to a crimson blush that raced up from below the neckline of her dress.

The column of her throat moved as she swallowed nervously. "Could you be a little more precise?"

Rian gave a nonchalant shrug. "Not so very long, I suppose. I marked your journey from the bedpost."

"Of course you did," she muttered more to herself than him. Though she kept her eyes firmly fixed on the pillow she was shredding, Rian could see her brows pull together. "So it is possible," she said, "that you might have heard me…talking to myself?"

"Talking to yourself?" He rubbed his chin with his thumb and forefinger appearing to ponder her words. "Talking to yourself, hmmm? Well, I suppose that's one description for what I heard."

She began to pluck furiously at the decorative tassel on the pillow. Rian was apparently not going to do the gentlemanly thing and spare her feelings by pretending he had not heard her cursing.

"I don't suppose you could be persuaded that you had been mistaken in what you might have thought you heard?" Her attention was focused entirely on the tassel and its apparent demise.

He shook his head. "No, I don't think that will be possible. Some things once heard, can never be forgotten, and it's well known that I am blessed with excellent hearing."

"Of course you are," Catherine muttered.

"Besides it's not every day I get to hear a young woman use language that would make a sailor blush. And trust me, I would know. About the sailor," he clarified.

Catherine may have known she was cursing, but she was completely naïve about what she was saying. The plucking now became anxious tugging. The tassel was doomed. "What I said…was it really so bad?" she finally asked him.

"Quite dreadful. I feel certain Mrs. Hatch would faint on the spot if I were to repeat your words to her, poor woman."

Catherine blanched. "Could I prevail upon you to not tell her? Could we not keep this a secret…between us?"

Rian walked over to the window, hands clasped behind his back, his mind mulling over this unexpected turn of events. Whether she meant to or not, Catherine was opening a door and inviting him in. He wasn't about to let her close it again if he could help it. He turned back around and gave her a thoughtful look, and watched as the color on her cheeks deepened even more. "I might be persuaded," he offered, doing his best to suppress a grin, "if you will answer a question for me."

She raised her head and he felt himself take a mental stumble. Even from across the room her eyes held him, pinning him fast and holding him down. "What do you want to know?"

"Who taught you to swear like that?"

"Oh, that was Edward," she answered easily, without hesitation.

The hairs on the back of Rian's neck began to prickle. Had Catherine even realized the significance of what she had said? A name from her past, someone she clearly remembered.

"And who is Edward?" Rian probed, keeping his tone conversational. *Husband? Brother? Lover? Friend? Please God, let it be the last.*

Catherine continued to gaze up at him, her eyes as dazzling as a summer sky and Rian felt his heart drum inside his chest. And then, just as quickly, her eyes darkened and she shook her head. "I don't know. I can't remember."

"Don't worry. It will come back to you."

"Will it?" The look on her face said she did not share his confidence.

"Yes, it will," he affirmed. "These things take time, and you must be patient."

Her sudden snort said patience was not a virtue she held in high esteem, but before further assurances could be offered, they were interrupted by Mrs. Hatch, who bustled into the room, followed by a maid with a tray. The housekeeper stopped and looked from one to the other, taking note of Catherine's flushed face.

"Why Miss Catherine, however did you get to the chaise?"

"Oh, um, Mr. Connor happened by, and kindly offered me his assistance," she answered innocently.

"Well, that was indeed fortunate," the housekeeper said giving Rian a knowing look.

The maid placed the tray on the small table close to the chaise. Mrs. Hatch dismissed the girl and settled herself on the adjacent chair.

Taking this as his cue, Rian said, "If you ladies will excuse me, I have some matters to attend to." He inclined his head toward each of them, and had almost reached the door when Catherine stopped him.

"Mr. Connor, did my answer suffice?" A small frown marred her brow and he saw the worry in her eyes. "Will you keep my secret?"

Out of the corner of his eye he saw the housekeeper raise her brows, but wisely made no comment. If Catherine chose to share the details she was free to do so, but he doubted she would repeat her salty language word for word.

"Of course," he said, giving her what he hoped was a reassuring smile, "but I think, as we are now sharing a confidence, you really should call me by my first name."

Catherine looked at him in shock. "But that would make me your equal," she blurted out.

"After what we have been through, how could you think of yourself as anything less?"

Chapter 24

Rian needed air, lots of air. With no destination in mind, he left the townhouse on foot. The best thing for him to do was walk. It didn't matter where he went as long as he kept moving. It always helped whenever something was weighing on his mind. Even something as delightful as Catherine. As he walked he carefully considered every moment of their recent interaction. Not just the words they had shared, but every glance that passed between them, every intake of breath, and every flush on Catherine's cheeks. It all became a ringing confirmation that it wasn't his imagination playing fanciful games *of what if.* What Rian felt for her was very real. Catherine triggered an elemental desire that no woman, not even one as skilled as Isabel, had been able to make him feel before. A need that had taken him by surprise with its intensity, but one he was more than willing to yield to. Not just physically, but with passions he'd thought were buried too deep to make themselves felt again.

When he had caught Catherine in his arms as she was about to fall, he had told himself the heat he felt rushing through him was an echo left over from the time she'd been delirious with fever. It was foolish to think that such an intense experience would not leave its mark. In the days and nights that had passed since then, he had repeatedly told himself the stirring hunger he was feeling was a mistake. Whatever spark had been ignited at that moment had to be extinguished because nothing would come of it. That he would never forget the feel of her body was his secret to keep.

And then with one faltering step Catherine had let him know there was a reason he still felt drawn to her. Expecting her to rebuff him, he'd been surprised by the inviting warmth of her smile. The spark was fast becoming a flame that Rian knew would quickly turn to an inferno unless he practiced restraint. What was it about her that was having such a profound effect on him, and who would have thought the key to bringing them closer would be delivered by a string of profanity? Profanity that even now made him grin at her appalling misuse of the salty phrase.

His own response to her was both exhilarating, and bewildering. Catherine was not the type of woman he was normally attracted to, or whose company he actively sought. Admittedly her beauty took his breath away, but his grief at losing Sophie had made him seek the company of women with experience. They offered far fewer complications, and he told himself he had neither the patience nor the temperament to deal with the anxieties of an inexperienced lover. An opinion he had seen no reason to change, until now. It seemed his set ideas regarding the opposite sex were being flung rudely out the nearest window. Instead of being dismayed at Catherine's apparent lack of experience, Rian found himself wanting to be the man to change that situation. As much for his own pleasure as for hers.

But did Catherine want the same thing? Had they met when she had the full measure of her own mind, capable of making informed decisions regarding her future, would she have welcomed him as a suitor? There was no way to be sure, not with her memory in such flux, and suddenly Rian felt he was taking advantage of a situation he had no right to be in.

A sudden gust of wind chilled him, and he pulled up the collar of his coat as he thought back to the first conscious interaction between them. Was it possible he had been mistaken? What if Catherine had not been repulsed by his touch, but the opposite had been true? What if the feel of his hand elicited in her the same desire she had awakened in him? Of course she would have pulled away, especially if she had never experienced such feelings before. Fear of the unknown was a powerful motivator.

If his intuition was correct, Catherine would need time to understand the longing stirring within her. Understand and accept it. A precarious condition considering her terrible assault. Being able to see both as two separate events, entirely unconnected, would be paramount to her mental well-being. Perhaps it was just as well she had no memory of her attack, although Rian had to admit her reaction to him might be very different if she had. Thankfully with maturity came understanding, and he was prepared to temper his growing ardor with patience. He knew she was not yet ready to see the mirror image of her own desire reflected in him. To recognize that he was both the cause and the cure for the growing ache inside her. If pushed too hard, too soon, she might not be able to reconcile the two. He needed to wait, and hope that once Catherine was completely well, she would want to pursue whatever she felt for him.

He did not concern himself with any notion of a husband looking for her. Family possibly, but his gut told him there was no husband. His own involvement with women of experience proved that, more often than not, they were also married. Their words were laced with sly innuendo, their deportment a promise of carnal pleasure, and looking at a man brought a very particular hunger to their eyes. Of course not all married women conducted themselves in this way, but those seeking a temporary respite from their marriage vows invariably did.

Catherine shared none of these indicators. The naive way she had blurted out the possibility of their being wed was proof enough she had no idea what it meant to make such a commitment. The absence of a gold band on her ring finger simply confirmed this belief, but should any of Liam's inquiries yield results, then whoever came to claim her had best be able to prove his relationship to her. Although even that might not be enough. Rian would not turn Catherine over to anyone she didn't want to go with, no matter how undisputable the claim.

A voice in his head spoke, *and what if she decides it is you that she wants?*

As delightful as that prospect was, he would still have to be cautious. He had no idea of Catherine's past. What influences may have shaped and molded her, and, if his estimation was correct, he was older than she by more than ten years. A sobering thought that brought with it a warning that their coming together might still be disastrous.

And yet…and yet…

You're looking for reasons that aren't there, the voice in his head scolded.

And still the possibility existed that all his speculations could be completely wrong. What if Catherine's feelings for him were quite different? What then?

Rian was reminded of his conversation with Liam, and his statement that he would accept full responsibility for Catherine. If that meant he had to absent himself in order to keep his word, then so be it. He would remain a distant figure until his need and hunger for her had faded. It would take a strong will to ignore his feelings, but he believed he could do it, no matter how much the idea filled him with misery. Catherine's well-being was all that was important, and Rian was determined to do whatever was best for her.

The voice in his head turned skeptical. *Didn't you tell your brother you didn't want a commitment? Why so eager to bind yourself now?*

In truth Rian knew the reason. Hesitation about a commitment to Isabel had been the subject of his discussion with Liam. A commitment to Catherine had a very different feel about it, although he couldn't say why.

Perhaps it is because the 'something' that is lacking in the one is what draws you to the other. The connection already exists, and even if Catherine cannot remember the details, she is aware that something happened between you. Give her the time she needs to discover it again. Offer help only if it is asked for, and above all be patient.

"And what if she never remembers?" Rian murmured inside his head, voicing his fears.

Then you will have your answer. The heart cannot be forced to feel what is not true.

The sense that his future was somehow entwined with Catherine's did not seem at all preposterous to Rian. Her presence alone was enough to ensnare him, but he had not felt this with Sophie, whom he had loved enough to make his wife. And that love would be a tragedy he would carry with him until the day he died. In his heart he knew what he had felt for Sophie had borne with it all the passion and desire of a young man's dreams, but the feelings rising now had nothing in common with the romantic yearnings of his youth. Now he had the raw, demanding appetites of a grown man.

Be patient with her. Give her the time to find for herself what you already know.

"And what is that?" Rian asked aloud, but the only answer he got was the wind rustling the leaves of the trees overhead.

* * * *

Mrs. Hatch had taken to spending an hour at some point of each day taking tea with Catherine. After discovering his housekeeper preferred tea over coffee, Liam made certain an ample stock was always kept on hand in both residences. And tea was always offered over coffee. But it wasn't just the beverage that both women enjoyed. It was also each other's company, and the housekeeper welcomed the opportunity to fuss quietly over the younger woman. For Catherine, it was a chance to envelope herself in a maternal warmth she could not remember experiencing.

"Mr. Connor must have a great many matters to attend to, I imagine," she remarked after Rian had departed. Despite his request, it would take some time before she had the confidence to call him by his first name. Except in her dreams.

"No more so than any other gentleman. Why do you ask?"

"No particular reason. I was just surprised to see him. It was the first time he had visited with me since"—she hesitated—"that other time."

"I suspect he thought it best to wait until you were a little better," Mrs. Hatch told her as she poured their tea. "You should have told me if you wanted to see him."

"No, I didn't—I mean it's not—I—" Catherine did her best to ignore the housekeeper's raised brow as she took the cup being held out to her.

"Well, don't fret, my dear. You'll have your fill of Master Rian soon enough."

And unexpected thrill surged through her. "Oh, why is that?"

"When you leave for Oakhaven, Master Rian will be going with you."

Startled by this unexpected development, Catherine paused with her cup halfway to her mouth and an unsettled look on her face. "I'm to be sent away?"

"There now, lass, don't look so worried."

The housekeeper's manner matched her words, but as Catherine set her cup back on its saucer she hoped the slight rattle went unnoticed. "What is Oakhaven?" she asked.

"Ah, that's the family estate. It's where Master Rian grew up." Mrs. Hatch cut a slice of bread, and set it on a plate alongside a generous dollop of damson jam. "Master Rian is of the opinion that good country air will help you to get better."

"Do you think he's right?" Catherine took the plate of bread and jam.

"Most definitely. The air in the city is dirty," Mrs. Hatch added, wrinkling her nose for emphasis.

Catherine gave a concurring wrinkle. "I suppose it is."

"Besides, I shall soon have my hands full with the preparations, and won't have hardly any time left over for such pleasant diversions as this."

"Preparations?" Catherine asked. "Preparations for what?"

"Why the wedding of course."

The bite of bread and jam threatened to choke her, forcing Catherine to wash it down with a most unladylike gulp of tea. "Mr.—Mr. Connor is to be…married?" she asked once she could speak again.

"Yes dear, that's right." Refilling her own cup, Mrs. Hatch did not notice the look of abject misery on Catherine's face. "Didn't I already tell you that?"

"No, no you did not."

No wonder Rian had looked so uncomfortable when she first asked if they might be husband and wife. And now he'd caught her cursing. Obviously his playful teasing had been to prevent her from being embarrassed. What must he think of her? No wonder she was being sent away. Although in all fairness, she didn't know he'd been watching her as she tried to cross the room. At least not to begin with, but by then it was too late. She'd already uttered the fateful obscenities. But why hadn't anyone told her he was to be married? Then again, why would they? It was a family matter, and she had no connection to anyone inside this house. There was no reason for her to know.

Mrs. Hatch continued to talk, a frown creasing her brow. "To my mind Master Rian will only be able to spend a day or two at Oakhaven before having to turn around and come back here."

Suddenly the idea of being with Rian in the confined space of a carriage was not as appealing as it had been only moments ago. In a single heartbeat a wondrous possibility had become a nightmare. It was more than Catherine could bear. "Surely, if I am to leave, there is no need to bother Mr. Connor with my departure. Could I not travel with you?"

"Lord bless you, child! I cannot dare to imagine the uproar that would take place if I was to leave." Mrs. Hatch chuckled softly. "No, it is best that I remain here. I will come to Oakhaven once the happy couple are wed."

Catherine's misery now plummeted to new depths. She couldn't imagine herself going to a strange place without the gentle comfort of this woman who had, in a short time, become more important to her than she realized. Noticing her expression, the housekeeper patted her arm, reassuringly.

"Tilly will go with you, and you will be quite safe with Master Rian. He was most insistent that no one else was to accompany you to Oakhaven." Gently, she brushed a stray curl from Catherine's forehead. "It is a beautiful house, and I will be there before you have a chance to miss me."

"Do you promise?"

"I do," Mrs. Hatch said solemnly, taking hold of Catherine's hand and giving it a reassuring squeeze. "Feel better now?"

She nodded, and both women sipped their tea until Catherine broke the companionable silence. "Mrs. Hatch, may I ask you something?"

"Of course, lass, anything you like." The housekeeper spooned a generous helping of sugar into her cup, and began stirring.

"What did Mr. Connor mean when he said I should think of myself as his equal because of what we had been through?"

For a few moments the only noise heard was the gentle clink of a spoon tapping against the inside of a cup. It seemed to Catherine that the housekeeper was trying to decide if she should respond at all, but a glance at the older woman's face said her question was not unexpected.

Mrs. Hatch had wondered if Catherine would ask what she knew about that particular time, and the housekeeper had told herself she would be honest with the young woman, just as she had in answering all of Catherine's other questions. But it didn't make the telling of it any easier.

"Before I answer, lass, you must believe me when I say you were very ill. So ill you were not aware of anything you said or did. And no one knows that better than Master Rian."

"Master...Rian?" Catherine's voice dropped to a tremulous whisper. Whatever this kindly woman was going to tell her, she was certain of two things. It would be the absolute truth, and it would be bad. Very bad.

"I know your memory has not yet come back to you," Mrs. Hatch started, "but can you tell me if you remember anything about when you first met Master Rian, or when he brought you here?"

Catherine shook her head. "In truth, I don't remember anything, but you told me he saved my life."

"Aye lass, he did."

And so the motherly woman explained how Rian had, by chance, come across her down by the docks, and stopped her from throwing herself into the river. Then, because she had fainted, he'd brought her here, to his brother's house, where the full extent of her injuries was made known to them.

"But...who would have done such a thing to me?" Catherine asked fearfully, unaware this was the first time she had ever asked about the person responsible for assaulting her.

"That is something we don't know, lass." Mrs. Hatch's eyes were sympathetic, but the hesitancy lingering in her words told Catherine she was keeping something from her.

"Tell me all of it, Mrs. Hatch. I need to hear it all. Please do not spare me the smallest detail, for not knowing will do me more harm than good, I assure you."

Taking hold of Catherine's hands, the housekeeper spoke softly about how Rian was the only person Catherine would allow near her while her fever raged.

"You did not stay with me? He made you leave?"

"Oh no, lass, it wasn't the master that made me leave. It was you."

Had Catherine realized the details of her illness would fill her with mortifying shame, she might have reconsidered asking for such an honest account. It made no difference that she had been out of her mind, with no conscious knowledge of her actions. She had been naked and ranting in the presence of a man who had no business seeing her in such a state. Her behavior was worse than that of a common streetwalker, if what she knew about those women was to be believed, and Rian was to be married! He must have been as horrified by her behavior as she was now. No wonder he had been avoiding her.

"As I said," Mrs. Hatch continued gently, "you were very sick, and unable to think clearly. Believe me we were truly grateful for the moments when you were so tired you no longer had the strength to fight him."

"I fought Mr. Connor?"

"Aye lass, but when you tired he was able to persuade you to take a few sips of broth and let me change your dressings."

"And he stayed with me? Through it all?" Catherine's voice was low and her cheeks burned furiously.

"You would not let him leave you. Not until your fever had run its course."

A rapid flurry of images suddenly appeared in her mind, and Catherine gripped Mrs. Hatch's hand tightly, her eyes glistening with un-spilled tears. "I thought it was my imagination," she said in a horrified whisper. "I thought he was someone I had conjured up, not a real man made of flesh and blood!" Her grip tightened, making the older woman wince. "What else did I do? You must tell me."

Pulling her hand free, Mrs. Hatch drew Catherine into a gentle embrace. "Only two people know what took place in this room during that time"—her eyes flicked toward the bed—"and I know Master Rian will never speak of it to anyone."

No wonder Rian had described their *intimacy* as exhausting. To learn that she had been with him in such a way was unbearable. How was she supposed to ever look at him again?

As the full impact of the housekeeper's words flowed over her, Catherine gave a stifled sob, and buried her face in the woman's shoulder as the sea of tears she had been holding back finally broke free.

"There, there, lass. Let it out. Let it all out," Mrs. Hatch soothed.

Chapter 25

Lying in the big bed, Catherine let her mind recall the day's events. It seemed as if an eternity had passed since she had first awoken in this room. Her concerns about her physical well-being had quickly been dispelled. She was healing at a remarkable rate thanks to the diligent care she was receiving and her own body's healthy constitution. Dr. MacGregor, whom she liked very much, had been honest enough to tell her that despite his best efforts, she would carry a permanent reminder of her ordeal. One of the lash marks across her back had been particularly deep, the wound unable to heal without the aid of stitches.

"I tried my best to close the edges as neatly as possible," he apologized, "but my mother did nae think sewing was a skill required of any of her sons."

Catherine assured him a scar on her back was no cause for distress, and she had no reason to be vain. Her comment made the physician wonder if she had been raised without a looking glass in her home. Apart from the occasional itch as the healing process continued, Catherine's only complaint about the scar was not being able to sleep on her back. The puckered skin still chafed at the pressure. Still, she recalled the scar had not bothered her at all when Rian held her in his arms. But even if it had, she suspected she would not have noticed. Her thoughts had been fixed on a very different place.

She was already far too aware of Master Rian's comings and goings. It had not taken her long to identify each set of footsteps that passed by her door. There was Tilly's girlish skip, Mrs. Hatch's no-nonsense tread, and then a certain long, easy stride that caused a strange fluttering sensation in her chest. At first she told herself it was her imagination that made her think the footsteps slowed as they approached her door, but when it happened three nights in a row she knew it was not a mistake. What did he do as he stood on the other side? Did he regret saving her? Did he wish her a good night's sleep? A speedy recovery? Catherine had no idea, but each night she found herself waiting for the sound of his footsteps to pause before continuing down the hall.

What was it that drew her to him? Even now, as she lay on her pillows with only the pale flicker of candlelight to keep away the shadows, there was a dryness in the back of her throat, a quickening of her pulse when she brought the image of his face to her mind. A single look was enough to make an unexplainable ache manifest within her. A sensation that had exploded on seeing him standing in the doorway. Was this what desire felt like? She didn't know, but she imagined it might be, especially as the hunger brought with it a heat that throbbed between her thighs.

Secretly Catherine had hoped Rian would confirm her preposterous idea of their being married, for she could not imagine feeling this way about a man she had no emotional tie to. But the crushing denial had been a declaration that he did not share the same feelings for her. Why then had he been so hurt when she snatched her hand away, and why allow her to see it in his eyes? It was more than a reaction to a lack of manners on her part. Rian might not be experiencing the same depth of feeling she did, but he felt something.

Mrs. Hatch's decision to spend time with Catherine each day was reaping numerous benefits. Not only did it ease the tedium of her convalescence, but talking with the housekeeper also stemmed the fear she felt at losing her memory. In the beginning their conversation revolved around the household. The number of boys to be hired to clean the windows, a new recipe cook wanted to try for dinner, the need to dismiss the laundry girl for ruining two of Master Rian's shirts. It was idle chitchat about the mundane in the hope a casual reference might open a door to the familiar. But as Catherine became more comfortable with the housekeeper, it was she who began to ask questions. Mainly about Mrs. Hatch and her children, and then about the Connor family. She did not, however, share her feelings about Rian.

Convinced that some unknown connection was behind her response to him, Catherine believed their pasts might be linked. But Mrs. Hatch had quickly refuted the possibility, telling her Master Rian had only recently returned from overseas. Was it possible Catherine's family had dealings in the Americas? She frowned and chewed on her lower lip in frustration. Anything was possible, but the suggestion did not feel as if it had merit, and so she discarded it.

In the beginning she had been grateful for Rian's continued absence. It made sifting through the chaos in her head easier to deal with, but then she found herself mired in a pit of conflicting sensations that both scared and aroused her. The only thing she was able to discern from the turmoil was the persistent sense of being connected to him. Yet she had no idea how…or why.

Until now.

She had believed the images in her head were a product of her own fevered imagination, or the good doctor's sleeping draughts, but Catherine now struggled to come to terms with the truth. The man she had fought with in her delirium had been very real.

It was Rian who had prevented her from harming herself, who comforted her when she collapsed in exhaustion, who held her tightly to him, allowing her soft curves to meld against his hard frame, and who whispered promises to her in the dark as he wiped down her burning skin. She recalled the muscular feel of his arms as he cradled her against his chest, and the easy way he held her seemed the most natural thing in the world. The warmth of his body had awakened the hunger which had turned into a raging torrent and she had been helpless to stop it from roaring through her.

Catherine was barely able to admit to herself that she dreamed about him. Dreams in which he touched her with a familiarity that could never be described as exhausting. She would come awake with trembling limbs and his name on her lips as she yearned for him. Only now she had to conceal such feelings. Lock them away deep inside her in a place where, given enough time, they would wither and die.

He was promised to another.

She fell back among the pillows. Perhaps being sent away was for the best. Rian would surely be relieved to have her gone. Distancing herself from him would help conquer feelings that she now knew were hopeless. She needed to focus her energies on other things. Her body was healing. Now it was time to heal her mind.

No one could imagine the anguish that came with having no recollection of her past. Though Mrs. Hatch felt a great deal of empathy, her response was that of a mother seeing her child in pain. Dr. MacGregor would be quite surprised at how often Catherine did gaze at her reflection in a mirror, but it was not to admire the handsomeness of her features. She was searching for recognition. The face that stared back was that of a stranger. There was nothing familiar about the shape of her eyes, the curve of her cheek, or the width of her mouth. Did she favor her mother or her father? Which of them had given her the color of her hair? She ran the tips of her fingers lightly over the calluses on each palm, but had no idea what had caused them.

Her mind was clear enough when it came to commonplace details, and she could function perfectly well on a day-to-day basis. But she was unable to recall any personal particulars. Sometimes she thought she saw images in her mind. Blurred pictures she knew were important, but when she reached out to examine them, they vanished like a will-o'-the-wisp. The only thing that had surfaced from the grey fog shrouding her memories had been her first name, and she knew intuitively that Catherine was her true name. But why was she unable to recall her family name? And now, apparently she also knew someone called Edward. A brother or a cousin perhaps? Surely only a relative would teach her such vile phrases.

She sighed. Sensibly she reasoned she had no future until her memory was restored and she could remember her past, but why did she feel so despondent at the thought Rian might not be a part of either?

Chapter 26

The clock on the mantel chimed the hour and the ache in her lower back told Catherine she had been sitting for too long. Almost a week had passed since her conversation with Mrs. Hatch and she had seen nothing of Rian. She did not inquire as to his whereabouts, and no one offered any information regarding his absence. She had no doubt, however, that he knew of her conversation with Mrs. Hatch. What he now thought of her she couldn't begin to imagine. She had absolutely no idea how she was going to be able to face him. All she could do was hope his forthcoming wedding would be enough reason for him not to seek her out.

She offered some advice to her reflection as she smoothed her hair. "Should Mr. Connor deign to converse with you again, you will simply have to follow his lead. Mrs. Hatch has assured you he will not refer to the matter, so stop imagining the worst, and hold your own tongue."

It was good advice, but Catherine had the oddest feeling that too often her emotions got the better of her, and advice in any form made a quick exit through the closest door or nearest window. She had the uncanny feeling it was something she experienced more often than she should.

Ignoring her own warning, Catherine decided a walk would be a good way to stretch out her back. Carefully she swung her legs over the edge of the chaise and pushed herself up off the seat until she was standing. She only winced a little with the effort, and was able to complete two full circuits of the room before making her way to the large picture window. Settling herself down on the cushioned window seat, she gazed with interest at the world beyond the glass. There was a good view of the street and the park beyond, and though there was now less pedestrian traffic due to the colder weather, there was always something to see.

She tucked a leg beneath her, her hand smoothing out a wrinkle in the skirt of her dress. She was still wearing the loose-fitting garments made specifically for her, and had been surprised to learn it was Rian who had given instructions to the dressmaker. But the sack dresses weren't all he'd requested to be made. His generosity had included the provision of an entire wardrobe.

The trunks had arrived a few days ago, and Tilly had squealed in delight at being allowed to open them. A mix of fashionable day dresses and evening gowns had been eagerly pulled out. All of them Catherine would delight in wearing, when she could suffer a corset once more. Holding up a pale blue muslin with lace embellishments at the neckline and sleeves, she could see it was almost a perfect fit.

"How on earth did he know what measurements to give the dressmaker?" she asked.

Mrs. Hatch, who had joined them, answered with an enigmatic smile. "Master Rian," she said, "has always been blessed with a most discerning eye." And she refused to say any more on the matter. If nothing else, Catherine could not fault his taste. The selection of colors and fabrics made him quite a connoisseur of women's fashion.

A frown now creased her brow as she stared out the window. Was it improper to accept such generosity? While it was true she needed clothes, surely only one or two of the plainer dresses would suffice. What need had she of ball gowns? She would tell Mrs. Hatch to have them returned. Her debt to Rian was already more than she could ever repay, and once she was no longer his concern, he would give her no more than a passing thought. Her frown deepened, and she instantly became depressed by the idea of leaving. Any hope that his renewed absence would help conquer her feelings was proving useless. She was ashamed to admit that not even knowing he was betrothed was making a difference. The flame within her continued to burn just as brightly, just as strong.

While she stared out through the pane of glass, movement caught her attention. She was surprised to see snowflakes, the first of the season. So delighted was she by their appearance she didn't realize a carriage had pulled up to the house until the coachman jumped down. The only visitor who had come thus far had been Dr. MacGregor, but this carriage was much too grand to belong to him. Curious, Catherine watched the coachman as he opened the carriage door, and put down the steps. The exhale of his breaths created puffs of smoke that wreathed about his hat as he now extended his hand to the occupant.

A deep red full-length cape, trimmed with white fur, enveloped the figure that emerged. The woman took a step forward, and then stopped and turned her face upward to gaze at the window where Catherine was seated. Even across the distance between them, Catherine could see the exotic face inside the hood, framed by dark curls. The woman was very beautiful. With no way to tell if her own face could be seen just as easily, Catherine remained still, unwilling to draw attention to herself. The visitor continued to look upwards a few moments longer, and then with a swish of her cape she turned and disappeared through the front door.

A sudden sense of foreboding had Catherine rubbing her forearms briskly. She scolded herself for her foolishness, but decided to return to the warmth of the fire nevertheless. Seated once more on the chaise, she wrapped a shawl about her shoulders, unsurprised by its ineffectiveness. The chill she felt had nothing to do with the temperature in the room.

Catherine could feel no connection to the woman from the carriage, and was convinced she did not know her. Unfortunately she could not say with any degree of certainty that the reverse was also true. Perhaps the woman knew her? She considered the look on the woman's face as she gazed up at the window. Someone like that Catherine would surely remember. Though confident the woman had no claim on her past, she could not, however, shake the unsettling feeling that she was inexplicably entwined with her present and her future.

* * * *

A knock on the study door rescued Rian from the reports he was reading. Liam had left a number of documents regarding a wide variety of holdings within the family's possession for his perusal. He had been both amazed and humbled at the extent to which the family wealth had been increased, as well as his brother's ideas for new areas of growth. However, even Rian could only take so much reading in a single sitting. The footman who entered bearing a note was a welcome interruption. Breaking the seal on the folded parchment, Rian opened the note. He looked thoughtful for a moment, and then asked, "Is Lady Howard's man waiting for a reply?"

The footman arched a brow. "*Her ladyship* is waiting in the drawing room, sir."

Rian grunted. He hadn't realized the note had been delivered in person, and for a moment wondered if failing to tell him had been deliberate on the servant's part. Deciding he was making too much of what was no more than an oversight, Rian thanked the man before dismissing him. Still his parting expression was worth taking note of. It told him he ought not to discount the possibility of fireworks.

As the door closed Rian's eyes dropped to the communication in his hand. Written in Isabel's bold, distinctive hand, it bore two words only:

Forgive me.

Unsure if the referral was to a past event or something yet to come, he placed the note on the desk. The only way to find out anything with Isabel was to ask her.

She was pouring herself a cup of tea, and paused to smile at him as he entered the room. The aromatic brew was quite pleasing, and he accepted when Isabel indicated a second cup on the tray. It was as if their last meeting had never occurred, and if Isabel chose not to raise the matter, then he most certainly would not.

"How nice of you to brave the cold," Rian commented. Isabel offered her cheek to be kissed and he obliged. To refuse would be rude, and he preferred to avoid a display of temper under his brother's roof. Still, he couldn't help but wonder if Isabel was going to make another attempt to change his mind regarding their relationship. If so, then she really was overdressed this time. Although it would do her no good no matter what she wore, Rian had the perfect foil against temptation: Mrs. Hatch.

"It was not snowing when I left. Had it been, I might have reconsidered," she added with a laugh, handing him the cup.

"Well, no matter, you are here now." Rian took a seat opposite her. The choice was deliberate. He did not wish to be reminded of what had happened the last time they shared the comfort of a couch.

As if reading his thoughts Isabel acknowledged him with a smile that brimmed shamelessly with the promise of sex.

"So what brings you to my door?" he asked.

"I thought perhaps you might be in need of a minor diversion from all your matrimonial duties."

Now it was his turn to smile. As far as he knew, none of Felicity's family disapproved of her choice so the notion of having to kidnap her back from disgruntled relatives, a primary function of the best man, was very slim indeed. But he was feeling generous so he said, "Actually, a diversion would be most welcome."

Rian had no need to be rescued from anything marital in origin, but he was in sore need of being saved from annual yields, percentages and ideas for projected increase in cash flow. He recognized the importance of such documents, and knew they demanded his full attention, but it was hard going. Especially when his mind refused to cooperate and insisted on drifting.

He had been somewhat vexed to learn that Mrs. Hatch had made Catherine aware of the 'history' between them. He'd wanted to wait until she was stronger before revealing his role in this part of her recovery, but once he got over his initial dismay, he realized the debt he owed the housekeeper. In truth he was completely ill-suited to deal with such a situation. With poise, and the innate empathy of her sex, Mrs. Hatch had managed to disclose the facts with far less damage to Catherine's fragile mental state than his telling would have caused. Now Catherine had time to absorb and hopefully understand his involvement.

"...and so I was thinking it might be helpful if I were to meet her."

Jolted back to the present, Rian realized he hadn't been listening to anything Isabel had said. "Meet who?" he asked.

"Your guest of course." Sipping her tea, Isabel looked at him over the rim of the cup. "Honestly, Rian, I should be insulted. You haven't heard a word I've said, have you?"

He had the decency to look sheepish as he apologized, and quickly caught up with the thread of missed conversation. "What benefit would be gained by meeting her?" he asked suspiciously.

Isabel shrugged and narrowed her eyes slightly. "Did it ever occur to you that I might know her? She wouldn't be the first young woman to have fallen victim to a love affair gone wrong. Perhaps the young man got cold feet, or perhaps she did, and is now too ashamed to face a disapproving parent or the threat of scandal."

Given the severity of Catherine's injuries it was obvious something had gone horribly wrong, but Rian had his doubts it was the type of affaire de coeur Isabel was suggesting. "I don't think that's the situation here," he said grimly.

"I was merely using that as an example." She placed her cup back in its saucer, and put it down. "The point I'm trying to make is that I may recognize her, may know her family. Unless of course there's some reason you don't want me to see her?"

"Have you heard of someone missing a daughter?" Rian asked, brushing aside Isabel's concern.

"That's hardly the sort of detail any family wishes to make common knowledge, Rian." Isabel got to her feet. "So it is settled then. Why don't you take me up to meet her?"

"Take you up?" He hesitated, unable to shake the feeling Isabel's motives were not as altruistic as they seemed.

She made a sound that was part impatience, part exasperation. "Rian, if the girl has injuries, I can hardly expect her to come to me."

Moving toward the door, she left him with no recourse but to follow.

Chapter 27

Having mentioned Rian's generous offer to search the library for something she might like to read, Catherine had been surprised when the young maid, Tilly, took it upon herself to find her a book. She spent the better part of a day running between floors, bringing one armful of books after another for Catherine's perusal. After the sixth or possibly seventh trip, Rian had intervened. Relieving the young girl of the half-dozen books in her arms, he gave her a single novel in their stead. Though nearly twenty years had passed since its first publication, when he had read it himself, Rian thought it would be something Catherine might enjoy. Tilly had tactfully placed it at the very top of the modest collection now gracing the table in Catherine's bedroom.

She had stared long and hard at the title, but *Travels into Several Remote Nations of the World. In Four Parts. By Lemuel Gulliver, First a Surgeon, and then a Captain of Several Ships* brought no spark of recognition. Neither did the name Jonathan Swift, who was not only the author but a clergyman, no less. Still, it proved to be a delightfully entertaining diversion, which Catherine knew she would have no difficulty in reading to the end. Now she lifted her head as a light knock on the door interrupted her. Mrs. Hatch entered the room followed by Rian, and the beautiful woman from the carriage. Marking her page with a length of ribbon, Catherine closed the book and set it aside.

Warmth flushed her face as she gazed at Rian, but the look he gave in return was one of bored indifference. Ah, so that was how it was to be between them now. She lowered her eyes in disappointment even though she was not terribly surprised. It was to be expected now that he knew she was aware of the part he'd played in the worst moments of her illness.

The least she could do was let him see she did not hold him at fault, and hope he gave her the same consideration. She raised her eyes in time to see the sudden change of expression on Rian's face. The fiercely arched brow, coupled with a look of exasperation said his show of unconcern had nothing to do with her. It was for the benefit of the woman now clinging to his arm. The same woman who had, until a few moments ago, been watching his face closely.

Unsure why Rian would feel the need to mask his emotions, if indeed that was what he was doing, Catherine nevertheless allowed a small smile to lift the corners of her mouth before turning her attention to his guest.

The smile on the woman's face was all wrong. It was too perfect, as if she had spent a great deal of time before a looking glass, and practiced how wide to stretch her lips to achieve the desired effect. It was a smile that carried no warmth. An impression verified by the glittering hardness of the brilliant green eyes that now looked back at Catherine. From the proprietary way she held Rian's arm there could be no doubt of her place in his affection. A fact that both surprised and disconcerted Catherine.

Since learning Rian was to be married, she had spent far too many moments imagining what his bride-to-be might look like. There was no denying this woman was beautiful enough, but Catherine had hoped his choice would also be...less polished. A glance at Rian's face made her think perhaps she had mistaken the nature of their relationship, but it was hard to ignore the physical familiarity he allowed the woman to enjoy. Such an obvious display of affection would only be granted under very specific circumstances. Mrs. Hatch interrupted Catherine's speculations by telling her, "Lady Howard has asked to meet with you in the hope she might be acquainted with your family."

Though the housekeeper gave away nothing by her expression, and her tone was respectful, Catherine could tell she didn't give a fig about anything Lady Howard hoped for. And she didn't like her. Not at all.

"Do you really think so?" she asked in a low voice as Mrs. Hatch came to fuss with the shawl about Catherine's shoulders. Her reply was a strange harrumphing sound. Whatever Rian's feelings for the beautiful woman, they were not shared by everyone with an interest in his life, which made Catherine wonder if the marriage was possibly an arranged match. Something Rian felt honor bound to go through with.

The man in question now stepped forward, and made the formal introduction. "Allow me to present Lady Isabel Howard."

Isabel seated herself in the chair placed close to the foot of the chaise, and Catherine stared at her with frank curiosity before looking back up at Rian. That was it? Just Lady Isabel Howard and nothing else? No explanation of her place in his affections?

She waited, fully expecting Rian to return the compliment by introducing her to his fiancée, but he seemed strangely loathe to do so. Catherine wondered if she had misread his expression. Could she really have fallen so low in his esteem that Rian no longer deemed her worthy of common politeness? A bubble of anger began to well up inside her. Pulling her brows together she was about to rectify the situation when she caught Rian's eye as he stood behind Isabel. Aware of her intentions, he stopped her with an alarming scowl. For whatever reason, he did not want the beautiful Lady Howard to know who she was, and it dawned on Catherine that Mrs. Hatch had also avoided using her name. Very well then, if they expected her to play along she would do her best.

Foregoing any pretense at manners, Catherine turned to the elegantly dressed woman and asked bluntly, "Do you know me? Am I familiar to you?"

"It is possible," Isabel said, glancing over her shoulder at Rian, who had replaced the scowl with an expression of mild concern. "I'm certain we have never met before, but there is a familiarity about your eyes and the shape of your mouth. Are you related to the Bristows of Pembroke, perhaps?"

Catherine shook her head.

"Ah well," Isabel continued, "let's see if you recognize any other families." She recited a number of names.

Some were prominent enough for even Rian to recognize, but most meant nothing to him, which was not so surprising when he considered how long he had been away. The rise and fall of aristocratic families was of little importance to him. But he couldn't fail to see none dislodged the blank look on Catherine's face.

"Not even one name is recognizable?" Isabel feigned surprise, though she would have fallen off her chair if Catherine had declared a kinship to any family she mentioned. The ones that Rian acknowledged had a direct claim to the throne, while the rest were complete fabrications.

"I'm sorry," Catherine apologized, "but I don't know any of them."

Unconcerned by the lack of success, Rian interrupted. "Well, it was certainly worth a try. Come now Isabel, we don't want to tire her anymore."

"Oh, I don't think she's tired at all, are you, dear?" Isabel parted her lips, and gave another version of the unsettling smile.

This time Catherine could see it was evasive and deceitful, and it sent a shiver down her back. She was unsure of what Lady Howard had in mind, but she doubted she would try anything with Rian present. Slowly she shook her head in response to the question she'd been asked.

Isabel rose from her seat and in another display of possessiveness, took hold of Rian's arm, and walked him to the door. "Darling, why don't you wait for me downstairs? This will only take a moment, I promise, but I want to ask the dear girl a few more questions that are more personal in nature. Questions I think she would prefer you did not hear."

Rian looked past Isabel at Catherine. It had been almost a week since he had last seen her, and he now had the unsettling feeling that allowing Isabel to meet Catherine was a horrible mistake he would come to regret. But Catherine stared back at him calmly enough. Blue eyes met his brown ones, and for a brief moment he let his concern show. The barest shake of her head, and he would escort Lady Howard from the room. But Catherine's own curiosity was gnawing at her, and she wondered what her ladyship had to say that she did not want Rian to hear. She gave him a small nod and an even smaller smile.

"Very well then," he said, turning his attention back to Isabel. "I will wait for you downstairs."

"There's a good boy!" Isabel ushered him from the room, and was about to close the door when she paused, hand on her hip, fingers drumming. "I'd prefer it if we were quite alone," she said icily, throwing her remark at Mrs. Hatch, who stood quietly, almost unnoticed, by the window.

Ignoring Isabel, the housekeeper stepped forward and took Catherine's hands in her own. "Do you want me to go, lass?" she asked.

As with Rian, Catherine knew she had but to ask and nothing her ladyship said or did would make the housekeeper leave the room. "It's all right, Mrs. Hatch. I'm sure I'll be perfectly fine." The older woman refused to acknowledge her ladyship's presence as she departed the room.

Isabel leaned against the closed door, and studied the face that now looked back at her from across the room. It was a calm and open countenance, seemingly incapable of any duplicity. With a soft rustle of skirts, she made her way to the window where Catherine had sat earlier. The snow continued to fall, forming drifts on the ledge.

"What was it your ladyship wanted to ask me?" Catherine asked as a prickle of unease skittered across her shoulders.

"Absolutely nothing," Isabel snapped in a viper's voice, "for you have nothing to say that is of any interest to me." She turned around, her entire demeanor changing as she glared at Catherine. "You're quite the jade aren't you? Still, this game you're playing will have only one outcome, ducky. A one way trip to Newgate."

Taken aback by Isabel's sudden transformation and the incomprehensible threat of jail, Catherine stammered, "G-game? I-I'm sure I d-don't know what your ladyship means."

"You think me soft in the head, girl?" All pretense of civility on Isabel's part vanished. "You're a clever harlot, I'll grant you that, and you seem to have fooled all the other simpletons in this house. Even the master is distracted by your questionable charm, but believe me when I say you possess neither the beauty nor the intelligence to command his affection for much longer. Continue with this charade of a memory loss for as long as you wish, but it will all come to naught." She dropped her voice and hissed, "You will never have him because he is mine, and I never give up what belongs to me."

Stunned by the enmity in Isabel's tone, Catherine shook her head. She needed to be certain she understood. That there was no possible misunderstanding. "Have who?" she asked with just enough bewilderment to enrage.

"*Rian Connor!*" Spittle flew from Isabel's mouth as she struggled with her temper. "He is mine, and I am not about to give him up to some dockside slattern!" Animosity morphed into pure, naked hatred and it oozed from every pore.

"Give him up?"

Catherine decided Isabel must have lost her mind, and it struck her that the fashionably dressed woman might also be dangerous. A sudden chill went through her. And then, as Isabel's words sank in, an unexpected revelation was born. Even though it made Catherine want to turn cartwheels, she kept her expression fixed. It would not be to her advantage to let Lady Howard see she knew the truth.

This was not the woman Rian was going to marry.

The temper tantrum Isabel was currently throwing was proof enough, and for that Catherine was secretly elated, but even so, Isabel must surely know Rian was about to be married. What was she hoping for? That whatever relationship she had with him would continue after he had taken his vows? Catherine felt her own temper beginning to rise. She might not know Rian as well as Isabel, and most certainly not as intimately, but she would go to her grave sure of one thing.

Rian Connor was not the type of man to bed one woman after pledging himself to another. And there was something else. Catherine decided she was not going to let her ladyship get away with making false accusations regarding her own reputation. A fierce burning need within her would not allow her honor to be sullied by a woman of questionable character and morals. Even if she did have a title.

It took some effort, but Catherine was able to keep her voice at a moderate, conversational level as she spoke, "Lady Howard, you accuse me of trying to win a place in Mr. Connor's affections, a place you believe is reserved for you alone. But from your obvious distress it would seem the feeling is one sided and tenuous at best." She ignored the high spots of color that now appeared on Isabel's cheeks. "Believe me, Lady Howard, when I tell you that this is no game on my part. If you have any knowledge of my identity, then surely it would be in your own interest to reveal it, thus removing the obstacle that prevents me from leaving this house."

Isabel balled her hands into fists, and shook both of them at Catherine. "I may not know *who* you are, but I know only too well *what* you are!"

Catherine arched a brow. "Then I beg of you to share your insight. I'm certain it will be more than enlightening."

As if suddenly realizing how close she was to losing control of herself, Isabel took a deep breath. "You're nothing but a trollop," she said in a voice that did little to disguise her cold fury. "A doxie who has managed to wheedle her way beneath this roof with some ridiculous tale of woe in order to gain sympathy, and the hope of bettering her situation." Isabel's voice turned hard. "I know very well the lengths a woman such as you will go to in order to win over a man like Rian Connor."

Unable to believe her ears, Catherine stared at Isabel, aghast. This was too much. Who was this woman to dare speak to her like this? What gave her the right to make such wild, inflammatory allegations? Catherine stood, grimacing at the sudden shooting pains in her legs, and turned her back on Isabel.

"Tell me, your ladyship," she snarled over her shoulder as her own temper flared, "if you believe this to be some sort of trickery."

Loosening the ties on the bodice of her dress with trembling fingers, Catherine pulled her heavy braid aside and exposed her back to Isabel. There was a deafening silence as Isabel took in the still vibrant crisscross pattern of healing welts, and the jagged scar that burned an angry crimson flame in Catherine's pale skin.

"A pretty piece of work to give weight to your story," Isabel commented with no show of emotion. "Though it appears the hand you employed had more enthusiasm than actual skill."

Shocked by Isabel's words, Catherine pulled her dress closed and refastened the ties as Isabel continued her venomous attack.

"If you expect to lie with a member of this household, you should confine yourself to one of the stable boys, or mayhap all of them. Do not delude yourself into thinking the master of this house will ever welcome you to his bed, or come to yours. You are nothing but an obligation he will relinquish at the earliest opportunity, and be relieved to do so."

An angry swish of taffeta accompanied Isabel as she stalked across the room, and her hand was stretched out, reaching for the door handle, when Catherine's voice stopped her.

"Lady Howard?" With her emotions still running high, Catherine's voice cut like steel.

"What?" Isabel ground out between clenched teeth.

"I fear I owe you an apology." Isabel turned her head, a triumphant look on her face as Catherine continued. "You made it quite plain that there was a whore in this room, but never having made the acquaintance of such a person, forgive me for not knowing what I was looking at."

Chapter 28

Mrs. Hatch returned to the master suite with a tea tray and a maid carrying a vase of colorful blooming flowers. Unfortunately Catherine was still too upset to appreciate either. Although no longer in danger of letting her temper get the better of her, she was hard pressed to say which troubled her more. Isabel's horrid accusations or the fact she had actually called a woman who boasted a title a whore. Catherine told herself she should be scolded for not having apologized immediately and begged forgiveness, but in truth she knew she would never apologize, and she felt absolutely no remorse.

The housekeeper was more pleased than alarmed by Catherine's agitated state. It was proof that her chick had the mettle to stand up for herself, but it still took some coaxing before Mrs. Hatch was able to get Catherine back into the big bed. It was hard to continue to feel angry when pillows were being plumped and someone was concerned enough with your agitated state to fuss over you. Exhaustion replaced her anger, leaving Catherine feeling wrung out, like a limp rag.

"Why would she say such horrible things to me?" she asked, momentarily forgetting the housekeeper had not been present during her conversation with Isabel.

It was obvious Catherine was upset, and, despite a burning curiosity about whatever horrible things Isabel had said, Mrs. Hatch decided having the conversation repeated would serve no good purpose. Besides, the housekeeper did not need to know the details. As far as she was concerned Isabel Howard never had anything good to say, and could upset a person simply by being in the same room.

"Some women are just born spiteful," she told Catherine, "and there's no changing them."

Accepting the hot drink being offered, Catherine caught the older woman's expression over the rim of the cup. "You don't like Lady Howard very much, do you?" she asked.

"Oh, I wouldn't say that." Mrs. Hatch caught a wayward curl and tucked it back into her charge's thick, blonde braid. "It would be more truthful to say I don't like her at all."

"Neither do I."

"Then let's not talk about her anymore."

Mrs. Hatch's words and solicitous gestures worked as a balm to soothe the barbs left by Isabel's vicious tongue, and before long Catherine's mood, while not fully restored to its usual good humor, definitely showed signs of improvement. She looked across the room at the colorful blooms the maid had placed on the table. "What beautiful flowers!" she exclaimed.

"They most certainly are," Mrs. Hatch agreed.

One of the books Catherine had kept from Tilly's excursion to the library was a botanical volume. Though she found the text somewhat difficult, she had been delighted by the large detailed drawings of many of the flowers, and had spent hours simply looking at the pictures. The colorful blossoms had stirred her interest because she could recall some bed curtains embroidered with flowers. Whom the bed curtains belonged to she could not say, but there was no denying the warmth surrounding the pale, vague memory. Apparently the young maid had not kept this revelation to herself, because now Catherine had a vase filled with similar blooms. A rich display of color to please the eye, and make her think perhaps Rian still held her in some measure of favorable regard.

"Please thank Master Rian for me," she said.

Mrs. Hatch chuckled. "Oh lass, these are not his doing." She began to reposition the few stems that had been disturbed by their journey, and seeing the puzzled look on Catherine's face, the housekeeper smiled. "These are from the hothouse at Pelham Manor. I recognize Miss Felicity's hand when I see it."

Catherine frowned. The name was one she had not heard before. "Who is Miss Felicity?"

"Why, Mr. Connor's betrothed."

Catherine's stomach roiled, and whatever joy she had derived from the lovely floral display suddenly soured. It mattered not that what she was hearing was a confirmation that Isabel was not Rian's intended, Catherine would have been quite happy to remain ignorant of any details about his bride-to-be. Knowing her name made her all the more real, only she didn't understand why Isabel would think Catherine was a threat when it was actually a woman named Felicity. It made no sense, but whatever the reason, she didn't want to think about it. A wave of anguish began to rise, threatening to drown her, and she wanted nothing more than to bury her head beneath the covers and wallow in self-pity.

"No doubt Master Liam told Miss Felicity you were here, and acts of kindness such as this only go to prove he's a very lucky man."

It took Catherine a moment to realize another new name had just been thrown at her, but she was too dismayed to be curious. "What makes him so lucky?" she asked instead.

Finally satisfied with the floral display, Mrs. Hatch turned around. "Why marrying Miss Felicity, of course."

"*He's* marrying..." Catherine was confused. "Who is he?"

"Master Liam is Master Rian's younger brother. His marriage is the reason Master Rian has come home, and I thank God for it I can tell you."

"*His* marriage?" The words tumbled out of her mouth before she could stop them, and Catherine felt light headed. It was always possible, but surely there would not be two weddings taking place. "But I thought—is it not Master Rian who is to be married?"

"Bless you lass, no. Whoever ever told you such a thing?" Mrs. Hatch stood at the foot of the bed, hands on her hips, wearing a look of exasperated amusement on her face.

"Well, you did actually."

"I did?" Now it was the housekeeper's turn to be confused. "No, surely not. Why would I say such a thing?" She paused and frowned, trying to recall the moment. "When did I tell you Master Rian was getting married?"

"Um, when you first told me I was being sent away." Catherine recalled the details of their conversation to see if she had been mistaken.

"And I told you that it was *Master Rian* who was getting married?" Mrs. Hatch repeated suspiciously.

"Well, not in those exact words," Catherine clarified. "We were talking about Mr. Connor, I mean Master Rian, and you said I was being sent away to Oakhaven, but you couldn't go with me because you were making wedding preparations, and so I just assumed—"

"That it was Master Rian who was about to take a wife," Mrs. Hatch finished for her.

Catherine made a squeaking noise as her face turned red. "I didn't know there was another one."

Mrs. Hatch opened her mouth and then shut it with a snap. The only time Liam had seen Catherine was the same day she had been brought here, and she obviously had no recollection of him. "Well, lass, in all fairness the fault is mine. I should have been more plain. I suppose I just took it for granted someone had told you about Master Liam, although I can't imagine why they would."

"How many of them are there?" Catherine asked faintly, beginning to feel ridiculously giddy. Rian was not getting married, and no marriage meant no fiancée!

Mrs. Hatch chuckled. "Just the two of them, lass, though Lord knows when they were lads there always seemed to be one too many."

"You're very fond of them, aren't you?"

"Aye, well I've been in service to the family since I was a young lass, before they were born. I came with their mother so I've known them both all their lives. It almost broke my heart when Master Rian left like he did."

"I'm so sorry." Though she had nothing to do with it, Catherine still felt the need to apologize.

"Well, it's all better now that he's back where he belongs."

"So will you thank Miss Felicity for the flowers?" Catherine asked, now giving the blooms the appreciation they deserved.

"Well, I don't know as I'll see her before the wedding, but I'll make sure to send word so she knows you liked them." Seeing her chick trying unsuccessfully to stifle a yawn, the housekeeper began fussing once more. "Time to stop this chattering and let you get some rest. You'll feel much better after you take a nap."

"I don't know why I'm suddenly so tired." Catherine looked suspiciously at the teacup the housekeeper now held. "Did you give me one of Dr. MacGregor's sleeping draughts?"

"Aye, well after your to-do with Lady Muck, I thought you might need some help relaxing."

Whether real or simply the power of suggestion, Catherine felt a lethargy stealing into her limbs. She slid farther down the bed. "That woman said some truly horrid things to me," she admitted sleepily.

"I'm so sorry you had to listen to the wicked bitch!"

"She thinks I'm a threat," Catherine murmured, disbelievingly.

"Does she now?" Mrs. Hatch cooed softly. "And why would she think that, lass?" Catherine's eyelids fluttered closed and she gave a deep sigh. "She thinks...Master Rian...is interested...in me."

"Oh lass, we can only hope."

* * * *

Rian watched Catherine sleep. Dark lashes fluttering against her flushed cheek made him nervous, but the smooth contour of her brow, and the slight upturn at the corners of her mouth brought a measure of relief. Whatever the imaginings of her subconscious, they were pleasant ones. He had been concerned the effects of meeting Isabel might follow Catherine as she slumbered, and he was grateful to see it appeared not to be so. Sitting in the chair at the side of her bed, he allowed himself to relax.

He was furious with Isabel for having caused Catherine any distress, but he also needed to wait before addressing the incident with her. Painfully aware of his error in judgment at their previous meeting, Rian wanted to be sure there would be no misunderstandings this time. To say the encounter between the two women had not gone well was an understatement. He was actually of a mind to say it had ended disastrously if Isabel's departure was any indication. The sound of the front door being closed with enough force to bring him out of the drawing room had been startling, and the horrified expression on the footman's face left him in no doubt that waiting for Isabel to join him was no longer necessary.

"She wouldn't let me open the door," the man apologized, not wanting to be thought neglectful in his duties. "She—she closed it with her own hand." His face colored as he realized how disrespectful he was being. "Her ladyship, I mean," he muttered hastily.

Rian was uncertain if the man's demeanor was due to witnessing Isabel performing a menial task unaided, or if this was his first brush with a volatile temper in a member of the fairer sex. "They can be quite unpredictable when you get them riled," he said, deciding on the latter.

"Strong too," the man observed, having firsthand knowledge of just how much strength was required to make the heavy door rattle so.

"Indeed," Rian agreed.

The impulse to race up the stairs to Catherine's room and learn for himself what had happened was forestalled by Mrs. Hatch. She had remained in the hallway, only a few feet from the closed bedroom door, and had witnessed for herself Isabel's dramatic departure. Now the housekeeper counseled patience. If, as she suspected, Rian was the subject of whatever discourse had taken place, Catherine's temper might be such that seeing him would only agitate her further. It was good advice, but he did not return to the drawing room until he had been assured that the encounter had not reduced Catherine to tears.

"You're sure she's not weeping or upset?" he asked the maid who had taken in Felicity's flowers, and was now retuning empty-handed.

"Oh, she's upset," the girl had told him with a smile wise beyond her years, "but she's not weeping, sir, nor do I think she will be."

With no other choice, he returned to the drawing room to wait for Mrs. Hatch. It was frustrating not knowing the nature of Isabel's personal questions, or any answer given by Catherine in response. What had been said was a mystery, and would most likely remain so as far as Rian was concerned. Mrs. Hatch had refused to divulge anything that Catherine may have told her, telling him it was up to Catherine to share any or all of the conversation if she so wished. He'd given the woman his most ardent, penetrating stare, but she was not moved.

"That look didn't work when you were a lad," she reminded him with a shake of her head. Abashed, Rian apologized. "I'm not saying the lass hasn't been affected by the meeting," she said, offering him what sympathy she could, "but only time will tell how much." Her mouth pulled into a tight line of concern. "Tis a shame you had not already taken the lass to Oakhaven. All of this unpleasantness could have been avoided."

"What's done is done," Rian said with a grimace, "and that I cannot change, but I can take steps to ensure it will not happen again. How soon can Catherine be ready to leave?"

"Would first thing in the morning suit?"

He smiled. It would suit very well indeed.

Now it was close to midnight, and, as he had on almost every night since her fever broke, Rian sat by Catherine's bedside listening to the even rhythm of her breathing. She rolled onto her side, brows pulling together, lips compressed as pain flared briefly. Her body was still healing, and it would take some time before it was completely well, if it ever was. The thought suddenly occurred to Rian that Catherine might never be comfortable lying on her back. A sudden heat spiking in his groin brought to mind a very particular instance where such a position might be required. But no matter. He was an experienced lover with no qualms whatsoever about being the one to adopt a supine position. He ought to have been shocked by such a thought, but he wasn't. Instead he welcomed the opportunity to acknowledge the part of him that recognized how much he wanted Catherine to be a part of his life. Had wanted her since the first moment he'd seen her.

But would she desire him in the same way? Her behavior toward him during her fever told him yes. She might not be able to articulate her passions, and might even try to keep them repressed, but there was no denying the need that had been kindled. He knew that flame, once lit, was never truly doused again. It would be up to him to show her she had nothing to fear. To make certain her future was not tainted by the ugly specter of the past. He would need to earn Catherine's trust, make her see him as more than a rescuer from a watery grave. Gently he picked up the hand that lay on top of the covers, admiring the slender fingers resting in his palm, grateful that, in her sleep at least, she did not pull away from him. Taking advantage of the fact she was ignorant of his presence, Rian carefully raised her hand and pressed his lips against the soft skin.

"No matter what horrors are hidden in your past," he whispered to the sleeping girl, "trust me with your future, and I promise I will always keep you safe."

And when he felt her hand move, slender fingers curling around his own, he told himself it wasn't his imagination creating the answer he yearned for. Catherine applied enough pressure to tell him she heard his words… and would hold him to his vow.

Resolve

Corsets and Carriages
Part Two

The exciting continuation is available for preorder now!

"I am not so naïve that I don't know what happens between a man and a woman when they are lovers."

In the sanctuary of Rian Connor's magnificent ancestral estate, Catherine Davenport struggles to remember who she was before he found her wandering practically naked on the docks of London. She has little memory of the vicious attack that brought her there, but she can't deny the feelings Rian awakens in her. In danger of losing her heart to a man tormented by the dark secrets of his own past, Catherine questions what an innocent like her has to offer such an experienced man of the world.

"You have no idea what you are doing to me—how much I want you, how much I need you!"

On the night of his brother's wedding ball, Rian proves exactly how much he wants his beautiful young protégé, only to be lured by his former mistress into committing the ultimate betrayal. For Isabel Howard will stop at nothing to do away with Catherine and destroy her future with the man they both desire above all others...

Meet the Author

Carla Susan Smith owes her love of literature to her mother, who, after catching her preteen daughter reading by flashlight beneath the bedcovers, calmly replaced the romance book she had "borrowed" with one that was much more age appropriate! Born and raised in England, she now calls South Carolina home where she lives with her wonderfully supportive husband, awesome son, and a canine critique group (if tails aren't wagging then the story isn't working!). When not writing, she can usually be found in the kitchen trying out any recipe that calls for rhubarb, working on her latest tapestry project or playing catch up with her reading list. Visit her at www.carlasmithauthor.com

Printed in the United States
by Baker & Taylor Publisher Services